the wife who ran away

TESS STIMSON is the author of nine novels and two
non-fiction books, and writes regularly for the *Daily Mail*
as well as for several women's magazines. Born and
brought up in Sussex, she graduated from Oxford before
spending a number of years as a news producer with ITN.
She now lives in Vermont with her American husband,
their daughter and her two sons.

www.tessstimson.com

BY TESS STIMSON

Fiction

The Lying Game

The Wife Who Ran Away

What's Yours is Mine

The Nanny

The Infidelity Chain

The Adultery Club

Hard News

Soft Focus

Pole Position

Non-Fiction

Beat the Bitch:
How to Stop the Other Woman Stealing Your Man

Yours Till the End:
The Biography of a Beirut Hostage

tess stimson

the wife who ran away

PAN BOOKS

First published 2012 by Pan Books

This edition published 2013 by Pan Books
an imprint of Pan Macmillan, a division of Macmillan Publishers Limited
Pan Macmillan, 20 New Wharf Road, London N1 9RR
Basingstoke and Oxford
Associated companies throughout the world
www.panmacmillan.com

ISBN 978-1-4472-4089-1

1 3 5 7 9 8 6 4 2

A CIP catalogue record for this book is available from the British Library.

Typeset by Ellipsis Digital Limited, Glasgow
Printed and bound by CPI Group (UK) Ltd, Croydon, CR0 4YY

Visit www.panmacmillan.com to read more about all our books
and to buy them. You will also find features, author interviews and
news of any author events, and you can sign up for e-newsletters
so that you're always first to hear about our new releases.

For my father

Michael

I'm so proud to be your daughter.

You are the best and bravest man I know.

Kate

Whenever I read in the newspaper about a mother who's abandoned her children and run off to Spain, or a wife who popped out to the shops and never came back, I never think, 'God, that's awful. How *could* she?' I think, 'I wish I had the guts to do that.'

I suppress the thought, of course, and quickly count my blessings: two healthy children (well, teenagers now); good husband (loyal, certainly, a wonderful father); great job . . .

But seriously: how do these women have the *balls*?

Think of the young mother-of-three, blindly folding laundry while her taxi idles in the driveway, pathetically determined that at least the children will have clean T-shirts when she's gone. Or the devoted wife of twenty-seven years (with a suitcase that's been packed for nineteen), waving her youngest off to college and then calmly putting the dishes in to soak before slipping out of the kitchen and closing the back door behind her for the very last time.

It's awful for those left behind, of course; only one step

down from suicide in terms of selfishness, I suppose. But not a decision taken lightly. Not, in fact, a *decision* at all, it seems to me suddenly, but an imperative: an impulse as violent and impossible to ignore as vomiting or giving birth.

I'd never actually *do* it, of course. Responsible, happily married women like me don't just quit.

I put the emerald gloves down on the glass sales counter. The girl behind it – to call her an assistant would be to imply that she has, in some way, *assisted* me – stops texting and looks up. 'You want to pay for those?'

No, I think drily, I'd rather shoplift them, if only to spare us both the effort. But no doubt my mother will change her mind about the colour, and exchanging them will be so much easier with a receipt.

I realize my jaundiced inner voice sounds increasingly like Eleanor herself. It's not an uplifting thought.

The salesgirl pulls out her white earbuds and lets them dangle round her neck so the tinny back-beat of music scratches at my nerves. She prods the gloves as if I've presented her with a dead mouse. 'There's no price tag.'

As I approach my fortieth birthday, I've found a curious thing is happening: I finally seem to be growing a spine. I send back bottles of wine when they're corked, where once I'd have grimaced and politely choked them down; I tell queue-jumpers to take their place behind me instead of grumbling sotto voce in that peculiarly British way and permitting them to shove ahead. I'm a perpetual source of embarrassment to my children – no surprise there: it is, after all, part of my job description as a parent – but, less palatably, also to my husband, whose mission, I have discovered over fifteen years of marriage, is to find the line of least resistance and then set up camp there. None of my new-found courage extends to my family, of course. When it comes to standing up to Ned, the children or my mother, I have all the backbone of a minced jellyfish.

Resolutely, I hold my nerve and stare the salesgirl down. With an audible sigh, she yields and disappears. My head throbs painfully. *I just want to buy a pair of gloves*.

Of course I knew, when my mother asked me at breakfast to 'pop into Selfridges', that it wouldn't take the five minutes she blithely predicted. It took fifteen minutes, in fact, just to walk to the department store from my office in Curzon Street, another twenty to find the precise shade of emerald to match my mother's scarf, and five – so far – trying to pay. Which has left me just enough time to get back for my crucial two o'clock meeting and none at all for lunch.

I should have said no. I should have told Eleanor that my job is on the line, has been on the line for months now, and that if she wants me to continue paying *her* mortgage, never mind mine, I don't have time to go shopping for gloves.

Naturally, I didn't. I can cope, you see. I can do it all.

I check my watch. I could leave Selfridges now and brave my mother's stoic disappointment, or come back at nine, after work, and take the late train home, the slow train that stops at every single station between Waterloo and Salisbury. Or I can just wait.

I press the fingers of my right hand against the inside of my left wrist, fighting the sudden, unfamiliar flare of panic. Indecision is a new sensation for me. I've *always* known what to do. Instantly, no second-guessing. It's why Forde Williams pays me the big bucks. But for the first time in my working life, I'm starting to question whether it's worth it.

Work has been my sanctuary and salvation for as long

as I can remember. For the past eighteen months, however, Trey Hamilton, Paul Forde's new protégé, has worked tirelessly to manoeuvre me into the cold. Paul should have protected me, of course; quite apart from the fact that I've given his company fifteen years of loyal service, sixteen-hour days, truncated holidays and lost Bank Holiday weekends, I'm the best Client Service Director he's ever had, and – on merit – the natural choice to take over the advertising company when he retires in five years' time. But I'm a woman, and the new wunderkind is a man, and I'm thirty-nine, and Trey Hamilton has only just turned twenty-eight, and in the world of advertising, experience and loyalty are worth far less than a youthful penis.

It's difficult enough, in this economy, to see off our commercial rivals without having to worry about friendly fire. I'm tired, so *very* tired, of fighting the very people who should be watching out for me.

And not just at the office. Ninety per cent of my rows with Ned are because he thinks I work too hard. He's fed up with cooking his own dinner at night and waking to an empty bed in the morning. But what my happily-stay-at-home husband forgets is that it's my salary paying two sets of school fees – three when my nephew starts prep school in September – and two mortgages. And if my husband is really that keen to see more of me, he could always agree to move closer to London as I've begged him to do for the past nine years.

A dragging pain gnaws at my abdomen. There are days when I wish I could unplug myself like a computer; simply cease, for a while, to be. Would anyone actually notice if I wasn't here? I suppose they would when they were left standing in the rain, or if there was no food in the fridge, or warm, wet hole to thrust into in bed.

The salesgirl finally returns with a second pair of gloves complete with the elusive price tag. I hand over my credit card, praying it won't be declined again, and once more check my watch. I can't miss this meeting, much as I might want to; it's simply too important.

My mobile rings as I step onto the escalator. 'Eleanor,' I sigh, 'I can't talk now.'

'Oh, that's all right, dear. I was just calling to tell you not to bother with the gloves. I don't need them any more.'

It takes me a moment to find my voice. 'Do you have *any* idea how much trouble I've gone to?' I manage. '*Do* you, Eleanor?'

'Well, dear, that's why I asked Agness to pick them up for me when she went into Salisbury at lunchtime. To save you the trouble.'

'Agness? Agness is at school.'

'Agness is here with me.'

For the second time in as many minutes, I'm lost for words.

'They're the perfect shade,' Eleanor says contentedly, 'Saint Patrick green. I don't know where she found them, but—'

I reach the bottom of the escalator and step to the side, out of the way. 'Let me talk to her, please.'

'There's no need to get upset, dear. She has a half-day—'

'She does *not* have a half-day! Eleanor, please let me talk to her!'

'Really, Katherine. I'm sure she knows if she has a half-day or not.'

Agness is truculent and unrepentant when she comes to the phone. 'No need to have a cow, Mum. I told Dad I was going to Salisbury.'

'Your father knew you were skipping school?'

'Stu-dy day,' Agness sing-songs.

There are moments when I could kill Ned. He knows perfectly well Agness doesn't have study days. She's only fourteen; her school, wise to the ways of teenage girls, only grants study days to A-level students in their final year. But it's easier to pretend he believes her than to confront her and deal with the consequences. That particular pleasure is left to me.

My phone beeps with an urgent email from Paul Forde. If I don't get to this wretched meeting *now* and save my career, Agness won't be the only one with study days to spare.

'We'll talk about this when I get home,' I say tightly.

'Brianna said I could spend the night with her . . .'

'Well, *I* say you can't.'

'I don't know why you're picking on me!' Agness cries. 'Guy's smoking pot! I suppose you're going to let him get away with it just 'cause he's a boy?'

Guy's smoking *pot*? 'We're not talking about your brother—'

'*Half*-brother,' Agness snipes.

God give me strength.

'Agness, tell your grandmother I want—'

I'm talking to myself. Agness has hung up on me.

I don't have the energy to ring back and berate her. Pain drills behind my temples. Eleanor, work, the situation with Ned (yet to be resolved after this weekend's rows), Agness, the parlous state of our finances, even the discovery that my stepson is smoking pot – any one of these scenarios I could deal with in isolation. Two or three of them even. But all of them combined is suddenly too much, even for me. I need a break, a gap in the clouds, just for five minutes. If I could just get a decent night's sleep before the next crisis breaks, a chance to catch my breath . . .

But it doesn't work that way. There are no days off from motherhood or marriage.

Outside the department store, I turn the collar of my coat up against the freezing April rain. I'll have to flag down a cab: I'll never make it back to the office in time if I don't. Although in this weather, of course, I'll be lucky to find one.

But for once, luck is on my side. A taxi pulls into the kerb beside me to let its passenger alight, and I have one hand on the door before the previous fare has even opened it.

Five minutes' peace, that's all I ask.

Three days before

Ned

I'm having a pint with the boys at the Lamb and Flag when I remember I'm supposed to be at home celebrating my wedding anniversary.

Actually, to be strictly accurate, it's Joe who remembers.

'Mate,' he says, 'shouldn't you be getting back?'

'What are you, my mother?' I drain my glass. 'Your round, mate.'

'I'm not kidding, Ned. Chloe bumped into Kate at the farmers' market earlier today buying fancy bloody arti-chokes for your anniversary dinner.' He gives me a nudge. 'Looks like you could be in luck tonight.'

Christ! I nearly choke on my beer. Kate'll go fucking *nuts* if I miss our anniversary again.

Neil smirks into his pint. 'Better get your arse in gear, mate. You won't be getting any if you're late.'

I force a relaxed grin and wave to the barmaid. 'Over here, love. Just 'cause you're pussy-whipped, boys, doesn't mean we all are. It's sorted. We've got time for one more.'

Two more, as it turns out. I'm for the high-jump already, so there's no point going home to face the music sober. By the time I fall out of the pub and start back up the hill, it's nearly nine. I haven't got her a card or a present. *Shit*. I suppose I can't turn up completely empty-handed or I'll never hear the end of it.

I stop by the Shell garage and grab a bunch of yellow carnations from a bucket outside. They look pretty pathetic on their own, so I go back for the entire bucketful. Ripping off the cellophane, I cram them together and admire the result. Who needs bloody expensive florists? Might as well push the boat out and pick up a box of chocolates. The selection's pretty shitty, but it's the thought that counts, right? I'd buy her diamonds if I had the money, she knows that.

The house is in half-darkness when I get home. I let myself quietly in by the back door and get a whiff of something good on the stove. Roast lamb. My mouth waters. Kate's a great chef, but she only cooks properly twice a year: Christmas and our anniversary. The rest of the time I have to fend for myself. Never mind *It's in the oven, you just have to warm it up*. That's not what I call putting a meal on the table. I don't mind about me, of course: It's the kids I'm thinking of. They should be able to come home to a proper dinner, not some bloody warmed-over lasagne or shepherd's pie, even if it *is* home-made.

I lift the saucepan lid. Joe was right: artichokes. Though they look a bit over-cooked to me.

She's gone to town in the dining room, I notice warily as I go into the hall. Candles, napkins, posh wine glasses, the works. Lucky I stopped off for the flowers and chocolates. It's not a big one like our fucking twentieth or something, is it? I do the maths as quickly as four pints and a whisky chaser allow. Aggie's just turned fourteen, so that's what? Fifteen years. Relief floods through me. Yeah, it's just our fifteenth. I was still working at the *Reading Evening News*; I missed the Jerusalem bombing because we were on our honeymoon. There was a local connection with one of the victims, and some little arse-wipe on the sports desk got it while I was still stuck in sodding Barbados. Beginning of the bloody end of my career.

'Kate?' I call. I cough and try again. 'Darling?'

I track her to the sitting room, where she's curled neatly on the sofa. There's a book on her lap and a glass in her hand, but I'm not fooled. She's about as relaxed as a choir-boy in a room full of nonces.

I proffer my bountiful armful of flowers. They look a bit sad now. 'For you.'

'Thank you,' Kate says, ignoring them.

I lay them awkwardly on the top of the piano and hand over the chocolates. Kate tosses them on the sofa beside her. 'Lovely.'

'What time did you get back?' I try brightly.

'Four. I told you I was taking the afternoon off.'

'Did you?'

Kate swings her feet off the sofa. 'Are you hungry?'

Tension eases out of me. She can't be that pissed off, then, or dinner would be in the bin. I'll get a couple of glasses of wine into her, let her witter on for a bit about work, then take her upstairs and really make it up to her. Foreplay and everything. We'll be fine after that.

She bends to pull the lamb out of the oven, and I eye her arse appreciatively. 'Smells wonderful,' I enthuse.

'It's burnt.'

I reach over and tear a sliver of meat off the bone. 'Tastes great to me.'

Kate carves while I open the wine, then silently dishes up the artichokes and garlic roast potatoes. She doesn't bang or clatter round the kitchen, but I can tell I'm not quite off the hook yet. She hands me my plate and I meekly follow her back to the dining room and take my place opposite her.

'You look different,' I say brightly as she sits down. 'New dress?'

'You gave it to me last Christmas. Well. You gave me one *like* it. In a size sixteen.'

'Sweet sixteen . . .'

'I've been a size twelve for as long as you've known me.'

'Whatever. I like that dress. It makes your tits look *huge*.'

Kate bridles. 'When did you turn into such a boor?'

'When did *you* turn into such a prig?' I snap back before I can help myself.

She shoves her plate away. *Blast*. I'm the arsehole who's in the wrong here, not her.

'Sorry, sorry.' I hold up my hands. 'Forget I said that. It's just the beer talking.'

'How many have you had?'

'Just a couple.'

'You've had more than a couple. I'm surprised you managed to walk home.'

'Look,' I sigh, 'are you going to be like this all night? Because I could live without it, to be honest.'

'*You* could live without it? I spend all afternoon cooking your favourite meal and you can't even be bothered to—'

'Look, Kate. Darling. I'm sorry. I forgot our wedding anniversary. So does ninety per cent of the male population at

11

one time or another. You know I didn't mean to. It's not the end of the world. We don't have to let it spoil our—'

'It has nothing to do with *forgetting*. You remember the name of every bloody horse in the National going back twenty years without any difficulty.'

'For God's sake!' I exclaim, flinging down my napkin. 'It's just one *day*! I'm still married to you the other three hundred and sixty-four, aren't I? I'm still here, day in, day out. Why does one damn day out of the whole year have to matter so bloody much?'

'Because it shows *I* matter!'

Christ. What *is* it with women?

'Look. Is it your hormones?' I ask, striving for patience. 'Because ever since—'

'It's not my *fucking* hormones!'

Suddenly she looks like she's going to cry. Kate *never* cries. Or says fuck, for that matter. She's made of Teflon; no matter what gets thrown at her, it just slides right off.

I'm not a complete Neanderthal. I love my wife; though if I live to be a hundred I'll never bloody understand her. I get up from the table and go round to her side. 'Of course you matter to me,' I sigh, pulling her towards me. For a long moment she stays stiff and unyielding within the circle of my arms. 'I'm sorry I didn't buy you a proper present,' I murmur into her hair. 'I'm sorry I forgot to send you flowers. I'm sorry I stayed out late with the boys and ruined dinner. You're right. I should have made the effort. I won't make the same mistake again.'

'That's what you said last year.'

'And still you stayed with me,' I tease.

She buries her face in my shoulder. 'Only just.'

I stroke her hair, relieved that the storm has passed. Kate

angry I can cope with, but, as we discovered a few months ago, a Kate in tears is well beyond my remit. 'OK, where's my present?' I demand playfully, getting the night back on track. 'I know you've got me one. You might as well give it to me now.'

She hesitates and then disentangles herself, gets up and opens a drawer in the sideboard. I take the small wrapped package she hands me.

'Not the new Kawasaki, then?'

She cracks a small smile. 'Couldn't afford the wrapping paper.'

I open the gift. A William Henry pocket knife. It's awesome: a folded Damascus steel blade with a sheen on it that looks like oil on water, a mother-of-pearl handle and a hand-stitched ostrich-skin case. It's an heirloom knife, something passed down from father to son, and I know it cost more than I earn in a month. She might as well have sliced my balls off with the damn thing.

'You shouldn't have,' I say, and mean it.

'I know you've always wanted one,' she says, pleased.

I wanted to earn it, not be given it by my ball-breaking wife.

Suddenly I'm stone-cold sober. 'Let's go to bed,' I say, pulling her by the hand.

'We haven't had dessert—'

'Who needs dessert when I have you?'

'Ned—'

But I'm not in the mood for yet another brush-off. I propel her up the stairs ahead of me, my hands skimming the thin jersey of her dress, and her nipples jump to attention as I graze her breasts. My cock throbs painfully in my jeans, and I press myself against her arse, which I have to admit isn't as soft as it used to be. She could do with putting on some weight. She must have lost a stone in the past two months.

Kate twists away from me as we reach the bedroom. 'I can't. I've got my period.'

'So? You know I don't mind.' I slide my hand into her bra and pinch her nipple. Thank God her tits haven't shrivelled up too. She's always had such nice breasts. 'Throw a towel on the bed. Or change the sheets in the morning.'

'I'm really not in the mood . . .'

'You will be,' I say thickly.

I pull my shirt over my head and unbuckle my jeans. Kate's still just standing there like a shop dummy, so I ease her back on the bed and unbutton her dress, peeling it off her body. After a moment, her hands slide around my back, and her legs reluctantly open. I can almost hear them creak, it's been so bloody long. I push her thighs further apart with my knee, scooping her breasts out of her lacy bra and sucking on them as my fingers fumble between her legs.

'I thought you said you had your period?' I ask after a moment.

'I do. I mean, I *did*—'

Kate flushes. I laugh, totally unfazed; it's not often I catch my wife out in a lie. It makes a nice change for the boot to be on the other foot.

My fingers probe her pussy. She's wet and ready for me, even if she won't admit it.

'You know you want this as much as I do,' I say hoarsely. 'Stop being mad, Kate. What happened wasn't my fault, you know that. I'm a good husband. I don't look at other women. I take care of our kids. I love you—'

'You don't notice me.'

'I *notice* you. I'm noticing you right now,' I add, sliding off my boxers. I run my hand down her body, still more or less firm in all the right places. 'God, you're beautiful. Just as beautiful as the day I married you.'

Despite herself, she moans softly as I finger her clit. I smile to myself. I knew it. Needs to get back on the horse, that's all. Women like Kate are so bloody independent, wanting to be in control all the time. Something goes wrong and they see it as a personal failure. Kate bitches that I never take responsibility for anything, but the truth is she never bloody *lets* me. Except in the bedroom. The one place I've always called the shots. She's never had much confidence between the sheets. Like too many bloody women, she's obsessed with the way she looks, but the real problem isn't in the mirror, it's in her head. She just can't relax. When we met, she'd never had an orgasm she hadn't given herself. It took me two years to get her to chill out enough to come; and trust me, it wasn't lack of experience on *my* part.

I thrust two fingers inside her, and as her juices flood into my hand, I position myself between her legs, my cock nudging her wet cunt. She's hot and tight when I enter her, and I cover her body with mine, lifting her legs onto my shoulders so I can fuck her harder.

A telltale flush spreads across her cheeks and she lets out short, sharp little barks, clawing the sheets. Her head goes back like she's crossing a finishing line, and I feel her cunt clench around my cock as she comes. Moments later I shoot my own wad. Short and sweet, the way I know she likes it.

I roll off her and grope for my boxers, wishing she wasn't so fucking anal about smoking in bed. Fifteen years, and I still miss that post-shag fag.

She doesn't move, and for a moment I wonder if she's fallen asleep.

'It's my hair,' she says into the darkness, her voice thick. 'I had it cut. It's my *hair* that's different.'

Kate

You don't run out on your husband because he's forgotten your wedding anniversary, even if it is for the third year running. If that were the criterion for divorce, we'd all be going it alone.

I'm not running out on my husband, though he certainly deserves it. I just want some peace and quiet to think for five minutes.

The cab driver twists round in his seat. 'Which terminal, love?'

Well, perhaps a little more than five minutes.

'Terminal Four,' I say, as if I know where I'm going.

Terminal Four? The airport? Are you insane?

No, but if I don't get a break from my life, I soon will be.

It's as if there are two people in my head: the stranger in charge of this ridiculous teenage escapade, this *escape*, and normal Kate, responsible Kate, the Kate I have known myself to be for nearly forty years.

This is crazy. Any moment, I'm going to tell the cabbie

to do a U-turn and head back to the office. For God's sake, I have a *meeting* to get to.

Where you can watch some spotty teenager steal everything you've worked for in the last sixteen years?

A sign for the M4 and Heathrow flashes past. As soon as we get off the flyover, I'll tell the cabbie to head straight back into town. Married women of nearly forty don't walk out of their lives because they're having a bad day. At least, not women like me. I'm not a teenager any more. I can't just take off because things are getting on top of me. I'm an adult. I have children. A husband. Responsibilities.

My chest tightens again and I press the pulse point on my wrist. *Breathe, Kate.*

The Monday mid-afternoon traffic is surprisingly light. Before I know it, we're actually on the M4. Somehow another mile goes past, and another, and still I sit mutely in the back of the black cab.

The driver takes the exit for Terminal Four. I try to think calmly. I don't have to get out of the cab when it pulls up at the airport. I can just tell the driver there's been a change of plan and go back to the office and no one will even know this happened. It's not too late. I can still stop this.

Except that I'm not sure I can. Crazy Kate, Rebel Kate, is in control, and she's not listening to me.

As if from a distance, I watch myself get out of the cab and pay, and then carefully tuck the receipt into my purse and put it back in my handbag, next to the passport I've kept zipped in there since the day I started work, just in case. In case of what, I've never stopped to ask myself.

I walk into the terminal with absolutely no idea what I'm going to do next.

Hail another cab or get the Tube back into town, of course. This nonsense has gone on long enough.

And then what? Go back to work so you can witness the death of your career? Back to a life in which you're important to your family not for who you are but for what you do?

Back to Ned, who couldn't be bothered to remember your anniversary and wouldn't notice if you served dinner stark naked as long as there was ketchup with it?

My sensible low-heeled court shoes click confidently across the marble concourse as if my feet know where they're going. Despite everything, I still love my husband, but if I have to stay and listen to him lie to me one more time, I'm not sure how long I will. Two months ago, he let me down when it mattered most, and it has taken everything I have to forgive him. I know, too, what he does in Winchester, even though I pretend not to. I realize how close the house of cards is to tumbling down. What I don't yet know is what I'm going to do about it.

I stop in front of a bank of monitors, staring at a flickering screen of destinations. Abu Dhabi, Houston, Moscow, Tokyo, Belgrade, Casablanca. *Casablanca!* Imagine if I actually went through with this and got on a plane. *Play it once, Sam. For old times' sake.*

I need to find my way back to the Tube. It's after three; Paul Forde's probably spitting feathers, wondering why I'm not at the meeting.

I'm suddenly caught up in a wave of excited chattering Italian teenagers heading towards the check-in desks. I try to get out of their way, but it's like battling an undertow, and after a moment I give up and drift.

Suddenly I realize I've known where I'm going all along.

*

The address isn't stored in my iPhone. I haven't looked it up in years, yet it's there, on my tongue, as familiar as if I've asked for it every day. '*Via Appia Antica, duecento settanta, per favore.*'

A thousand fragmented images and tastes and smells kaleidoscope in my mind's eye. Twirling a forkful of spaghetti puttanesca, the rich, spicy sauce dribbling down my chin. Scooping up a handful of cool water and splashing my face from a fountain in a shadowed courtyard, sweat trickling between my shoulder blades. The sudden scent of lemon and thyme as a door opens in a city wall and unexpectedly reveals a hidden garden. The hollow sound of feet running up stone stairs, a couple rowing in a language that makes even the most furious insult sound like a Shakespearean sonnet. The sewing-machine song of a Vespa zinging down a narrow side street. The taste of rough red Chianti. Strong arms easing me back against a picnic blanket that scratches my sunburned legs even as they open. The giddy, unquenchable, intoxicating feeling of falling in love for the first time. *Alessio*. Not my first lover, not quite; but certainly the first man to break my heart.

The taxi driver repeats the address back to me and swerves from the kerb into the hectic Italian traffic. I brace myself against the door and open the window a crack to let in the balmy night air. Rome in April is ten degrees warmer than London, already holding the promise of summer, and I gratefully pull off my wool suit jacket and undo several of the buttons on my grey silk blouse.

The driver catches my gaze appreciatively in the rear-view mirror, and I quickly do two of them up again.

I lean my head against the cool glass. Whatever fever

drove me to this recklessness has passed just as suddenly. Now I need to find a way to put it right. It's nearly nine o'clock in England, but Ned won't have missed me yet since I'm rarely home before ten on a weeknight. He won't notice I'm not there until the morning, when there's no one to drag Agness and Guy out of bed, but it won't strike him as strange. He'll think I came home after he went to bed, and then went into the office early, before he got up, as I often do. I can spend the night with Julia and get a taxi back to the airport first thing in the morning. I'll square things with Paul Forde somehow. I'll be back in London before anyone but the cat notices I'm gone.

Stop kidding yourself. You haven't come all this way just to stay for a few hours.

For more than half my life, Julia was the person dearest to me in the world. From our first day in nursery school, we were inseparable. I never had to ask if she was on my side; it was a given, as fixed as the sun rising in the east. We had more fun washing dishes together to pay our way through university than I've ever had at Forde's. I used to think you earned serious money for doing a serious job. In actuality, it's just to make the bullshit easier to swallow.

Julia was the one who made Italy happen. That glorious, hedonistic summer the year I turned twenty-one, before Ned, before work, before Guy and Agness. The summer I finally escaped from my father, the summer Julia and I claimed as our own, my first – and last – taste of real freedom.

I don't usually dwell on the past, but suddenly I miss being young; not for the taut skin and firm breasts and high-powered metabolism, though I wish I'd known then that that was as good as it gets, but for all the unwritten pages that lie ahead. I miss the belief that the world is essentially good, and that those parts of it that are not can still be changed.

It's not just my body that was more resilient then. My spirit was, too.

We pass through a small village on the outskirts of Rome, and jolt over cobble stones the size of dinner plates, as we reach the ancient Appian Way. Five minutes later, the driver slows to a halt in front of a pair of large wrought-iron gates with the number 270 written in white paint on the boulder to one side.

'*Duecento settanta*,' the driver says firmly as I hesitate in the back of the cab.

I pay him and climb out. I'm still standing in the driveway wondering if I should get back into the cab and go back to the airport after all when the driver roars off, making the decision for me.

There was no dramatic row or parting of the ways. After she decided to stay on in Rome at the end of that magical summer, Julia and I simply grew apart, divided in the end not by geography or lifestyle, nor even by Ned, but by motherhood: I had children, and she did not. We belonged to different tribes, each speaking a language the other couldn't understand. For a year or two after Agness was born, we tried; Julia sent her new goddaughter impractical Tiffany bangles and hand-painted porcelain cups, and I responded with gummy photographs and newsy letters, but we both knew the heart had gone from our friendship. All we had in common was the past. The last time I saw her was when she came back to England for her father's funeral, not long after Agness's second birthday. She didn't stay long.

The fact that she disapproved so strongly of Ned certainly didn't help. The only time her opinion ever chimed with Eleanor's was on the subject of my husband. Both tried to talk me out of marrying him, right up to the moment I walked down the aisle; quite literally, in Julia's case.

'He's a decent guy, Kate, but the two of you are running on completely different tracks,' Julia pleaded as she straightened my train in the church sacristy. 'It's not too late. Your career is just taking off, but he's never going to set the world on fire. You'll end up carrying him if you're not careful, and he'll hate you for it.'

'That's not fair. You don't know him like I do. He loves me. And I love him.'

'He's an escape route,' she said tartly, 'not a soul mate. If it wasn't for your father, you wouldn't look at him twice.'

She'd hit the nail on the head, of course. What I felt when I first saw Ned in the supermarket, struggling to pick up cereal boxes as fast as his small son could tumble them to the ground, wasn't love, or even lust, but the recognition that here was a man who needed me more than I needed him. As I stepped in to help, scooping up the child and organizing the man, I knew instinctively that I'd be safe with him. I was used to being needed. It was what *I* needed to survive.

Ned was the one who asked me out, but I sensed from the beginning that it would never go any further unless I took charge. Ned was still reeling from the surprise of finding himself married once; to have expected him to take the initiative a second time round would have been hoping for the moon. So it fell to me to organize our first date and our first weekend away, to raise the subject of living together and, later, marriage. I didn't mind; I'd had enough of being bossed around by a man to last me a lifetime, and had no intention of jumping from the paternal frying pan into the marital fire.

I didn't ever fool myself into thinking we were Romeo and Juliet, but Ned was practical and masculine. He could fix a car and build a kitchen cabinet and replaster a wall. An investigative reporter with the *Reading Evening News*, back then he had zeal and energy and determination. I thought Julia was wrong. We *were* a good match, even if our relationship wasn't the most passionate in the world. I *did* love him. We were comfortable, compatible. Ned would look after me without threatening my hard-won independence. He was proud of my fierce ambition and burgeoning career. I had no idea then that it had nothing to do with me. He just wanted someone to take care of him, to pick up where his indulgent mother had left off, and I stepped into the breach.

I love my husband, even now, despite the casual cruelty of his betrayal two months ago, or the recklessness that nearly wrecked all our lives. I know that, if asked, he'd say he loved me too. But the truth is that he has no idea who I am any more: how I feel, what I think. Worse still, he makes it clear over and over again that he doesn't care. Fifteen years of marriage and he still forgets that I hate chocolate. He's watched me dress and undress a thousand times, but couldn't begin to tell you my size, and wouldn't think to check the clothes in my wardrobe so he'd get it right. He believes sex is the answer to everything, but still pushes his fingers inside me just as I'm starting to get aroused, even though I've told him how much I hate it. He couldn't name a single person I work with, or the colour of my eyes. He gave me a fax machine for my last birthday, and he refuses to see why his failure to remember our anniversary matters. How can he love someone he doesn't know?

Julia was right. I've carried not just Ned but the entire weight of our marriage since the day I walked down the aisle.

I push open the old iron gates, still unprotected by locks or alarms, and close them behind me. Julia and I could never have afforded to rent a place in this upscale part of town if she hadn't bewitched the nephew of an old lady who owned a huge estate here. Vincenzo was clearly the apple of his aunt's eye, and thanks to him, the old lady offered us an artisan cottage on her property in return for a peppercorn rent and the dubious pleasure of our company as we occasionally wheeled her around the grounds. She must have been in her seventies back then. I wonder if she can possibly still be alive, or if all this now belongs to Vincenzo.

I stumble up the unpaved driveway in my court shoes, tripping occasionally in the dark. As far as I remember, it's about a quarter of a mile from the gates to the main house the old lady used to live in, and then another quarter of a mile to the artisan cottage at the rear of the estate. I can't see any lights in either the main house or the cottage. It occurs to me – a little late in the day – that the whole estate may have long since been sold, and that Julia may have moved. It's been three years since we even exchanged Christmas cards.

I'm suddenly aware just how tired I am. I have no idea what I'm going to do next if Julia isn't here. I don't have the energy to walk several miles to the nearest village and call another taxi. I don't know what possessed me to come here. I don't know what possessed me to do any of this.

The door to the cottage opens abruptly and a gold wedge

of light spills across the garden. Julia steps out onto the brick terrace of the cottage and looks intently into the inky darkness as if she can sense I'm here. I shrink back into the shadows, suddenly afraid, though I can't think why.

This is a mistake. I shouldn't have come. Once Julia sees me, it'll all be real. I need to go back home to my children, to Ned . . .

'Kate,' Julia calls across the moonlit lawn. 'I've been expecting you.'

Two days before

Ned

Kate's side of the bed is already empty when I wake up. Not unusual, even on a Saturday; she's always up first. At least once or twice a week she doesn't get home from work till long after I'm in bed. Days can go by with the two of us just passing in the night. I only know she comes home at all because the kitchen's been cleaned and the wet towels are no longer on the bathroom floor.

I get up and take a leak. Kate started the job at Forde's the week after we got back from our honeymoon. If it had been the week *before*, I swear I'd have left her standing at the altar. In fifteen years, we haven't made it through a single family holiday without my wife having to cut it short for work. Bank holidays, evenings, weekends: she's glued to her fucking iPhone. She likes to think she's doing it for us, but it's not like any of us give a shit if she's CEO of the bloody company. We'd settle for having her home once in a blue moon.

Giving my dick a brisk shake, I leave the yellow to

mellow and turn on the shower, waiting a moment for it to run warm. Might take the bike out later. It could use a run – the weather's been too piss-poor this winter to go anywhere on it. Not that Kate gives a damn. She hates my bloody motorbike.

I step into the shower, then swear and leap back out again.

'Kate!' I yell. 'What the fuck's happened to the hot water?'

Grabbing a towel, I wrap it round my waist and go in search of my wife. She'll be in her study, no doubt. *My* study in theory, except that Kate takes it over whenever she's home, regardless of whether I have an urgent deadline or not. Although, as she frequently points out, I haven't actually had an urgent deadline in all the years I've been freelance. I'm not exactly a hold-the-front-page Watergate kind of journalist; more your grubbing, get-it-to-us-when-you're-ready sort of hack.

The flowers are still lying on the piano, I notice, as I pass the dining room.

'The water's stone cold!' I exclaim, flinging open the study door. 'What's going on?'

'Didn't you call the plumber?' Kate says without looking up.

I hesitate. Now she comes to mention it, I vaguely remember her mentioning something about the boiler having a leak and asking me to give the plumber a call.

'Ned? You promised you'd take care of it.'

'You always deal with the plumber,' I say defensively. 'I thought you'd called him.'

'I asked *you* to handle it last week. I *told* you – I've got a lot on at work. You said you'd deal with it. "Consider it done" were your words, I believe.'

There are times when my wife makes me feel about two inches tall. She's worse than my fucking mother.

In the beginning, I liked the fact that Kate told me what to do. It was such a relief after Liesl's hippie flakiness and flower-power bullshit. I'd married my first wife for the mind-blowing sex; as soon as Guy was born, I realized that if I stayed with her any longer, she'd blow my mind in every other sense too.

The very first time Kate and I met, she saved my arse. It was my second access weekend after Liesl and I had split up. I had made the rookie mistake of taking Guy, who was then about sixteen months old, to the supermarket and had forgotten to lock him down in the trolley. Naturally, I had only turned my back for a minute and he had two shelves of cereal down. As fast as I stacked it back, he pulled the next row off, and I was soon up to my knees in a sea of Kellogg's. He was heading towards the pickle aisle with evil in his eye when a tall goddess with waist-length, honey-streaked dark blonde hair cut him off.

'This one yours?'

Huge tits and legs to die for. *Come to Papa.* 'Sorry. I'm still on probation when it comes to kids. Not literally,' I added quickly. 'I'm not a child-beater or anything.' Oh, Christ, even worse. 'I just meant I'm a bit new to flying solo. His mum and I only split up a couple of weeks ago. I haven't quite got used to going it alone.'

She laughed. 'We all have our bad days.'

'You don't understand. This is a *good* day. I'm Ned, by the way,' I added as she laughed again.

Her handshake was firmer than mine. 'Kate. Kate Drayton.'

I was still holding on lingeringly when Guy lunged for

the confectionery stand, scattering Mars Bars and Wrigley's to the four winds.

'Look, why don't I take him to the family room while you finish up?' Kate said, briskly scooping him up with one hand and righting the spilled stand with the other. 'We'll be fine for five minutes.'

'The family room?'

She pointed to the end of the store where there was a playroom filled with small children at various stages of anarchy. 'Come and get us when you're done.'

She took charge of our relationship just as efficiently. I asked her out, but she was the one who booked the restaurant – 'I know this great little place in Chinatown, and the manager owes me a favour' – and organized the Eurostar to Paris a month later for our introductory fuck. Within six months we were living together, and less than a year after we met, we were married and Agness was on the way. It seemed only sensible to go along with her suggestion that I quit the *Evening News* to go freelance (something I'd been banging on about for ages) and take care of the kids while she went out and earned the big bucks.

It was only much later that I realized I'd sacrificed my balls as well as my career.

I tighten my grip on the towel as icy water trickles down my back. 'Give me the plumber's number and I'll call him now.'

'Forget it. I'll call him myself,' Kate snaps. 'At least that way I know it'll get done. And tell Agness I want to see her. She owes me some chores before she goes to that party of hers.'

'What about your bloody mother?'

'What *about* my mother?'

'I suppose she'll be gracing us with her presence *again* this weekend?'

'I've told her she'll have to go to Lindsay for Sunday lunch instead,' Kate says tightly, turning back to her screen. 'I've got too much work to do.'

'Remind her to pack her cauldron,' I mutter.

'Ned, I really don't need this.'

'Fine. *Fine.* You just do whatever it is you do to keep the world turning. We'll fend for ourselves. As usual.'

I stalk upstairs, send a simmering Agness down to her mother, and fling on a polo shirt and my jeans from yesterday. Screw Kate. I *had* been planning just to take the bike into Salisbury. Now I'm going to head over to Winchester, and she can just deal with the kids on her own.

I'm not breaking my promise to her if she never finds out.

Two days before

Agness

This is *so* lame. Everyone else gets to do what they want on a Saturday, but I have to stay home and help my mother clean the house. Like, *seriously*. Actually get down on my hands and knees and scrub the floor! I've told her I could call ChildLine. You can't use your own children as slave labour. There's a law. We have *rights*. If someone doesn't stop her, she'll be shoving us up chimneys next. It's not fair; everyone else at school has a *proper* cleaner. Lucy Hemmings has a housekeeper *and* a maid, and she hasn't turned into a spoilt little brat. Well, not much of one, considering her Dad actually *knows* Simon Cowell. Seriously, my mother is paying thousands for my education, and she wants me to waste my time cleaning the loo? Has she *seen* it after Guy's been in there?

I turn on the tap and throw the toilet brush into the sink to soak. I don't care what she says. I'm not cleaning up after my brother. She can't make me do this. It's not the Dark Ages!

'Agness! Watch where you're going!'

Dad stomps down the hall wearing just a towel. *Gross.* Does no one ever think how I feel? This is my house, too. I should be able to walk around without running into my pervert father wearing practically no clothes *in public*.

'Your mother wants to see you,' Dad says as I pointedly cover my eyes.

'Well, I don't want to see her. Seriously, Dad. Could you, like, put some clothes on?'

Dad goes into their bedroom and picks his jeans up off the floor, then slams the door shut. I loll against it, picking at the chipped blue polish on my nails as the cat stalks past, his tail in the air.

'Are you going out?' I call.

'In a bit.'

'Where?'

He opens the door, buttoning his shirt. 'Thought I'd go over to Winchester, take the bike for a spin.'

'Can I come?' I plead. 'Oh, *please*, Dad. We could have a really nice time, just the two of us. It'll be like the old days. We hardly ever spend time together any more.'

I wrap my arms round his neck and give him my sweetest little-girl smile. Mum's been wise to me since I was about three, but I can still twist Dad round my little finger. He'll do anything for a quiet life.

But to my shock, he just kisses the top of my head and disentangles himself. 'Sorry, sweet-pea. Another time.'

'Da-a-ad! You can't just *leave* me here!'

'Don't be silly, Agness. I have things to do. Anyway, your mother's banned me from taking you on the bike again.'

I roll my eyes. My friends thought it was super-cool

when Dad gave me a lift to school on the bike a few weeks ago, but as soon as Mum heard about it, she had to play the heavy as usual and ruin everything.

'She doesn't have to know. I won't tell her. Please, Dad. She's only going to spend the day working – she won't even *notice* I'm not here.'

'Aggs, you promised you'd help out around the house so you could go to that party this evening. Your mother will kill me if I let you skive.'

I scowl. 'Even Cinderella had, like, mice to help her!'

'Your mum makes the rules, you know that.'

'Can't you talk to her?'

'Not when she's in one of her moods. Now come on, Aggs. Let me get going.'

I slouch out of the room. Naturally, Guy doesn't have to waste *his* weekend scrubbing toilets. He's always been Mum's favourite, which is, like, *so* unfair when he's not even her real son. He's Dad's kid from his first marriage to the Flake, aka Liesl. She's, like, this New Age freak, with weird hemp skirts and recycled tyre sandals. She doesn't believe in leather or make-up or deodorant, and she even uses one of those disgusting plastic cup things when she has her period instead of tampons, I saw her showing it to Mum once. (Clean, obviously; even Liesl isn't *that* yukky.) Frankly, I can't imagine her ever being married to Dad. My father would eat raw steak for breakfast if he could, and the only thing he's ever recycled is himself as a husband. Plus he's *beyond* disorganized. I love him and everything, but if he didn't have Mum to sort him out he wouldn't know how to get out of bed. How he and Liesl ever got it together to make a baby is beyond me.

Guy spends a weekend every month with the Flake. I

swear he only goes to top up his stash. Liesl believes in letting everyone 'make their own choices', and she grows weed in her back garden 'for medicinal purposes'. Guy says she hides it in with the tomato plants so the neighbours don't know. She may be nuts, but at least he gets out of this labour camp once in a while. I'm the one stuck here in solitary with Kommandant Kate.

I mooch into the kitchen to make myself a sandwich (seriously, does she expect me to do all this hard physical labour on an empty stomach?) and am just sitting down for, like, the first time in *hours* when Mum storms in.

'Agness! What the hell are you doing?'

'Eating breakfast. What does it look like?'

She snatches the sandwich out of my hand. 'You left the tap running in the basin upstairs with the toilet brush blocking the plug hole! There's water all over the floor. It's a miracle you haven't flooded the entire house!'

Seriously. If I could leave home *right now*, I would.

'So? At least the place would've been clean,' I mutter.

'Do you have *any* idea how much damage you could have caused?' my mother shouts. 'If the ceiling had come down it would've cost *thousands* to repair!'

'You're insured. Can I have my sandwich back, please?'

'No, you can't!' she shrieks, tossing it into the bin. 'I've told you before, peanut butter and jam is *not* breakfast! If I hadn't heard the water running upstairs, the kitchen would've been ruined! Do you realize how much it would cost to fix it? The insurance wouldn't begin to cover it! We'd have been living in a building site for *months*, the premiums would've gone through the roof – oh, for God's sake, why am I even bothering to explain?'

She said it. Defiantly, I get up and start making myself

a new sandwich. My mother immediately confiscates the bread.

'You're grounded,' she says furiously. 'You can forget about Sam's party tonight, or any other night!'

I fling my peanut-butter knife on the counter. 'That's not fair! Dad said I could go!'

'Well, you should've thought about that before you flooded the bathroom.'

'It's not like I did it on purpose!'

'Oh, really?' Mum snaps. 'If you think doing a job badly will get you out of doing it, young lady, you're sadly mistaken.'

'It's not up to you! Dad said—'

'Your father isn't here,' she says tightly. 'Frankly, if he'd said no to you a little more often when you were younger, we wouldn't be having this conversation now.'

'Yeah, well, maybe if you'd been *home* a little more often, you could've pointed that out.'

She jerks her head back like I've slapped her, and for a second I feel bad. Well, so what. *She's* the one who should feel bad. She's ruining everything. *Everyone'll* be at the party and I'll look like a complete loser if I can't go.

'Agness—'

'Leave me alone! I hate you! I wish I'd never been born!'

Sobbing, I run upstairs to my bedroom and slam the door. I don't bother to answer when she knocks at the door later and asks super-nicely if I want lunch. Only when I hear the sound of Dad's motorbike on the gravel do I close my laptop and slip downstairs to find him before Mum realizes he's back.

One-nil to me, I think later as I sit on the stairs and listen to them shouting in the kitchen. Serves Mum right for being so *selfish*. It's all right for her, she's *had* her life. She can't stop me from living mine just because hers is over.

Suddenly the yelling stops and Mum comes out of the kitchen and walks right past me without even looking in my direction. Her mouth is sucked in like a monkey's bum. She hates it when she doesn't get her own way.

I bounce up excitedly from the stairs. 'Dad?'

'You can go to the party,' he says tiredly.

I fling my arms round him. 'Thank you, Daddy! That's *so* cool! I promise I'll clean my room as soon as I get home! *And* the bathroom.'

'Never mind that. I went out on a limb for you, Agness, so you'd better not blow it. Just make sure you're ready to go when Mum comes to get you at eleven-thirty.'

'Eleven-thirty? Can't I stay till midnight? Everyone will think I'm such a baby if—'

'Don't push it, Agness. You're lucky she's letting you go at all.'

'Fine,' I mutter.

'And you'd better be on your best behaviour,' Dad warns. 'If you come home reeking of booze and cigarettes, I'll never hear the end of it with your mother.'

I widen my eyes. 'Daddy, it's not that sort of party! I promise I won't even have a sip of wine!'

As if.

'Eleven-thirty,' Mum snaps as she drops me at the end of Sam's road. 'If you're not right here, I'll come in and find you.'

'I'll be here,' I mutter. Anything but that.

The party's in full swing when I get to the house. Sam's

37

parents are in Morocco for Easter and have left her eighteen-year-old brother in charge, though *obviously* I didn't tell Mum that or she'd have, like, seriously flipped. Someone tweeted about the party, and now there's like a thousand people here. Some of them are a lot older than us. Nearly everyone's drinking and smoking, and for a moment I feel kind of freaked out.

'Aggs! Over here!'

Mica waves to me from the end of the terrace. I force myself to look bored as I walk over, like I come to this kind of party all the time. She hands me a plastic cup filled with some kind of home-made punch, and I knock some back, even though it tastes disgusting. There's nothing else on offer, and anyway I don't want to look lame.

'You see the hot guy in the Low Water T?' she whispers. 'He's *totally* eyeing you up right now.'

'Low Water suck,' I say without looking round.

'Seriously, Aggs, he's super-cute and he's been staring at you for, like, five minutes already.'

'Whatevs. Is Harry here yet?'

She shrugs. 'Inside.'

I finish the punch and then feel sick and wish I hadn't. 'I'm going to find him.'

'I don't know what you see in him,' Mica says crossly. 'He's just a kid. The guy in the Low Water T has his own car – I saw him parking it. I bet he'd take us out in it if you asked!'

Sometimes I wonder why I bother with Mica. She's been my BFF since nursery school, but she can be super-annoying sometimes. I *like* Harry. OK, he's kind of weird, and he dresses a bit EMO, but he's cool really. His mum died when he was a kid and his dad acts like he doesn't exist. He says he lets people think he might top himself any minute because it keeps them from bothering him. Maybe I should try acting suicidal. Might get Mum off my back.

It's totally dark and smoky inside the house. They're playing some kind of indie music so loud it's just, like, *noise*, and I can smell grass. I check out the rooms downstairs for Harry, then go upstairs. The nearest bedroom is locked, but voices are coming from the second, so I crack the door. A guy is standing by the bed with his pants down. Between his legs, a girl is sucking on his dick like it's an ice-lolly while he tells her she's a dirty bitch, over and over.

'Hey, baby,' the guy says, leering at me. 'You want some? Plenty to go round.'

I give him the finger and slam the door. I'm not a kid, I know about blow-jobs and a lot of other kinky stuff that wasn't in our Sex Ed classes, but seriously, he *pees* out of that thing, and if my brother is anything to go by, he probably has a shower, like, once a month. How can she put it in her *mouth*?

I finally track Harry down outside, sitting alone on a low wall a little way from the house. As I go over to join him, I pass Mica deep in a clinch with the Low Water guy.

'How's it going?' I ask, sitting down next to him.

He shrugs. Harry doesn't talk much. It's one of the reasons I like him.

'I was looking for you,' I say. 'I thought you were inside.'

Harry shrugs again. Then he reaches under his parka and pulls out two cans of ginger ale and hands one to me.

'Cool. Thanks.'

For a long while, we just sit in the dark and look out across the downs. I remember coming out to a place near here last summer with Mum for a picnic, before things got all weird between us. We often used to go for drives and not talk and it'd be *nice*, instead of strained and tense like it is now. These days, she's so stressed about her job and Gran and money and all that other stuff with Dad, she never has time to just hang out with me.

'Have you told your mum yet?' Harry asks suddenly.

It's like he's read my mind. 'No. I will, though. I just . . . you know. Need to wait for the right time.'

He nods. 'She's all right, your mum.'

Harry's the only person I've told about the paper I found on the floor of Mum and Dad's bedroom last week. It probably fell out of Dad's jeans or something. I don't know whether to give it to Mum or just put it back where I found it. I really wish I'd never read it. There are some things about your parents you just don't need to know. Harry says I've got to tell her, or at least leave it somewhere she'll see it. It's too big for me to hide, he says. Mum needs to be told. But things have only just started to get back to normal at home. Mum and Dad think I don't know why she's been crying so much lately, but I do. I'm a kid, not a moron. I can see what's happening under my own roof.

As it gets later, more people start arriving, friends of Sam's brother, and they're standing around smoking weed and drinking vodka and jeering, and it's getting a bit freaky, so Harry and I go inside to find Mica and the others. The other girls don't normally bother with Harry, but I make it clear he's with me, so they stay off his case. Mica even offers him a beer, which he doesn't take, but that's, like, a serious breakthrough. Sam takes us down to the games room in the basement, and we play a few games of foosball and basically just hang out and chill.

I'm curled up in a massive beanbag next to Harry and

kind of falling asleep when I hear shouting upstairs. I sit bolt upright and check my mobile. *Shit*. It's after midnight. My mother must be going *mental*.

'Agness Forrest! Where the hell are you?'

I'm already halfway up the basement stairs, but there's no stopping my mother.

'Do you have any idea what time it is?' she yells. 'I've been sitting in the car for thirty-five minutes waiting for you to come out, because I didn't want to come in and *embarrass* you in front of all your friends! *Thirty-five minutes!* D'you think I've nothing better to do than sit around half the night waiting for you?'

Everyone is watching. I totally want the floor to open up and swallow me. She's only ruined my entire life! I'll never be able to face anyone again. I just want to *die*!

My face burns as I push my way through the sniggering crowd towards the door, and my eyes sting with tears of humiliation and rage. I hate her! Why do I have to have such a bitch for a mother? I wish I was an orphan!

I'll never forgive her for this, *never*!

Kate

No mother abandons her family because her teenage daughter is thoughtless and selfish, even if the girl plays you off against her father with Machiavellian expertise. If that were the case, every child in the world would grow up motherless.

I'm not abandoning my family, or Agness, for that matter. I'm just taking a day or two to regroup.

A day or two? Absolutely not. I'll be on the first flight home.

Another day or two won't hurt. I'll be home by the end of the week. They won't even have time to miss me.

Footsteps echo on the outside staircase and I put down the photo of Agness and quickly knot the belt of my borrowed bathrobe. A moment later, the wooden door latch clicks up and Julia reverses into the room bearing a breakfast tray laden with fresh bread, olives, ripe tomatoes and hunks of fresh parmesan cheese.

'You didn't have to do this,' I exclaim.

She sets the tray on the dresser and flings open the

peeling blue shutters, flooding the narrow whitewashed room with sunlight. 'You didn't eat a thing after you arrived last night, and I know what plane food is like.'

I'm surprised to find I'm suddenly ravenous. 'Are these tomatoes from the garden?'

'And the olives.' She perches on the edge of the high single bed and picks up the creased school photo I've left on the side table. 'Is this your daughter?'

'Agness,' I mumble through a mouthful of fresh bread.

'Agness, of course. She's changed so much. I'd never have recognized her.'

'Well, she was two the last time you saw her,' I point out.

Julia returns my smile and hands me back the photograph. 'What's she like now?'

I brush the crumbs from my fingers and tuck the picture carefully into my purse. If Julia had asked me that question a year ago, my answer would have come easily. Bright, hardworking, full of enthusiasm, happy. As generous with her affections as her smiles. A child-woman with pictures of Robert Pattinson on the walls and rows of teddy-bears on her bed. She likes pink and *Mamma Mia!* and writing plays and performing all the parts for us. She spent six months nagging me to let her get her ears pierced, and when I finally agreed to it for her thirteenth birthday, held my hand as we went into the jeweller's to choose the small sapphire studs we'd decided on. Even though she's a Daddy's girl, she's also my best friend.

Now, I find myself searching for the right words. How to explain to Julia the overnight loss, as painful as bereavement, of the sweet-natured, affectionate daughter I cherished for thirteen years? I barely recognize the sullen stranger who's taken her place. The daughter I knew would never have told me she hates me, or despised me for working to put a roof over her head. She wouldn't have deliberately pitted her parents against each other, or made me feel like an unwelcome stranger in my own home. She wouldn't have set out to goad me, to turn everything I hold dear on its head out of spite.

I know it will pass, of course. It's her hormones; just a phase. She'll grow out of it as surely as she used to grow out of her clothes. In the meantime, I have to carry on biting my tongue when she comes downstairs looking like a cross between a ghoul and a hooker and tell myself she doesn't mean it when she says she wishes she'd never been born.

'She's a teenager,' I sigh. 'It's curable.'

Julia throws me a sharp look but leaves it there for now. 'How did you sleep?' she asks. 'I'd have given you back your old room, but it's full of my canvases.'

'Don't be silly. I'm fine here.' I hesitate, fiddling with the bowl of olives. 'Look. Ned hasn't called, has he?'

I can't help feeling an irrational wave of disappointment when she shakes her head.

'Did you *really* not give him a clue you were leaving?' she asks curiously.

'I didn't plan any of this,' I say defensively.

She smiles. 'Well. I doubt he'd think to look here.'

'Last night, when you said you were expecting me, I thought he must've called you. I was terrified he was already on his way.'

'I told you. I meant it in a general sense, not a literal one. I've known for years things weren't right between you and Ned. It was only a matter of time before you ended up here.' She gets to her feet. 'If it's all right with you, I'll leave you

44

to it. Alessio's waiting for me in my studio now. I need to show him some rough sketches so he can give them the OK.'

'Alessio?' I ask sharply.

'Oh yes. Of course. I'd forgotten about that. Yes, Alessio Ricci. He's mellowed since he got married,' she adds. 'He and his wife moved back to the village after their first son was born, to be near his parents. They've got three boys now, I think.'

I absorb this. It doesn't hurt. It's been nearly twenty years, after all, and it was a summer romance, not Hepburn and Tracy. But I feel a brief pang of pity for my heartbroken twenty-one-year-old self.

'Alessio opened up an office in the village a couple of years ago,' Julia adds. 'He commissioned some artistic renderings of a development he was working on and came to me. We've worked together quite a few times since then. You'll probably run into him if you hang around.'

I'll need something new to wear, I think instantly and chide myself for it.

'What about you?' I ask, quickly changing the subject. 'Ever come close to settling down?'

'Not at the moment. It took me a while to get over you, but I managed it,' she teases with a graceful smile. 'I lived with a man, Marcello, for nine years, but we split up eighteen months ago.'

'I'm sorry.'

'Don't be. He wanted kids, and I didn't.' Julia opens the stiff wooden bedroom door and starts down the external staircase. 'Take your time,' she calls. 'I'll be in the studio if you need me.'

I finish my breakfast, mopping up the last olive with a piece of bread, and stack the empty dishes neatly on the tray. Gathering my crumpled clothes from yesterday and the towel Julia has left out for me, I'm about to go downstairs to the bathroom when my phone beeps on the dresser.

I freeze, my stomach alive with butterflies. I haven't yet heard from Ned, but it's only a matter of time before the bomb drops. I've already had four increasingly irate emails from Paul Forde; I haven't dared listen to his voicemails. I urgently need to call him back and tell him I'm taking a few unscheduled personal days before my career detonates in my face. He won't like it, though I suppose it's marginally preferable to my vanishing off the face of the earth without a word. But somehow I can't bring myself to do it. It's as if making contact with the outside world will somehow open a portal through which I can be reached and yanked back to the chaos. I can feel my throat closing and my chest tightening at the thought.

My mobile beeps again. Gingerly I pick it up and check the incoming number as it goes to voicemail. It's not Ned, of course, but another message from Paul. Stupid of me to think my husband would actually *miss* me. Clearly that's not going to happen until he runs out of beer or feels randy again.

I give myself a mental shake. I should be relieved that I haven't sparked a panic at home, not piqued that my absence hasn't been noticed. I'll send Ned a quick text later, and with any luck I'll be back in London in a few hours, before he's any the wiser.

Surely the whole point of leaving was to make *him wiser?*

This isn't some sort of childish game. I didn't leave to prove a point.

Then why did *you leave?*

I deliberately leave my phone on the dresser and go down to the small bath house set a few metres behind the main cottage. Like my bedroom, it's as simple and ascetic as a nun's cell, the plain white walls unadorned apart from a carved wooden crucifix and an icon of the Virgin Mary. Julia never used to be religious; perhaps they came with the house.

The shower is no more than a high tap over the stained claw-foot tub. There's no curtain, and I quickly discover it's not necessary as I struggle to rinse shampoo from my hair in the feeble trickle of tepid water the tap produces. I'd forgotten the inadequacies of Italian bathrooms. Hard to believe this is the same country that had perfected aqueducts and under-floor heating while the inhabitants of Albion were still squatting round campfires and daubing themselves with woad.

When I dress, I feel instantly grimy and dishevelled again in yesterday's clothes. My knickers haven't quite dried after I rinsed them out, and my wool suit, appropriate for a cold, rainy spring day in London, is far too heavy for Rome. I wish I had time to buy a clean shirt to travel home in. Julia's clothes are several sizes too small for me to borrow, even if she had anything remotely suitable for me to wear back to work. I do my best to make myself presentable using the few bits of make-up rattling around in the bottom of my handbag, then take the tray down to the kitchen, where I find Julia cranking the handle of an old-fashioned coffee grinder.

'Espresso?' she shouts over the noise.

I clear a space on the counter for the breakfast tray with one hand, scattering several skinny cats who've been lolling on the work surface, then pull out a rush-seated kitchen chair, dislodging yet another offended feline. 'Tea, if you have it.'

She finishes grinding. 'This is Italy, Kate, not Tunbridge Wells.'

'Espresso, then.' I smile as a tiny ginger kitten leaps onto my lap and starts kneading my thighs. 'Has Alessio gone?'

'He was sorry to miss you, but he had a meeting. He'll be back on Friday, if you're still around.'

She boils some coffee on the ancient enamel stove and then puts the dented iron coffee pot and a couple of cups on a small tray. She leads the way to a shady cobbled courtyard at the back of the cottage, bounded on two sides by the kitchen and bath house, and on the other two by high, dense hedges. I scoop up the ginger kitten and follow her. The courtyard is much smaller than I remember, overgrown with bougainvillea and lilacs, their heady scents filling the small space. We settle in a pair of wrought-iron chairs beneath vines already laden with tiny grapes. An old grey-muzzled black Labrador resting in the shade stirs briefly and then rests its heavy head back on its paws.

I sip my espresso, the tension in my body easing as the kitten settles himself in my lap. For a few moments I'm Kate Drayton again, single and carefree: no ties, no responsibilities. I have all the time in the world for espresso and olives from the garden and soaking up the mellow, goldwashed sunshine. For the moment, however long it lasts, I don't have to answer to anyone.

'Now,' Julia says gently. 'I think it's time you told me what's happened, don't you?'

The day before

Eleanor

I stand at the turn of the staircase, carefully holding on to the banister. I don't like to take matters into my hands like this, but Katherine's left me no choice. There's really only so much of Lindsay one can take. If Katherine were a good daughter, I wouldn't have to go to such extraordinary lengths. She has no one but herself to blame.

Lindsay was James's favourite child, but never mine. Frankly, my younger daughter bores me to death; she hasn't half Katherine's brains, and none of her spunk. She scraped through teacher-training college, and then took a job teaching at a third-rate public school (arranged by James not long before he died). Even at this she failed, getting pregnant by a married teacher before being summarily dumped by the lover and then fired by the school for bringing its name into disrepute. I was rather sorry James didn't live long enough to see that.

But Lindsay is malleable and obedient, so I make the best of things. I stay at her dreary council flat when the loneliness overwhelms me because it's better than rattling around my own home alone. Unlike Kate, she doesn't complain she's too busy when I ask her to take me to the dentist or drive me to bridge, and she cooks the kind of plain, wholesome food I like. But I don't appreciate having to share a bathroom with a seven-year-old boy who seems incapable of aiming *into* the lavatory and leaves Lego all over the floor for me to step on in my bare feet. Lindsay has no concept of discipline; her son is utterly unruly. And she's so desperately *needy*. Dealing with her constant desire for attention is quite draining. It's as if I don't count at all. Life is so much more congenial at Katherine's. Particularly as she's so rarely *there*.

When Katherine's children were younger, I was welcome in her home. My son-in-law may have been looking after the children in theory, but in practice, *I* was the one who dropped them off at ballet and football, helped them with history projects, babysat when both their parents were off working. Free from James's malevolent shadow, I loved my grandchildren in a way I hadn't dared love my daughters. And Katherine knew her husband's limitations; she was *grateful* to have me to stay. These days, you'd think I was bringing the Black Death across her threshold.

My stockinged toes curl over the edge of the top stair. Katherine really should have helped me buy that lovely ground-floor apartment in Salisbury. At my age, I shouldn't have to deal with stairs. I can't believe she couldn't manage the bigger mortgage, given the amount she's earning. She was just being contrary.

With my free hand, I pat my cardigan pocket. Wouldn't do to lose my phone now.

I close my eyes, take a deep breath and let go of the banister.

*

Katherine isn't the child I should have had, because James Drayton isn't the man I should have married. I knew the wedding was a mistake even as I walked up the aisle, but at just eighteen years old I had little choice in the matter. My parents didn't approve of the local boy I loved, so they bundled me into marriage with my father's business partner, and that was that.

James wasn't a bad man. I didn't love him, but that's not necessarily a prerequisite for a good marriage. The problem was, James *did* love me. Quite horribly, in fact; and he never forgave me for it.

Perhaps if I hadn't been quite so young, I'd have known better than to spurn him so openly. I'd have understood how to handle his ardent approaches in bed without humiliating him, and to turn his passion to my advantage. Who knows, maybe I might have learned to love him back, given time. But what girl of eighteen either knows or cares about such things?

At forty-one, James seemed like Methuselah to me, so grey and lined and *old* in comparison with Robert, the boy I loved. When Robert kissed me, I felt it in every part of my young body: my nipples hardened, my legs buckled, and I burned with hot, throbbing need. At James's clumsy touch, I felt nothing but revulsion. Robert was strong and virile, and if he was penniless, he still made my heart beat faster and my breasts ache. How could James, obsessed with his investments and his businesses, dry and dull as ditchwater, possibly hope to compete?

But my father was teetering on the edge of bankruptcy. His property business had been driven to the wall by a mixture of bad luck and foolishness; he owed far more than he could hope to repay in two lifetimes. When James Drayton offered to invest in his company in return for 'encourage-ment' in his marital hopes, my father leaped at the chance. Knowing he'd had no choice didn't make his betrayal sting any less.

London might be swinging, but decent girls still obeyed their parents in those days. Robert called me a coward and ran off to join the army. Bitter and lovesick, I determined to make my husband as unhappy as I was. I was more successful than I could have hoped: his ardour quickly coalesced into cold, implacable hatred, and with divorce out of the question, our marriage became a war of attrition. Every night, James came to my bed to demand his rights. I lay there as cold and stiff as a board, refusing to give him the satisfaction of letting him see me cry. With no job, and as yet no child to distract me, I had plenty of time to sit at home and brood.

And think about Robert, the man I *should* have married.

A year later, Robert came back. He gave me a simple choice: leave James now and run away with him, regardless of the consequences, or I would never see him again.

I had twenty-four hours to choose. I was up all night, literally sick with fear and indecision. The thought of spending the rest of my life without Robert, locked into this appalling marriage for ever, was unbearable. But if I left, James would withdraw his financial backing, and my par-ents would be ruined. He'd fight divorce tooth and nail; in the end, I might win my freedom, but I'd end up penniless.

Leave James, and I would destroy those I loved. Stay, and I destroy myself.

When he returned for my answer, I chose Robert. As James watched, white-faced with shock and anger, I ran upstairs to throw skirts and blouses into my suitcase, dizzy with the enormity of what I was doing. Once more I was overwhelmed with nausea, and yet again ran to the bathroom to vomit.

And then realized I'd never be able to leave.

The balance of power in our marriage changed for ever with my daughter's birth. James had won, and he went on winning. I couldn't ever leave him and risk losing my child. So I bit my tongue and accepted defeat as graciously as I could. When Katherine was born, I let James name her after his viper of a mother and ignored his snide remarks about the baby having Robert's eyes. I knew he didn't really believe she was Robert's child; for a start, the dates didn't fit, and as she grew older, it became obvious she was James's spitting image. True, he greeted Katherine's arrival with complete indifference, but that was hardly surprising. James was a cold man at best, and babies are the province of women, not men. I told myself he would show interest in his daughter when she was old enough to become interesting.

But three years later, when Lindsay was born and James fell in love at first sight, I realized James's dislike of Katherine *was* personal.

James had discovered the best way to hurt me was through my elder daughter, and he never missed a chance to twist the knife. He lavished time, money and affection on Lindsay, but never so much as glanced Katherine's way. Her Father's Day gifts went unopened, her childish paintings were consigned to the bin. If Lindsay brought home a C, she was celebrated as if she'd won a Nobel Prize. Katherine earned straight As year after year, but never received a single word of praise. The harder she worked to make her father proud, the more he criticized her.

I never interfered. I loved Katherine, of course I did; but she was also the anchor trapping me in this miserable marriage, the reason I'd lost Robert. And so I kept silent and watched my daughter struggle to understand why she didn't deserve to be loved.

Only once did I speak up: when she brought Edward home. I knew he wasn't the man for her, and was initially confused by James's uncharacteristic enthusiasm for the match; he even offered to pay for the wedding, the first time he'd ever willingly given his elder daughter anything. But then I realized James could see in Edward precisely what I saw. James realized his prospective son-in-law was a reed that would break in the wind. He'd weigh Katherine down, stop her from following her dreams. I couldn't bear my daughter to follow me into a dead-end marriage with a man who didn't deserve her. Katherine was twenty-three and had more courage in her little finger than I'd ever possessed. She'd defied her father to put herself through university, and again when she took the summer off to travel to Italy. The world was her oyster, if she wanted it.

I did everything I could to dissuade her from marrying Edward, but without success. 'You've never taken an interest in anything I've done before,' she said coldly. 'Why should I listen to you now?'

It has given me no satisfaction to be proved right.

'It could've been a lot worse,' I tell Katherine brightly when she comes to collect me from the hospital on Sunday afternoon. 'No bones broken, that's the main thing.'

Katherine frowns. 'You still haven't explained what really happened, Eleanor. Did you have some sort of turn? Were you feeling dizzy?'

'I'm perfectly fine, dear. Ask the doctors. I tripped, that's all. Loose carpet probably. Lucky I had my phone on me to call for help, or it could've been a lot worse. I did *tell* you I was having trouble with stairs.'

Katherine eases my wheelchair down the ramp towards the hospital car park. 'Well, obviously you'll have to come home with us now,' she sighs. 'I can give you Agness's bedroom, and she can take the sofa-bed in the den.'

'Oh, I couldn't, dear. I wouldn't want to put you out . . .'

'Eleanor, what will put me out is having to drop everything and dash to the hospital on another mercy run,' she says crisply. 'I need you at home, where someone can keep an eye on you.'

'I'm not a child, Katherine.'

'A *child* would be easier to deal with. A *child* would do as it's told.'

'How did Agness enjoy her party last night?' I ask disingenuously.

Katherine jolts the wheelchair to a halt. 'Clearly you know the answer to that,' she says tightly.

'She's fourteen, dear. You can't expect to wrap her in cotton wool, not these days. Of course she wants a little freedom and independence, it's only natural. She works hard at school, she deserves a little fun. All work and no play, remember.'

'Agness certainly *doesn't* work hard at school,' Katherine snaps, 'as you'd know if you ever actually read her school reports. As for all work and no play, I brought home straight As every single term and I wasn't allowed to join the Youth Club, never mind stay out at raves all night! She's *fourteen*, Eleanor! I was still playing with dolls at that age!'

'Things are different these days, dear. You have to move with the times. You can't get stuck in the past, Katherine, or you'll be left behind.'

Katherine grasps the wheelchair handles and pushes me through the car park to her ancient Land Rover with rather more vigour than necessary. I realize she didn't have the easiest time growing up, but this sort of chippy grudge-bearing does no one any good.

Nor am I in the least surprised that Agness is behaving badly, once I have a taste of the atmosphere at home. One could cut the tension with a knife.

'This isn't good for the children,' I tell Katherine as Edward finally storms out of the house following a taut, whispered 'discussion' in the kitchen that fools no one. 'No wonder Agness is upset. I may not always have agreed with your father, but we never argued in earshot of you children. We showed a united front.'

'No, *you* never argued with Dad,' Katherine says bitterly. 'You left that to me.'

'You get more flies with honey than vinegar, Katherine. You never did learn.'

She slams the empty kettle on the stove. 'Would you like to know what Ned and I were arguing about?' she challenges.

'I'd prefer not to get involved, dear. It's none of my business.'

'It never is, is it? Look the other way, pretend everything is fine. That's you all over.'

'I'm not one to air my dirty linen—'

'Ned wants me to put you in a home,' she interrupts fiercely. 'He wants us to sell the house I bought you so we can pay off some of our debts. I'd say *that's* your business, wouldn't you?'

'He's just upset,' I say serenely. 'He doesn't mean it. Where would I live?'

She stares at me for a long moment.

'How do you do it?' she demands finally.

'Do what, dear?'

'Sail through life without ever having to get your hands dirty. Letting everyone else take care of you, take care of the *mess* and the *chaos*.' Her body is rigid with anger. 'When was the last time *you* worried about paying the mortgage, Eleanor? When did *you* last lie awake wondering if you were doing the right thing sending your son to a school you couldn't really afford, when he'd probably be much happier at the local comprehensive anyway? You've never taken responsibility for anything in your life. You've never even held down a *job*!'

Her voice shakes; I can't determine whether it's with fury or tears.

'You've no idea what it's like to work a seventy-hour week just to keep a roof over your family's head when you'd much rather be at home making jam tarts with your babies! You sit there like a cuckoo with your beak open, take, take, *take*, expecting me to buy you a house, pay your bills, jump whenever you snap your fingers. Lindsay's just as bad! *Katherine's the one with the big job, she can afford another set of school fees.* When do *I* get any say in the matter? What if I don't *want* the big job any more? What if I want to give it all up and go and . . . go and keep bees?'

'Do you *want* to keep bees?'

'No, of course I don't want to keep bees!'

'Then why mention them?' I reach for my biscuit and dunk it in my cooling tea. 'We all make choices in life, Katherine. And we all have to live with them.'

'But that's just it! I *didn't* have a choice! Dad didn't give me a free ride like Lindsay! I had to fight for everything. And you never stuck up for me, not *once*!'

'I really don't see what any of this has to do with me.'

Her voice is scathing. 'Of course you don't.'

I sip my tea. Katherine is more like her father than she imagines. Best to ride the storm and let it blow itself out.

'Don't you think I'd like to stay at home baking pies while someone else worried about how to pay for the apples?' Katherine exclaims. 'Every day I go into work *sick* with worry in case this is the day I'm fired and I have to come home and yank Guy and Agness out of school. Do you know how long we could survive without my salary before we lost the house – yours too? Four months. That's it. I've got enough put by for four months. I spend my life battling to keep my head above water at work, and then I come home and have to start all over again. Sort out the car insurance. Check the council tax has been paid. Book the cat into the cattery while we're away this summer. Make Guy an appointment at the dentist. Organize the boiler to be serviced. It never stops!' She sucks in a deep breath. 'I'm just a glorified skivvy and no one ever, *ever* offers to help!'

My daughter needs to learn to count her blessings. She's pushing forty, and she's suddenly realized her life hasn't turned out the way she thought it would. Well, we could all say that.

'Do you,' I ask equably, 'ever actually *ask*?'

Kate

'It had nothing to do with Eleanor,' I insist. 'What happened was hardly *her* fault.'

'Oh, I think Eleanor has to shoulder some of the blame,' Julia says evenly.

Eleanor has spent her life wrapped in a cocoon like a spun-glass ball, too precious to be exposed to real life. It would be foolish to expect her to change now.

Why did she never, ever speak up for me? Not once? What did I do that was so wrong?

Despite myself, I start to cry again. I press the heels of my hands into my eyes, already ashamed of my emotional meltdown. Until now, I haven't told a soul what happened two months ago; apart from Julia, Ned is the only other person who knows. I don't whine or cry; certainly not in front of other people. I pull myself together and get on with things. I'm a *coper*. 'Ned knows how much pressure I'm under,' I mumble. 'It's not like I wanted Eleanor to come and stay. It's bad enough Agness kicking up such a fuss about giving up her bedroom without Ned taking her side.'

Julia picks up the tissue box and silently hands it to me.

'This is ridiculous.' I blow my nose firmly. 'I'm so sorry. I don't know what's the matter with me . . .'

'Kate. Darling. Quite aside from what happened in February, at the ripe old age of not-quite-forty you've just done something utterly impulsive and selfish for the first time in your entire life. You haven't thought about the effect it might have on your husband and children. You haven't even put work first. You've behaved completely out of character, and now you're wondering if you've lost your mind.' She sits back with a sigh. 'I'm not surprised. It'd be a miracle if you weren't in a mess.'

I screw the tissue up into a ball. 'I hate to ask, but do you think you could take me to the airport? Or drop me in the village so I can get a taxi? If I leave now, I can probably make it home in time for dinner . . .'

'Everything's suddenly fine, is it?'

I drop my eyes to my lap, nervously shredding the tissue into pieces.

'You can't brush this under the carpet,' Julia says softly. 'Less than ten weeks ago, you lost someone you loved. Maybe it was for the best, but it's still a major deal. Ned should never have reacted the way he did—'

'That had nothing to do with me leaving,' I say sharply.

'Of course it did. It's the only reason. You haven't forgiven him,' she says calmly.

I should never have told Julia the truth. She knows me too well.

'Thousands of women have it much worse than me, and they don't just down tools and run away,' I protest. 'I don't know why I got into such a state. Not enough sleep, I expect. Working too hard.'

'Look, Kate. I'm not going to tell you what to do. You can tell yourself you're under pressure at work and the kids and your mother and Ned all drive you mad, but we both know that's not why you're here. Everyone thinks about walking out of their lives now and again, but most of us never actually do it. Something tipped you over the edge.' She sighs. 'What happened to you was *huge*. You've been burying your head in the sand for weeks, but sooner or later, you'll have to deal with it. Until you do, there's no point going back.'

I can't go back. I feel dizzy with fear at the mere thought. I drop my head between my knees. I can't breathe. *I can't get any air . . .*

'Kate? Kate, are you OK?'

Julia thrusts a glass of water into my hand. I gulp it gratefully, forcing the panic back down. *Don't let the fear win.*

'Oh, Kate. Look at you.' She puts her hand over mine and smiles gently, her blue eyes filled with pity. 'You're a wreck. What use do you think you'd be, going home like this? You'll end up having a nervous breakdown. You can't go anywhere until you sort yourself out.'

I take another sip of water as the little ginger kitten rearranges himself on my lap, his tiny chest throbbing like a motorized toy. Absently, I stroke his ears. I've always despised people who couldn't cope. Since when did I become one of them?

'I'm sure Ned and the kids can cope without you for a day or two,' Julia presses. 'Why don't you just take a little time to get your head together before you go rushing home? A couple of days to yourself might be all you need.

Then you can go back and face the music. Doesn't that make more sense?'

'But what about the children? I can't just *abandon* them.'

'You're not abandoning them. Come on, Kate. They're teenagers, not babies. I think they'll survive a few days without Mummy there to hold their hands. It'll be good for them. Anyway, it's not like they'll be on their own. Ned and Eleanor will be with them.'

'A few days,' I echo.

'At least stay till the weekend. Blame me if you want to. You can tell Ned I had some sort of emergency.'

'I don't want him to know I'm here,' I say quickly. 'He'll have a fit if he thinks I've dumped everything in his lap to come out here on some sort of girls' weekend.'

Julia snorts. 'If you ask me, it's about time he had everything dumped in his lap, but have it your way. Tell him you had to go away on business, and let your boss know you've taken a few days off so they don't compare notes.' She picks up our empty coffee cups. 'It'll be OK, Kate. Stop making such a drama out of this.'

She's right. I'm blowing this way out of proportion. Everything got on top of me for a bit, and I snapped. Walking out the way I did was a bit sudden and unorthodox, but at the end of the day, I'm just spending a couple of days with my oldest friend, catching up on the past and reliving a few happy memories. No need to make such heavy weather of it. Of course it doesn't mean I can't cope.

'As long as I'm home before the weekend,' I say, suddenly feeling better than I have in a long time. 'Ned would never cope with the kids on his own.'

Still stroking the ginger kitten, I follow Julia back into the kitchen with the tray. She's right. Agness and Guy are teenagers now, not babies. They don't really need me. They'll probably enjoy the freedom for a few days.

I don't suppose they'll even notice I'm gone.

Day zero

Guy

You can't take a frigging crap in this house without being interrupted. Cursing under my breath, I stop texting as my sister hammers on the bathroom door.

'Get a move on!' Agness yells. 'You're not the only one who wants to take a shower!'

Hunching my shoulders, I ignore her and turn my attention back to the small screen, my thumbs moving rapidly across the keys.

Need gear. Got any?

Sorry bro all out hv u tried Ben?

No go. Any1 else?

MayB. Get back 2U l8r.

Fuck. It'll do my head in going to school without a buzz on. I need something to take the edge off.

I chew my lip. Maybe my mum'll have some over at

hers. I meant to bring some back this weekend, but I forgot. Bet Liesl will have a bit of weed, at least. Can't hurt to ask.

Agness gives the door a final bang and thumps down the stairs. 'Mum! Guy's locked himself in the bathroom! Can I use yours?'

I put the phone down and yank off a fistful of paper. If I get out of the house before Kate notices, I can take the bus into town and then walk to Mum's instead of going to school. Kate won't know any different.

Turning on the tap, I stick my head under it for a few seconds so Kate'll think I've taken a shower, and rub some toothpaste round my gums. Dad's left his aftershave on the side of the sink; it stinks worse than cat piss, but it'll hide the fact that I'm wearing the same rank T-shirt I've slept in for the last two days, so I slap some on. At least I don't have to wear a fucking uniform like Agness. It's bad enough dealing with the psychos in my year without getting jumped on my way home by the losers in the village because I'm dressed like Little Lord Fauntleroy.

The kitchen's empty when I get downstairs. I open the fridge and chug half a pint of milk straight from the plastic container, then peer at the crammed shelves. For a moment I think I'm SOL, but lurking behind Gran's weird bionic yoghurts and Agness's low-fat low-sugar low-fucking-taste crap is a box containing the remains of a pepperoni pizza from last week. I pull it out and open it. There's at least a third left; it's got a bit of blue fuzz round the edges, but that's, like, penicillin, right? It can't be any worse for you than the yoghurts.

Standing over the sink, I munch the pizza and stare out of the window. Kate's chasing the cat round the garden in her fancy wool suit and a pair of wellies, trying to get the dumb furball to come in for breakfast. Gran must've let it out again. Stupid fucking animal. One of these days it'll end up as roadkill.

Kate looks up and beckons to me to come and help. I pretend I haven't seen her and help myself to another slice of cold pizza. Maybe I should text Ivan. We could go and hang out at the Mall, or maybe even take off for the coast. I quite fancy spending the day slinging rocks from the pier.

My phone buzzes. Wiping my hand on my jeans, I slide it out of my back pocket. My thumb hesitates over the name illuminated on the small screen. *Monkeyboy69*. Who the hell is that?

Warily, I click on the message. *Hope ur dick shrivels up ponce.*

Angrily I hit delete. Seconds later, another email appears in my inbox. *Fuckin loser u deserve 2 die.* Arseholes can't even spell.

The phone spazzes in my hand as more messages hit in quick succession.

Y dont u just kill yurself now.
Yur mutha sucks cock.
U sad fuck its all ova 4U now.

Delete. Delete. Delete.

I don't recognize any of the user names, but that doesn't mean anything. A few clicks and you can be anyone. I know who's really behind it. I could change my own email and phone number, but what's the point? I've done that before, and sooner or later they always find me again.

A message appears from Ivan and I open it.

A-holes tweeted ur number.
Sorry dude. Wanna borrow my fone?

Screw em, I text back.
Meet me at Eddies in the Mall?
Cant. Rents on my case.

Fuck. Ivan's dad is OK, but his mother's a frigging Nazi. She's on his case twenty-four-seven like a fucking stalker. He won't be going anywhere this morning but double chemistry.

I turn my phone on to vibrate and slide it back into my jeans. The Mall's out; no point going on my own.

There's a whoosh of cold air as the back door opens and Kate comes in, the cat squirming in her arms. 'Can you feed Sawyer for me, Guy? He's been out all night again. He must be starving.'

'That's Agness's job.'

'Come on, Guy. Agness is already upset over giving her room to Gran. Don't make my life more complicated than it has to be.'

Scowling, I open the cupboard under the sink and get out a tin of Whiskas. I hate that fucking cat. A couple of years ago, I sneaked up on him when he was sleeping with the vacuum cleaner hose and sent him yowling four feet in the air. He retaliated by spraying all over my favourite leather jacket like a fucking skunk. These days, he stays out of my way, and I stay out of his.

I fork some of the goop into his bowl and mix in some dry biscuits. He gives me a dirty look, then stalks over to the bowl, taking his time.

'Have you had breakfast?' Kate asks me.

I shrug.

'How about some porridge? Or eggs? You've got time for an omelette if you're quick.'

'Already ate,' I mutter.

'Cold pizza? That's not breakfast.' She opens the fridge. 'Come on, let me make you some—'

I grab my jacket from the back of a chair. 'Gotta go. I'll be late.'

'I told you I'd give you a lift this morning. You don't need to take the bus.'

She doesn't get it. My life *sucks*. I don't need my *mother* – stepmother, whatevs – dropping me off like a fucking mummy's boy at the school gates.

'I'll take you now,' Kate says, picking up her bag. 'Dad'll drop Agness off later. Gran wants me to pick up some gloves for her at lunchtime, so I could use an early start myself to get a jump on the day.'

Fuck it. I pick up my backpack and steam out to the car. I'll have to sneak out by the fire escape after registration. Maybe Ivan and I can go across the back fields to the abandoned farmhouse near the chalk pit and hang out. No one'll notice if we're not there after lunch; they never take afternoon roll call.

'There's lasagne in the oven for tonight,' she says over her shoulder as she reverses her clapped-out old Land Rover out of the drive. 'You'll need to put it in at a hundred and eighty for forty-five minutes – I've written it down. I've got a big meeting this afternoon, so I may not be back in time for dinner.'

'With that wanker who's trying to steal your job?'

She glances at me in surprise. 'I wish your father paid as much attention. Yes, with the wanker, as you put it, who's trying to steal my job.'

'You'll be there tomorrow night for my presentation?' I blurt suddenly. Heat rises in my cheeks. I hadn't meant to say anything.

'It's tomorrow?'

'Doesn't matter if you aren't,' I mumble, embarrassed. 'It's only a stupid PowerPoint thing.'

'Of course I'll be there,' Kate says warmly. 'I'll have to move a couple of things, but I promised, didn't I? A promise is a promise.'

I settle back in my seat, feeling a bit better. Kate's all right. I love my mum, obviously, but Kate's the one who takes care of stuff and gets things done. She makes sure I've got clean rugby kit, and she gets it when I tell her I *need* a new pair of Nikes. When I was on the cross-country running team, she came to every single meet, even when it was pissing with rain. Dad didn't even bother coming to the championship race. Kate's about the only grown-up who's never let me down.

When all the crap started going down at school a few months ago, I told Vance, my year advisor. I figured he'd, you know, keep an eye out. Maybe have a quiet word with some of the bastards without letting on he knew the score. Instead, Vance makes this big song and dance during our advisory class about 'valuing each other' and 'non-aggressive dispute resolution' and all the rest of the bullshit, and looks at me, like, the whole time he's talking. It got a thousand times worse after that.

Vance is on top of me the second Kate drops me off, and I don't get a chance to sneak out across the playing fields after assembly. But it means Dessler and his mates can't get near me either, so I'm OK for now.

At break, I catch up with Ivan by the lockers. 'I'm out of here. You coming?'

'Nah. I've gotta get my biology project sorted.' He slams his locker door shut. 'Come on, Guy. You can't keep skipping school. Dessler isn't worth it.'

'Forget it. Catch you later.'

'Guy—'

I walk away from him, waving without turning round to show there's no hard feelings. But the fact is, it's not his arse on the line. He's not the one having his head shoved down the crapper every frigging day.

I don't intend to wait around for Dessler to make his move. I'll head out to the old farmhouse and hang out for a while. Maybe Ivan will grow some balls and join me later. I don't have any weed, but I've got a stash of Jack Daniel's and some fags and porn hidden in the abandoned place. Better than double frigging chemistry, I know that much.

I almost make it.

Dessler's waiting for me in the corridor by the fire escape, leaning against the grey wall. I glance desperately over my shoulder as he steps forward, but I already know there's no way back.

His sidekicks grin nastily at me as I back up, my head swivelling as I try to keep all four bastards in view.

'What's the matter?' Dessler sneers. 'Looking for Teacher?'

I raise my chin. Fuck 'em. I can take whatever they dish out.

Seconds later, they're bundling me into the girls' bathroom. Break is over, so it's empty. I brace myself for another dunk in the shitter, praying some minger hasn't left a used tampon lying around. But before I realize what's going on, they bend me over the sink instead and a wad of bog roll is shoved in my mouth to stop me from crying out. One of them twists both my arms painfully behind my back, while another yanks down my jeans. I struggle as my arse cheeks are pulled apart, choking on the wad of paper in my mouth. There's an agonizing, invasive pain and I almost pass out.

'Did you get it all?' Dessler asks. 'Cool. That'll do.'

Someone kicks the back of my knees and I collapse, banging my forehead on the basin. Then, as quickly as they came, they're gone.

Slowly I spit out the paper and pull the bloodied toilet brush from my arse, crying with pain and humiliation. Snot runs down my face, mingling with blood where I've bitten through my lip. *Fucking bastards. I'll kill them for this.*

I yank up my jeans, wipe my face and stagger out of the bathroom, every movement agony. Vance is passing down the corridor as I emerge, and his eyes narrow suspiciously when he sees me.

'What are you doing in the girls' bathroom, boy?'

'Fuck you,' I say.

Kate

No mother should have a favourite, but if I'm honest, and against the rules of biology, I have a particularly soft spot for Guy. He was an easy child from the first day I became his mother. There were no terrible twos or childhood dramas. I can't remember a single family crisis that involved him. He didn't fall out of trees, electrocute the cat, shove gravel up his nose, play with matches, wear his wellies to bed for three months or trigger the car airbags in the throes of a tantrum, all of which Agness managed before she was six. At least I can rest assured that he'll be fine while I'm gone.

Julia's right: Agness and Guy don't need my constant attention. In fact, they're probably better off without me fussing round them all the time. I'm sure they'll cope beautifully without me for a few days. And it's not as if they're on their own: like Julia said, Eleanor and Ned will be there to look after them.

I check my iPhone again as I walk back to the Metro

station in the centre of Rome's upmarket shopping district, a clutch of glossy cardboard carrier bags dangling from my fingertips. Ned still hasn't called. Dozens of emails from work, but not a single message from my husband. I haven't spoken to him for two days, but he hasn't even noticed I'm gone.

I put the phone back in my bag and rearrange the carriers in my hands. Suddenly I no longer feel guilty about the money I've just splurged. I have *never* spent this much on myself before, let alone on the kind of frivolous, non-work-related, impractical clothes I've just bought: a delicate sea-green chiffon summer skirt from Armani, a Pucci jersey sundress with its trademark swirls, several tissue-soft T-shirts from Kenzo and a gorgeous pair of high gold strappy sandals from a tiny Italian boutique I found tucked away in a side street. But I refuse to feel bad about any of it, despite the stacks of brown envelopes I know are waiting for me at home. Surely I deserve a little bit of retail revenge? I earn six figures; I *should* be allowed to spend a tiny fraction of it on myself. If we're in debt, it's not because of *my* spending.

I can't believe I'm thinking like this. What have I started?

Stop beating yourself up. You've bailed Ned out enough times. If it wasn't for him, there wouldn't be any brown envelopes.

When I arrive back at the nearest Metro stop to Julia's house, I decide on impulse to walk home. It's a beautiful day, and I can't help enjoying the fact that I don't have to rush to be anywhere. For the first time in years, I have no deadline to meet or schedule to follow. It's a novel sensation. I stop off at a couple of local shops in the village and take my time buying some fresh bread, mozzarella, tomatoes, Chianti and salad, noting with slight alarm that I have less cash left than I'd thought. I can't sponge off Julia, even if it's only for a couple of days. I need to pay my way.

By the time I get back to the cottage, I'm hot and sweaty and I have blisters on both heels, but I feel more relaxed than I have in a long time. Julia isn't yet home, so I take another brief, inadequate shower in the bath house and then slip on a pale green T-shirt and the chiffon skirt, feeling absurdly frivolous.

I pour myself a glass of white wine from the open bottle in the fridge and go upstairs to the brick terrace outside my room. I brush dead leaves off a battered rattan basket chair and curl up in it, gazing across the gardens towards the seven hills surrounding Rome. The late afternoon shadows are lengthening into dusk, and the soft susurration of cicadas floats towards me on a warm breeze along with the scent of jasmine, thyme and mint. Despite a dozen family holidays in destinations as far-flung as Florida and New Zealand, it's been nearly twenty years since I had a moment like this.

The little ginger kitten appears again and twines himself around the legs of my chair. I put my glass down and pat my lap. In an instant he leaps up, kneading my thighs until he settles himself. I smile and stroke behind his ears.

'Don't you have a home to go to?' I scold.

The kitten mews softly and closes his eyes. I feel strangely comforted by his presence.

I pick up my glass again, slowly sipping the wine. I had so many dreams and ambitions when I was twenty-one; not just in terms of my career, but for all the things I wanted to do with my life. Surf in Hawaii, ski in South America, visit the Taj Mahal with my lover, any lover. Keep bees, throw a pot, learn about wines, write a screenplay, experience multiple orgasms. When did the limit of my hopes become the private schools my children attended or a bespoke Smallbone kitchen? What happened to me?

At the sound of a car on the gravel drive, I jolt out of my maudlin reverie and unfold myself from the chair, cradling the kitten in my arms. Julia's ancient orange Fiat bounces erratically down the long drive. I've never envied Julia her trust fund or even her happy family background, so different from mine, but for the first time I feel a faint pang of jealousy. She's the architect of her own life. She has a job she adores, and she answers to no one. If she wants to spend a day gazing up at the ceiling of the Sistine Chapel, she can. If she decides to lie in bed all day, no one will come in demanding to know where their rugby shorts are or when dinner will be. She can party all night, take a new lover every night of the week, or get a tattoo on her forehead if she feels like it. I can't remember the last time I was even able to choose the TV channel.

My mobile beeps suddenly, signalling that the battery is low, and I jolt, spilling my wine. I didn't bring my charger with me, of course, so I'll have to go back into town and try to find one tomorrow. I should have thought about it when I was in Rome earlier.

I'm still holding the phone when it suddenly rings. I stare at the number illuminated on the screen. Ned. *Finally.* More than twenty-four hours since I fled the country, and nearly two days since we last exchanged a word. *Two days.* Has it really taken him that long to notice his wife is missing, or does he just not care?

My stomach tightens with a combination of nerves and suppressed fury as I hit the answer button. I still don't know what I'm going to say to him. I've never lied to my husband before, but the thought of telling him exactly what I've done leaves me breathless.

'Kate? Kate, is that you?'

I open my mouth to reply.

And then my battery dies.

Guy

No way am I telling anyone what happened. Not even Agness, and she pretty much knows the score about what goes on at my school. But I still wish Kate was home when I get in. I wish she was just *there*.

I open the back door and hesitate just inside the hall, pulling out an earbud to listen. Over a backwash of *Carnival of Rust*, I hear Gran and Agness in the kitchen burbling on about a stupid pair of green gloves, but there's no sign of Dad. I put the earphone back in and bolt up the stairs before anyone notices I'm home early. I spent the day at Liesl's; I copped to bunking off, but she wasn't bothered. She never is. Agness won't let on, either. She's a fine one to talk, anyway. She bunks off whenever she feels like it, and no one says a thing.

Locking my door, I fling myself back on my bed, wincing with pain from yesterday's assault. I stare up at the ceiling, dread settling like a cold stone in my stomach. I can't take much more of this. If I have to go to that school much longer, I'm going to top myself.

I fiddle with my iPod, looking for something angrier. I settle for Nightwish and lean back on my pillows again, folding one arm under my head. Maybe if I talk to Kate and try to explain. I'm not *like* the rest of the kids in my class. I may be at a twenty-grand-a-year school, but I'm not a twenty-grand-a-year kid. We don't have a pad in Chelsea and a pile in Gloucestershire. We don't spend every Christmas in the Caribbean or have our photos on the society pages of stupid magazines. My dad isn't called Hector and doesn't have a job in the City or wear mustard-coloured cords and a blazer at Speech Day. For Christ's sake, Kate *works*. We're not broke or anything. But I know it costs her to pay our school fees. It means not having other stuff, important stuff like a new car. Dessler and the rest of the tossers have got no idea what it means to *earn* money. They think it just arrives like magic on your twenty-first birthday.

I'd be just as happy in a council flat and an allotment; happier, probably. I could go to the local comp and hang out with other kids like me. I wouldn't have to listen to endless bullshit about Glastonbury and Henley and pretend to care. Why does anyone think this shit *matters*?

After a bit, I realize I'm hungry. Not just hungry: *fucking starving*. I haven't eaten in twenty-four hours. I knock back a couple of painkillers from the bathroom cabinet and wipe my face. Quietly, I go downstairs to the kitchen, careful to miss the stair that squeaks. The place looks like a bomb's hit it, with dirty plates and pans piled in the sink. Kate clearly didn't come home last night; she'd never go to bed and leave it like this. She must've worked late and stayed in town.

I lean against the counter and finish what's left of the

cold lasagne. I don't want to go to school for my presentation tonight, but Kate promised she'd be there, and I don't want to let her down. I couldn't give a shit if Dad turns up or not.

Gran limps into the kitchen as I swallow the last mouthful. I grab my backpack and bolt for the door.

'What about all this mess?' Gran demands.

I shrug: *Like, try tidying up, why don't you?* She's only sprained her ankle, though you'd think it was broken from the way she's carrying on. I hope she's not staying long. She drives Kate mental.

I help myself to a banana. 'Late.'

'But what about the dishes?' she wails as the door shuts behind me.

By the time the bus drops me off at school, the Founder's Hall is already starting to fill as parents arrive in their blazers and pearls. This is the last show before A levels start, so it's pretty packed. I don't see Kate, but I'm not worried. She's always running late because of work. She'll be here before it begins, that's the main thing.

I wait nervously in the wings, running over my presentation in my head as the other kids go out and present theirs. When it's finally my turn, I step out on to the stage, trying to catch sight of Kate in the darkened hall, but the audience is a blur of pink faces.

'Fucking cool, man,' Ivan whispers when I come off stage.

'It was OK,' I mutter, flushing with pleasure. It was bloody word-perfect.

After it's all over, I dive straight into the audience, trying to find Kate in the crowd. All around me, parents are hugging their kids and slapping them on the back. I thread my way through the throng, bobbing and weaving to try to see over people's heads. We're probably going round in circles looking for each other. Maybe if I keep still she'll come to me.

Gradually the crowd starts to thin. I still don't see Kate, and I start to get a bit freaked. She should've found me by now. *Where is she?*

I give it another fifteen minutes, just in case she's in the bathroom or something. Finally, when it's clear I'm on my own, I jerk my backpack over my shoulder and head towards the bus stop.

She promised she'd be here. *She promised*. Isn't that supposed to *mean* something?

She acts like she's on my side, but Kate's no different from every other grown-up after all.

Ned

'Come on, my son,' I mutter, leaning forward on the sofa. I need this damn nag to pull a fucking rabbit out of the hat or I'm in big shit. 'Come on, you – Christ!'

The horse falters as it lands the water jump, but his jockey manages to hold his seat, though the horse slips back from fifth to seventh place. I slam my fist on my knee, stomach churning with adrenalin.

I *need* this race. I've had a run of bad luck lately; nothing I can't handle, but I could seriously use a good result to get myself back in the black. Blind Beggar's won his last eight races; he's odds-on favourite. I don't even need him to win. All he has to do is place. *Place!*

Sweat trickles down my back. I've got a hard-on like a frigging flag pole. 'Come on. Come on, you bastard!'

The horse moves up the inside rail into fifth. Acid chews my gut. Neck and neck with the nag in fourth now.

They move into the final bend. If Blind Beggar places in the first four, I'm up eight grand. Doesn't sound like much, given the amount I owe, but it'll hand me back my stake and give me something to play with for the four-thirty at Kempton this afternoon. If the horse wins, I'll walk away with a cool forty. More than enough to wipe out the losses at Winchester this weekend.

The third option doesn't bear thinking about.

'*Yes!*' I shout as Blind Beggar edges into third. 'You can do it, you fucker! Come on! *Come on!*'

The last straight. He's just a length behind the lead now, in second place. Talk about taking it down to the wire. I'm on my feet, willing the horse forward.

'Come on! Come on, you beauty! You can do it!'

He's barely half a length behind the lead when he stumbles. The jockey struggles to keep it together, but the rest of the field is bearing down behind him. In a split second, everything falls apart. The horse staggers again, throwing his jockey, who tumbles into the path of the field and curls into a tight ball to protect himself from their hooves. Blind Beggar keeps running, effortlessly moving into the lead without the weight of the jockey to hold him back. He passes the winning post, empty stirrups flapping against his flanks.

I fling myself back on the sofa. Eighty grand. *I just lost eighty fucking grand.*

Jesus Christ. How the fuck am I going to cover this? I don't have eight grand, never mind eighty. My bowels are suddenly liquid. What in God Almighty was I *thinking*?

I was so *sure* my luck was going to change. The law of averages said I couldn't keep on losing. Sooner or later, the tide would turn. Blind Beggar was a dead cert to win. Guaranteed to place. *Guaranteed*.

Eighty grand on a single race. Plus what I already owe

the bookies. And the loan I took out at Christmas. The second mortgage on Eleanor's place. The money I borrowed from my brother. We're talking close to two hundred thousand all told. *Two hundred thousand!*

Kate swore she'd leave me if I got into trouble again. She had to cash in half her pension and her share portfolio to bail me out last time. She went round all the bookies in Salisbury and threatened to have their balls on a plate if they took another bet off me, which is why I ended up at the Tote in bloody Winchester. No way is she going to bail me out again. I'll be out on my ear the moment she finds out. I forged her signature on the mortgage application, too; she could actually get me thrown in jail if she really wants to be vindictive.

I can't believe it has snowballed like this. It was just a few hundred quid in the beginning. I made some money, lost some, made some more, lost it again. That's the way it goes. Luck of the draw and all that. Then I hit a bit of a losing streak, I'll admit. Not enough to start a panic, but I needed to make it back. Every time, I had to lay out more to make enough back to cover my losses. I didn't dare stop and think about the numbers.

It's not like I'm an addict, for God's sake! I could stop if I felt like it. I went two years without placing a single bet, and I was totally fine. Then two months ago the rest of my life went to hell in a hand-basket and I figured, why not? In for a penny, right? It's just a harmless thrill to take my mind off things, that's all. Kate buys a lottery ticket every weekend when she goes to Tesco; what's the difference?

Except Kate doesn't blow two hundred grand on scratch cards. Jesus Christ. *What the fuck am I going to do?*

I sit on the sofa till it gets dark, too paralysed to move. When the back door slams, I leap half a foot with shock.

Agness sticks her head round the door. 'Mum didn't leave anything out for dinner,' she scowls. 'I'm ordering pizza, OK?'

She storms off before I have a chance to reply.

My brain is working furiously, searching for a way out like a rat in a trap. I've got to find the money from somewhere. I've tapped every place I can think of: the bank, the house, anyone who'll lend me a fiver. Only way I can get two hundred grand together is to win it. There's no other way.

Maybe if I sold the Suzuki, got some seed money together. Placed a few spread bets, small and cautious. It's not impossible. If I can just keep Kate from finding out for a bit, until I get things sorted, I've got a chance.

A couple of hours later, the door slams again and I hear the kids bickering in the hallway.

'Why's the kitchen still trashed?' Guy demands. 'Where's Kate?'

'How should I know?' Agness retorts. 'I haven't seen her.'

'What d'you mean, you don't know?'

'What are you, deaf?'

'That haircut really makes you look fat,' Guy yells as Agness storms back upstairs. The only response is the sound of a bedroom door slamming overhead.

A few minutes later, Guy slouches into the room and hovers near me. 'Where's Kate?'

'No idea.'

'Is she home yet?'

'Work,' I say shortly.

'Did she come home last night? She's not away or anything?'

For crying out loud. How the fuck should I know? I'm just her husband. 'No, not that I know of.'

'Are you sure?' Guy presses.

'What is this, twenty questions?' I say irritably. 'I don't know what time she got in last night, I didn't see her, and I haven't seen her today. What's so urgent it can't wait?'

'She missed my presentation,' he mumbles, sounding about five years old again. 'So did you.'

Shit. Kate should've reminded me. I can't be expected to remember these things on my own. 'Yeah, well. I'm sure she meant to be there.'

'She wouldn't have missed it for no reason.'

'Oh, there'll have been a reason,' I mutter. An important one, no doubt. After all, Kate is a very *important* person. She has *important* reasons for missing things, unlike me. I'm just a fuck-up with nothing better to do than bankrupt his family.

Guy chews his thumbnail. 'It's just the kitchen's still a mess. And she didn't turn up to my presentation, and she promised.'

I heave a sigh and point the remote at the TV to turn down the volume.

'Look. I'm sorry we missed it, all right? Kate's been flat out at work. I'm sure she'd have been at your presentation if she could. And quit worrying about the kitchen. She's just been too busy to sort it, that's all. She'll get to it when she can.'

He slumps on the sofa next to me. 'Yeah. Right.'

'Another time, mate. OK?'

'Can you call her?' he blurts suddenly.

'What the fuck for?'

He shrugs.

'For God's sake. Fine. *Fine*. If it'll make you happy, I'll call her.' I fumble in my pocket, flip open my phone and hit speed-dial.

She answers on the third ring. 'Kate?' I demand. 'Kate, is that you?'

Silence. And then suddenly I'm listening to the dial tone.

I grab the remote and whack the TV volume back up, steaming with fury. *Who the fuck does she think she is?* Where in shit does she get off *hanging up* on me?

I'm damned if I'm going to ring her back. The ball's firmly in her court.

She can bloody well call *me*.

Kate

My hand hovers over Julia's ugly green seventies push-button telephone. I just have to tell Ned I'm away on business for a few days, apologize for the short notice, and ask him to hold the fort till the weekend. He won't question it. As long as I'm back before Saturday, he probably won't even care.

Bile churns in my gut. I should've called him straight back last night, as soon as my mobile died on him. He's probably beside himself with anxiety, wondering what on earth has happened to me. For all I know, he's already got the police out dragging rivers and searching ditches. The longer I leave it before I call, the worse this is going to get. I've already passed the point where no one will notice my absence; even if I go home now, straightaway, there'll be explanations, consequences. Paul Forde has abruptly stopped emailing and calling me, which is a bad sign. I've probably been fired already. Which means no money coming in to pay the mortgage, the school fees, the bills . . .

Don't go there. I'll sort everything out when I go back. I've given Paul everything; he won't hang me out to dry when I need him most.

Ned did.

The ginger kitten twines himself around my ankles and then suddenly runs up my capris and T-shirt, perching like a parrot on my shoulder. Laughing, I reach around and stroke him. He reminds me of my cat at home. 'Sawyer two-point-O. Is that what we'll call you? What would you do, Sawyer 2?'

My newest friend purrs loudly in my ear. 'That's what I thought,' I sigh.

Picking up the green receiver, I twine the curly plastic cord round my index finger. I'm desperate to know how Agness and Guy are. I missed Guy's presentation last night; I'm sure he won't have minded, but it'd be nice to see how things went. And Eleanor had a nasty fall a few days ago; I really ought to check she's OK. It's not fair to leave her frantic with worry.

It's not fair to run away in the first place.

Yet still I don't dial, and suddenly I realize I actually *can't*. I need Ned to make the first move. What he said two months ago cut deeper than either of us knew. Only he can put it right. Until he does, I can scarcely look after myself, let alone the children. They need me whole, healed. In the truest sense, I'm doing this for them.

My stomach actually fizzes with tiny bubbles of relief as I put down the ugly phone.

He'll call me. He'll miss me, and then he'll call me, and we can put all of this right.

Ned

It's not difficult to keep out of Kate's way, since she's apparently working all the hours God sends: getting home after I've gone to bed, and up and out before I wake up. There are times when I wonder if she even comes home at all. It pisses me off, but I don't really have a leg to stand on; she's the one actually earning money, after all.

I'm in the shower, listening for the results from the race at Lingfield, when the phone rings. I'm tempted to leave it, but I've just listed the Suzuki for sale in the local paper, so I turn off the water and hop out, grabbing a towel as I run into the bedroom.

'May I speak to Kate, please.'

A man's voice, crisp and impatient.

I knot the towel at my waist with one hand, water dripping onto the carpet. 'She's not here, I'm afraid. D'you want me to take a message?'

'Can you tell me where she is?'

Jesus. What am I, her social secretary? 'At work. Look, who is this?'

'Paul Forde,' he says tersely. 'Kate's boss. She's not here.'

'What d'you mean, she's not there?'

'Precisely what I say, man. Kate isn't here. No one's seen her for three days. She missed an extremely important meeting on Monday afternoon, and a crucial pitch with a client yesterday. We've probably lost the account, if you must know. Now, if there's a family matter I should be aware of, or if she's ill—'

'You haven't seen her since Monday?'

'That's what I said.'

'But it's Thursday,' I say stupidly.

'Dear God,' Forde mutters under his breath. 'Look here. Do you know where Kate is or not? Because, frankly, I'd like to know what the hell is going on.'

'You and me both,' I retort, pulling myself together. 'I assume you've tried calling her?'

'Of course I have. I've left a dozen messages.'

'And she hasn't replied to any of them?'

There's a silence. 'No,' he says finally. A note of concern enters his voice for the first time. 'Are you telling me you don't know where she is either?'

'It's been a pretty hectic week,' I say quickly. 'Ships passing in the night, you know how it is.'

'Well, quite.' Another pause, longer this time. 'Look, when you do manage to track her down, would you mind asking her to give me a quick bell?'

'Absolutely.' Christ, he's got me talking like a public-school prat too. 'I'm sure she'll be in touch.'

I put the phone down and stare at it uneasily. I've never known Kate play hooky. Ever. Even when Agness was born, she was back at her desk less than three weeks later. If she hasn't turned up for work, there's got to be a damned good reason. Life or death, nothing less.

I pull some clothes over my damp skin. 'Eleanor?' I call from the bedroom doorway. 'Eleanor, have you heard from Kate today?'

Her voice echoes faintly up the stairs. 'If you need to speak to me, Edward, please come to where I am and don't yell.'

Gritting my teeth, I go down to the kitchen. 'D'you know where Kate is?'

'At work, I imagine. Why?'

'I've just had a phone call from her boss. He says she hasn't been in to work since Monday. She's missed several important meetings. Did she say anything to you about going away?'

'Away where?'

I shrug. 'Anywhere.'

'No, but I'd hardly infer anything from that,' she says tartly. 'I'm not exactly my daughter's confidante.'

I finish buttoning my shirt and look round, taking in the mess for the first time. Dirty plates are piled in the sink and the rubbish bin hasn't been emptied. Pizza boxes spill out of the recycling container, the cat's bowl is encrusted with old food, and a carton of milk sits out on the counter. Kate wouldn't let things get this out of hand, no matter how hard she was working. My anxiety ratchets up a notch.

'She missed Guy's presentation on Tuesday. Are you *sure* she didn't say anything?'

'Really, Edward. Why would she tell me and not you?'

I pull on my lower lip. 'You really don't know where she is?' I ask again.

'Shall we call the police?' Eleanor says calmly.

I snort. 'Oh, I don't think there's any call for that!'

'Don't you?'

Her faded blue eyes meet mine steadily. I'd feel less worried if she was hysterical.

'I'm sure there's an explanation,' I bluster. 'No point panicking. She probably forgot to diary an appointment or something. Maybe she's interviewing for another job.' *But she's not answering her phone. She missed Guy's presentation. No one's seen her for three days.*

'If you say so,' Eleanor says.

'Perhaps,' I say carefully, 'I should just make a few calls.'

'I wouldn't be bothering you,' I say brightly, 'only it is a little . . . well, *odd*.'

'Let me be sure I've got this straight. You haven't seen your wife for three days. She hasn't been in to work since Monday, and you say she's normally very reliable. Not the type to disappear on a whim. None of her friends know where she is. She isn't answering her mobile—'

'Well, *someone* answered it,' I interrupt, 'but they didn't actually speak.'

Plod nods and corrects his notes. 'Someone, but not necessarily Mrs Forrest, answered her mobile. She hasn't responded to text messages or emails, and as far as you're aware, she hasn't taken anything with her: clothes, laptop, that sort of thing.'

'Yes. Just her handbag.'

'And you think this is . . . *odd*?'

I start to get a bit hot under the collar. 'Well, more than odd, obviously. Worrying. I'm worried about her.'

'But not enough to report it for, let me see . . . three days?'

I feel bad enough about that without him rubbing it in.

'Look, I didn't realize she was missing until her boss rang this morning and said she hadn't been in to work. First thing I did was call all her friends and see if anyone had seen her, and then I came straight here. I didn't want to waste your time if there was no need.'

'Quite.' He writes for a few moments then glances up. I don't like the look in his eye. 'Tell me, Mr Forrest, is it normal for you to go three days without seeing your wife?'

'She works extremely long hours,' I say defensively. 'She's often away on business.'

'But that's not the case now?'

'No. According to her boss, she was supposed to be in London for some important meetings this week.'

He scrawls a few words in the margin of his notes and underlines them. He's left-handed; the heel of his palm crabs awkwardly across the page.

'When exactly did you last see her?' he asks.

'Monday. Look, I've *told* you all this—'

'Just want to be sure we get things straight,' he says calmly. 'What did you talk about?'

'Well, I suppose the last time I actually talked to her was Sunday night. I was still half-asleep when she left for work on Monday. I'm a freelance journalist,' I say before he can get another dig in. 'I work unusual hours. But as far as I can remember, everything seemed fine. Same as usual. I remember she said she might be late back because she had a big meeting. The kids had breakfast with her. She dropped my son off at school and took the train to London. Her car's still in the car park, I checked on my way here.'

'So you last talked to her properly on Sunday night. How were things between you?'

'Fine. Well, actually we'd had a few words earlier that evening—'

'Oh?'

I don't like his sudden flash of interest. 'Her mother had had a fall, and Kate brought her home to stay with us for a few days. I wasn't exactly happy about it, that's all.'

'Did you argue?'

Hardly. Kate lays down the law, and I put up with it. 'Not really. She knew how I felt.'

'What would you say her frame of mind was that night?'

'She seemed perfectly normal. A bit tired and fed-up, maybe. Look, are you going to—'

'No indication anything was amiss?'

Who uses words like amiss in real life? 'Nothing out of the ordinary. I *told* you. She wasn't very happy with work, some boy-wonder was treading on her toes, but nothing she couldn't deal with. And she'd had a bit of a run-in with Agness the night before – that's our daughter. They'd fallen out over a party, the usual teenage stuff.'

'Any financial worries?'

I hesitate. *Yeah*, I think, *two hundred grand's worth of worries*. But Kate doesn't even know about that. If she'd learned the truth, she'd have thrown me out, not abandoned the kids and disappeared.

'Things have been a bit tough for us recently, same as for everyone,' I admit. 'I don't see what that's got to do with anything.'

Plod leans back in his chair, his face expressionless.

'She was unhappy with work,' he recites, checking his

notes, 'she'd argued with her daughter and with you, money's tight, and she wasn't very pleased her mother had come to stay.'

I shift in my seat. Put like that, it makes Kate's life seem pretty bloody miserable. But then, Christ, whose life isn't these days? All things considered, Kate hasn't got it bad. Most of the time she loves her job. I don't screw around, and the kids are no worse than your average teenagers. We had a bit of a hiccup a couple of months ago, but there's certainly no real reason I can think of for her to bloody run away.

'Is there a *chance*, Mr Forrest, that your wife decided she wanted a little time away from it all?' Plod says, his voice laced with sarcasm. 'She may have gone to see a friend or—'

'I told you, I called all her friends. None of them have heard from her.'

'Is it possible there's a friend you don't know about?'

It's the way he says *friend*. I want to punch his fucking lights out.

'Are you trying to suggest my wife's having an *affair*?'

'I realize this is difficult . . .'

I shove my chair back from the table. 'It's not difficult, it's bloody ridiculous, that's what it is! Kate would never have an affair! She hasn't got the fucking time apart from anything else! And even if she was screwing around, she'd never walk out on the kids. Something must have happened to her. It's the only explanation.'

As I say it, the reality hits me. Kate isn't the sort of wife who'd run away. She wouldn't leave the kids, not without a good reason or a word of goodbye. It's just not her style.

I lean over the table. 'Something's happened to her,' I say again urgently. 'You need to find her.'

'We will, Mr Forrest,' Plod says, his tone loaded with meaning. 'Whatever's happened to her, we will.'

Kate

'Excuse me? Are you OK?'

I'm startled out of my reverie. All these Vatican statues and paintings and tapestries of the Madonna and child: no wonder it's getting to me.

The girl beside me tentatively touches my arm. 'Ma'am? Is everything all right?'

Ma'am? I suppose to a pretty girl of nineteen or twenty I do seem old.

'I'm fine,' I say. 'It's just a bit warm in here.'

'Would you like some water? Keir,' she says, turning to the boy behind her, 'we've got a spare bottle, haven't we?'

'Really, I'm quite all right—'

'Please. It's no trouble. You look terribly pale.'

I do feel a little giddy. I move to the deep stone window embrasure overlooking the Vatican courtyard and sit down. These apartments are terribly close. I don't know how those medieval popes survived without air conditioning.

The girl's boyfriend hands me a sweating bottle of spring water. I unscrew the cap and take a grateful swallow.

My two Samaritans regard me seriously as I drink, like anxious parents watching their baby feed. The girl is really very lovely, with clear blue eyes and honey-coloured hair rippling to her waist like a pre-Raphaelite maiden. A striped woollen messenger bag is slung across her chest, bisecting small high breasts, and her fringed skirt brushes the stone floor as she moves.

Her boyfriend isn't in quite the same league. Older, perhaps mid-twenties, his look is very Celtic, all long red-blond hair, pale skin and high, razor-sharp cheekbones. It's colouring that can be attractive in a woman, but I find it rather unappealing in a man. He's not particularly tall, probably my height, but his tawny eyes are alight with energy and interest. A long narrow scar runs the length of his left jawline. I imagine it gives him quite a bit of trouble when he shaves.

I proffer the half-empty bottle, but the girl waves it away. 'Keir's got another one in his backpack.'

'I've some trail mix, too,' the boy volunteers. His voice has the trace of a soft Irish accent. 'If you still feel a bit weird.'

I stand up, embarrassed by their concern. I must seem like a sad, menopausal old woman to them, despite the knock-off pink Converse trainers I bought in the village market yesterday and a new leather cuff bracelet. Agness would disown me.

The girl pulls out a leaflet and pores over it. 'Keir, did you figure out where we are?'

'Raphael's rooms,' he says vaguely.

'This was Julius the Second's library,' I say. 'It's the first of the rooms Raphael decorated, and the frescoes here were almost entirely painted by him, rather than his team. They're supposed to illustrate the three highest categories of the human spirit according to the neo-Platonic vision: truth, goodness and beauty –'

I break off, appalled. *Listen to me*. I'm turning into one of those women who rant to strangers on the bus.

'Are you, like, a guide?' the girl asks in confusion.

I gather my things. 'I'm sorry, I didn't mean to interrupt. Please don't let me hold you up any longer. I'm quite all right now.'

'I'm Molly,' the girl says suddenly, thrusting her hand forward. Slender silver bracelets chime the length of her tanned arm. 'We totally *do* want you to interrupt. We didn't get a proper guide book, which was dumb. I thought because Keir teaches archaeology, we wouldn't need one, but he's totally *hope*less. We've got no idea what *any*thing is.'

'I do ruins,' her boyfriend says mildly. 'Stones. I know nothing about statues and paintings. I did *tell* you.'

'I'm probably getting half of it wrong,' I sigh.

'That fresco,' the boy says, pointing. 'Do you know what it's supposed to be?'

'The *Disputa*,' I say, turning. '*The Disputation of the Sacrament*. See, in the centre is Christ, between the Virgin and Saint John the Baptist. That's God the Father above, and below there's the dove representing the Holy Spirit.' I glance at them, gauging their interest. Both are gazing raptly up at the fresco. 'Those men on the right in the papal vestments are Gregory the Great and Sixtus the Fourth, and behind them is Dante. During the Sack of Rome in 1527, soldiers left graffiti on the fresco, one in praise of Luther, the other of Charles the Fifth.'

'Can we follow you?' Molly asks eagerly. 'Can you tell us about everything?'

I feel a sharp pang. She reminds me so much of Agness. At least, the Agness I used to know.

'Molly!' Keir exclaims. 'I'm sure she doesn't – I'm sorry, we don't know your name?'

'Kate,' I supply.

'You can't possibly want us trailing after you, Kate. It wouldn't be fair.'

In other words, *My girlfriend has got us into this and I need a way out.*

'Unless you'd like the company, of course,' he adds.

His tone is unmistakably sincere. I have the feeling that this young man is not the sort to lie. Unlike my husband.

I smile. 'Actually, I'd love some company. When you get bored, you can go off and do your own thing – I won't take offence.'

'We won't get bored,' Molly promises sweetly.

Shyly, I lead the way towards the Borgia apartments, and, with a little prompting, explain their turbulent and bloody history, surprised at how quickly it comes back to me. I'd have quite liked to be a teacher. When Julia stayed in Rome to pursue her painting, for a brief moment I was tempted to go back and join her and teach art history. But I'd met Ned by then, and there was Guy, and then very soon Agness. It was only ever a pipe-dream.

We emerge into a long vaulted gallery lined with dozens of marble busts – men and women, Caesars and anonymous Romans, an eerie audience frozen in time.

'They were alive, once,' Keir says, echoing my thoughts so precisely that I'm startled. 'They lived and breathed and plotted and loved. We haven't changed in thousands of years, have we? We still have the same desires and passions. The same fears.'

'It's not history,' Molly says. 'It's *people*.'

The directed pedestrian flow around the museum finally leads us to its pièce de résistance, the Sistine Chapel. I watch Molly and Keir's faces change as they enter the vast chamber through a small door behind the altar and behold Michelangelo's masterpiece. These two are scarcely older than Agness and Guy. Why can't it be like this with my own children?

Agness would rather cut out her tongue than ask you to explain a fresco, and Guy's too wrapped up in his teenage angst. You're living in a fantasy world if you think they'd ever be company *for you.*

Maybe things will change now. Maybe my absence will make them realize that they miss me, too.

Keir worms his way to the centre of the huddle of spectators craning their heads upwards and lies down among them on the marble floor. I smile. That's exactly what I did the first time I saw it. I watch a museum guard shoulder his way through the crowd towards Keir. '*Alzi! Alzi!* Get up! Get up!'

'Hey, I'm just looking . . .'

'No talking! No pictures!'

'OK, OK,' Keir mutters, scrambling to his feet and brushing himself down. His pale skin blotches red with embarrassment. 'Keep your hair on.'

The guard throws a final scowl our way and then bolts off to harangue a pair of Canadian tourists taking forbidden photographs.

I nod towards the vast fresco on the wall behind the

altar. '*The Last Judgement*. I'm sure you've seen pictures of it a thousand times.'

'That's Christ, right?' Keir says, pointing to the figure in the centre. A worn friendship bracelet encircles his bony white wrist. 'The Virgin next to him, and that's Peter, with the keys. I'm guessing that's Saint Catherine with the spiked wheel.'

'Oh! Like the firework,' Molly murmurs.

'So who's the guy with the flayed skin?' Keir asks me.

'Saint Bartholomew. Michelangelo painted him with his own face, like a kind of self-portrait.'

'Very Hitchcock.'

I laugh. 'Exactly.'

'What's your favourite movie?' he asks.

'Hitchcock? *Lifeboat*,' I say instantly.

Ned hates old movies, by which he means anything that's out on DVD.

The kid tilts his head up to study the high frescoes, red-gold hair spilling across his collar. '*Vertigo* for me.'

I sigh. 'Yes, I do love that one too . . .'

'No talking!' the museum guard yells again. 'No pictures!'

The next hour passes quickly – we leave the Sistine Chapel to tour the remaining rooms and then wind up stopping for an espresso at the museum café. I'm surprised at quite how much I'm enjoying myself. Despite – or perhaps because of – the age gap between us, I'm energized by the conversation. I hadn't realized until today how much I miss my own children's company.

Molly impulsively flings her arms round me as they get up to leave. 'Thank you so much, Kate. Today has been lovely.'

I hug her back, touched. 'Honestly, it was my pleasure. Thank you for putting up with me for so long.'

'Look,' Molly says, 'I don't know if you like opera, but there's a production of *Carmina Burana* in San Galgano next Friday at the ruined abbey. We thought we'd drive up – it's only a couple of hours away. Maybe you'd like to come along? You could bring, like, your husband or someone . . .'

My stomach twists in sudden panic at the thought of Ned.

'It's really sweet of you, but I won't be here,' I say quickly. 'I have to get back home to my family.'

'Give her our number,' Molly urges her boyfriend. 'In case you change your mind,' she tells me.

I hand Keir my iPhone, watching as he taps in a number, fumbling, knowing I'll never call it.

'Thanks again for today,' he says, returning the phone. 'You were cool.'

You were cool. Agness and Guy will never believe it.

My smile fades. I won't be sharing this story with them. They aren't going to want to know how much fun I had after I ran out on them.

Given what I've done, they may not want to know me at all.

Ned

The husband is always the prime suspect. I get that. They have to look at the husband first. Of course I haven't bloody done anything to my wife, but as soon as they start digging, they'll find out how much money I owe the bookies. Kate has a massive life insurance policy; she's always said she needed it, given our financial responsibilities. Two mortgages, Eleanor's and ours, and the kids' private school fees, for a start. I'm innocent, but how's it going to look?

I should have clued in when the cop shop phoned at the crack of dawn and asked me to come down to the station to 'help further with their inquiry'. It's what they always say when they nick some poor bastard, isn't it? 'Dr Crippen is helping with our inquiries.' Never bloody occurred to me I was in the frame for something. That's the trouble when you're innocent. You let your guard down.

Funny. I've seen a thousand cop shows on TV, but nothing quite prepares you for the reality of starring in one.

I'm shown into a very different sort of interview room

from yesterday. No cosy sofas and boxes of tissues this time. There's worn lino on the floor instead of carpeting, and a two-way mirror where the pot plants should've been. They leave me to stew on my own for a good forty minutes, while I picture being banged up and buggered by some Kray wannabe. Finally the door opens and a cop strolls into the room without glancing up from the open folder in his hand. Mid-forties, fit, no more than average height but with an air of authority about him. Clearly a lot more senior than Plod yesterday. There's no smirking now. Suddenly everything is deadly serious.

'Have you found her?' I blurt, half-rising from my seat.

'Not yet, Mr Forrest.' He pulls out the chair opposite me and puts the folder down on the table between us. 'DCI Wooding. We were rather hoping you could help us with that.'

I stare at him. 'I've told you everything I know. I haven't seen her since Monday. No one has. I told you all this yesterday.'

'I'm aware what you told my colleague yesterday, yes.'

'So why've you brought me back here? Have you found something, or what?'

'What sort of something might you expect us to find, Mr Forrest?'

'Christ, I don't bloody know!' I rub my face with both hands, wishing I'd taken the time to shave. 'Look,' I say, trying to sound calm, 'I've been up all night imagining the worst. If you've found Kate's . . . if you've found Kate, I'd rather know. Whatever's happened, I'd rather know.'

'We haven't found anything, Mr Forrest. Frankly, we're as confused as you are.'

I wish he'd stop being so fucking polite.

'My wife isn't the sort of woman to just disappear,' I insist, leaning forward in my chair. 'She's not like that. She's got a good job, she loves our kids. She'd never walk out without a word. Something must have happened to her.'

'That's what we're here to find out,' Wooding says with infuriating calmness.

'I understand you have to consider all the options,' I say reasonably. 'I get that. I know you have to look at me as a suspect. But all the time you're doing that, you're not out looking for her. I haven't hurt my wife. I love her. She could be out there, in trouble, while you're wasting time with me.'

'I can assure you, we're doing everything we can to find her. Now, if we could go over the events leading up to her disappearance one more time . . .'

'For God's sake!' I cry, losing my patience. 'I've told you, you're wasting time! You should be out there looking for her!'

Wooding refuses to be deflected. Slowly, he goes over everything I've already told them, asking the same questions again and again. Eventually, after nearly an hour of this, he closes the folder.

'Come on, Mr Forrest,' he says kindly. 'We're not unsympathetic here. We all know how things can escalate. Before you know it – well, we do understand.'

'What's that supposed to mean?'

He pushes back his chair and comes round to my side of the table, perching on one corner in a familiar fashion. 'What was it? A row that got out of hand? It happens. You tell us your side of the story now, we'll work with you. Where's Kate, Mr Forrest?'

'Look,' I say, through gritted teeth. 'I've told you, *I have no idea where she is.* That's why I came to you, remember?'

His face hardens. 'Yes, but you didn't quite tell us everything, did you?'

'What are you talking about?'

Wooding reaches behind him for the folder and pulls out a sheaf of paper. 'Shall we talk about this?'

I take the paperwork, unable to stop my hand from shaking. It's all there: the debt to the bookies, the second mortgage with Kate's falsified signature, the loans, the credit card debts.

The life insurance policy.

I swallow. 'How did you get this?'

'The usual channels. Is there anything you'd like to add to your previous statement, Mr Forrest?'

'This has nothing to do with what's happened to Kate!' I fling the pages on the table. 'Look, perhaps I haven't been the best husband in the world. I'm crap with money, but so what? It doesn't mean I don't love my wife! I'd never do anything to hurt her!'

'Your wife knew all about your debts, did she, sir?'

'No, not all of them. Do you tell your wife everything?'

Wooding holds my gaze for a long moment, then returns to his chair on the other side of the desk.

'Is there anywhere you think she could be, Mr Forrest? Anywhere she could have gone?'

I bury my head in my hands. I can't think of a happy explanation for Kate's disappearance. I keep picturing her dead in a ditch somewhere, or decomposing in a shallow grave. Maggots, rigor mortis, blunt head trauma. Rape. Ever since yesterday, I've been praying for something simple like a car accident: a minor head injury, amnesia. Or a nervous breakdown. Another man, even – I don't care. Just as long as she's OK. Christ. I never thought I'd find myself viewing an affair as the lesser of two evils.

The door opens again and a young cop beckons Wooding over. The two of them exchange muted whispers and then Wooding returns.

'It seems we've found something,' he says.

I feel sick.

'Your wife would appear to be perfectly fine.' A beat. 'We've managed to trace a transaction on her credit card. Was your wife planning a trip at all, Mr Forrest?'

'What?'

'It seems she purchased a ticket to Rome on Monday afternoon. She also withdrew two thousand pounds in euros from a bank at Heathrow. You had no idea she was going away?'

'No, of course I bloody didn't!' I shout.

'We've checked the CCTV cameras at the bank. There's no doubt it's your wife, Mr Forrest. From what we can tell, she was travelling alone. There were no signs of duress.'

'I don't understand,' I say blankly. 'Why would she be going to Rome? Why wouldn't she tell me?'

'I don't know, sir. But it would seem this is no longer a Missing Persons case.'

'Why would she do something like this? Why would she leave without saying a word? Everything was fine between us! I don't understand . . .'

And then finally, *finally*, I do.

Four months before

Kate

'You can't be,' Ned says when I tell him. 'You're nearly forty, for God's sake.'

'Ned,' I protest, half laughing. 'You make it sound like I've got one foot in the grave. Thirty-nine is nothing these days.'

'You'll be forty in a few months.'

'Cherie Blair had a baby at forty-five. Kelly Preston was forty-eight when she had her last baby. I'm a spring chicken in comparison.'

Ned's shock is so absolute, I laugh again. Wanting to be quite sure before I raised his hopes, I've hugged this incredible secret to myself for three whole weeks, long enough for the surprise to wear off and the joy to sink in. A baby was the last thing I was expecting, the very last thing I'd thought I wanted, and yet joy is the only word to describe what I feel.

He shakes his head as if to clear it. 'But I thought you couldn't – all those years after Agness was born, when we tried for another baby . . .'

Suddenly I'm very busy with the kettle. No need to tell him now that I was on the Pill the entire time we were 'trying'; or that I came off it when I turned thirty-five, anxious about clots and strokes, and replaced it with the Mirena coil, which was supposed to last five years. Clearly it came up a month or two short.

Ned rubs his hands across his face. 'Are you *sure*? How do you know?'

'I've done two home tests and both were positive. I've been feeling tired, and my breasts are tender . . .'

'Those home kits aren't reliable,' Ned interrupts. 'You can get false positives, especially at your age.'

'Would you stop going on about my age,' I say, nettled.

'You can't be pregnant,' he says again. 'You must've made a mistake.'

For the first time, I start to feel nervous. This isn't how I thought this conversation would go.

Fifteen years ago, when I fell pregnant with Agness, Ned didn't take it well. He'd wanted to wait a bit, give our new family time to get to know each other before adding the complication of another baby. I hadn't been particularly thrilled by the timing either; the prospect of a second child, when I'd barely got used to parenting the first, filled me with dread. Besides, at that stage, I'd only been at Forde's a couple of months; the last thing I'd needed was to take time off to have a baby.

But a termination was out of the question. Ned had been educated by nuns, and you can take the boy out of the convent school, but you can't take the convent school out of the boy. I had no such religious constraints, but discarding a healthy baby merely because it was inconvenient timing had seemed too much like tempting Fate. What if I could never have another child? What if this was *it*?

What I'd needed then, for the first time in our relationship, was Ned's support and reassurance. But he responded in what I soon learned was his usual fashion: by burying his head in the sand and ignoring what he didn't like. I found myself a de facto single mother, attending doctor's appointments and prenatal classes on my own. Ned refused to discuss childcare arrangements or which room to use as a nursery. When I tried to show him the fuzzy black-and-white scan photos, he walked away. What should have been one of the happiest times of my life became the most miserable.

Two weeks before my due date, Ned accepted an assignment to the news bureau in Belfast, filling in for one of his colleagues who was, ironically, on paternity leave. I had no idea whether my husband was even planning to be home for the birth, and such was the froideur between us by this stage that I couldn't ask.

'If you don't like it, leave him,' Eleanor said briskly when I finally swallowed my pride and broached the subject to my mother. 'You haven't even been married two years. Do you think things are going to get *better* as the honeymoon shine wears off?'

Ned's own mother was equally appalled when she found out. 'I'll speak to him,' she said grimly. 'The divorce wasn't *all* Liesl's fault, you know.'

Humiliating though it was to have my mother-in-law intervene, by this stage I was desperate. When Ned rang and said he was coming home, I didn't care that he was doing it for his mother, not me; I was just grateful he was coming at all. As it was, he nearly missed Agness's birth. I was crossing my legs and cursing him in three languages by the time he finally showed up at the hospital with a hangdog expression, a wilting bunch of garage flowers and a cheap stuffed rabbit that went straight in the bin.

But the moment he saw his newborn daughter, red-faced and Churchillian, he had eyes for no one else. Cradling her head in his palm, her tiny body stretched along the length of his forearm, he gazed at her as if the rest of the world no longer existed.

My relief was intense. I'd been terrified he wouldn't bond with her; that his rejection of the baby would continue after her birth. I couldn't have borne it if history had repeated itself and her father had rebuffed her the way my father had rebuffed me.

But the intensity of his devotion to Agness soon became disconcerting. Naturally it didn't take the form of practical help – it was too much to ask for him to actually change a nappy or do the midnight feed – but he spent every free moment, of which he had rather too many nowadays, with his daughter. He bought so many ridiculous plush animals that the nursery resembled the toy department at Harrods. One evening he came home with a plastic bag filled with hundreds of ten- and twenty-pound notes he'd won on a race at Newmarket.

'For her college fund,' he'd said, counting it onto the table.

She wasn't even six months old when he started lobbying for another child. A playmate for Agness, he said fondly. I pointed out that she already *had* a playmate: Guy.

'She needs a *proper* brother or sister,' Ned insisted. 'A *real* family.'

'Guy is a proper brother!' I protested.

Ned shrugged. 'You know what I mean.'

I didn't want another child. As far as I was concerned,

we already *were* a real family, and two children under three was quite enough. I was still winning back ground my maternity leave had cost me and had no intention of scuppering my career for good with a repeat performance.

Quietly, I went on the Pill. I'd trusted Ned with condoms before, and look where that had got us.

Every month, when Ned saw the box of Tampax on top of the lavatory cistern, he'd sulk for days, as if *he* were the one with PMT. After five or six months, he started wondering aloud if I should get 'checked out', clearly assuming that if there was a problem, it couldn't be with *him*.

I explained, yet again, why I didn't want another baby. In his usual fashion, Ned listened to me and then brushed everything I'd just said under the carpet.

'Maybe this time one of my swimmers will make it through,' he'd quip jovially every time we made love. 'At least we know from Agness I'm not firing blanks.'

Whenever we visited friends with small children, he'd spend the next few days talking about how nice it'd be if 'the stork paid us a visit' before it was too late.

Which is why, when I found myself pregnant just before Christmas, I thought he'd be pleased.

'Ned,' I say, 'I know it's hard to believe, but it's not a mistake. My period is more than a month late, and you know how regular I've always been. I thought at first it was my age, same as you. I assumed it was the start of the menopause, but—'

'The menopause! Well, of course! That'd certainly put your hormones out of whack.' Suddenly he smiles and holds out his arms. 'Come here, darling. Put that kettle down. You poor old thing. No wonder you've been looking so peaky.'

There's no mistaking the relief in his voice. A chill ripples down my spine. 'Ned, are you listening to me?' I exclaim, pulling away. 'I'm looking peaky because *I'm pregnant*.'

He stares at me for a long moment and then bluntly turns away from me.

I gaze at his rigid back in disbelief. For years he's wanted another child, company for his precious Agness. I've tortured myself endlessly over denying him, and now, when I least expected it, nature finds her own way. A last-chance baby. A new beginning. The opportunity to get my mothering right, to make the right choice and put my family first. Now Ned's telling me he doesn't want it after all?

'Ned,' I say tentatively. 'Ned, I thought you'd be pleased.'

He whirls round. '*Pleased?*'

'But you always wanted another baby . . .'

'When Agness needed a playmate! When we were still young! Not *now*! Christ Almighty, Kate! I'm forty-three! I'll be over sixty by the time this kid leaves school!' His face is white, stricken. 'Do you have any idea what a new baby means? Back to the sleepless nights, the endless fucking nappies, the two of us wrung out like wet dishcloths!'

'What am I supposed to do?' I plead.

'Agness is fifteen this year!' he cries, as if I haven't spoken. 'She'll be off to university soon. Guy even sooner. We'll have a chance to get our lives back. Travel, do what we want, go where we like. Do you really want to exchange all that to go right back to the beginning?'

I sink into a chair, gripping the edge of the table so hard my knuckles whiten. On one level, I understand where he's coming from. I've looked forward to our liberation as much as he has. For years I've dreamed of trips to Californian wineries and walking tours of Tuscany, freed from the tyranny of school calendars and the endless demands of teenagers for nightlife, entertainment, lifts. In a couple of years, we'll have paid off our mortgage, and once the children leave university, we'll have more disposable income than we've ever had in our lives. Maybe, given time and space alone, Ned and I will rediscover each other, too.

I'm fully aware what a new baby will do to our lives. No more skiing trips to Whistler every winter. No early retirement to the south of France, as we'd fantasized. Bucket-and-spade holidays instead of pony-trekking down the Grand Canyon. Forking out for a babysitter every time we want to go to the cinema. Giving up my dressing room to make space for the nursery.

I've even debated with myself whether it's fair to burden a baby with ageing parents. It'll effectively be a single child, its siblings long since grown before it's even at school. We'll be pensioners by the time it leaves college. Many of the things we did with Guy and Agness, from piggybacks to white-water rafting, will be physically beyond us as we get older. Can we bear to repeat so much of the mind-numbing early years, the cake-and-ice-cream birthday parties, the trips to Disney? Will we have the energy to battle through the teenage stage, just as many of our friends are enjoying the indulgence of becoming grandparents? Will this baby grow up feeling cheated of a normal childhood?

And yet I don't hesitate for a second. I want this child more than I've wanted anything in my life.

I close my eyes. The milky, yeasty smell of a newborn. The warmth of a baby against my chest again, the feel of a small hand in mine. Isn't that worth a few missed holidays, an extra couple of years on the mortgage? How could a second home in Provence compete with the sound of childish laugher echoing round the house again?

I grope for Ned's hand. 'This wasn't what I'd planned, either, but it's happened,' I plead. 'C'mon, Ned. We're older, yes, but hopefully we're wiser, too. We can do this.'

He pulls free. 'I can't, Kate. I'm sorry, but I'm not ready to go back to the beginning. I can't do it all again.'

'I'm not asking you to. I'll give up work this time. Take a career break.'

Ned laughs shortly. 'You, give up work?'

'I mean it,' I say, realizing as I speak that it's true. 'Advertising is a young person's game. I've only got a few years left before I get overtaken or sidelined by one of Paul's new boy wonders. I've had enough. Once the baby's at school, I can think about what I really—'

'How can we afford for you to give up your job?' Ned cries. 'You're living in dreamland, Kate! We couldn't possibly get by on my salary!'

'We could if we made some changes. Economize a bit. Eleanor could easily manage a mortgage herself if she moved somewhere smaller. We've got some savings, and we could sell this house if need be. In a couple of years, we'll be done with school fees, and—'

'Jesus,' Ned says, burying his head in his hands. 'You're serious. You really want to go through with this.'

'What do you want me to do?' I demand shrilly. 'Get rid of it? Kill it, just because it's not convenient?'

Ned exhales slowly and looks up. 'I don't know,' he says tiredly. 'Christ, Kate. I don't know.'

*

I try to give him space and time to get to grips with the idea. I tell him when I go for my first scan the following week, but I don't ask him to come or show him the amazing 3D photographs afterwards. I stand in my dressing room and work out where the cot will go, and find a local handyman who can build me some new wardrobes in our bedroom for my clothes. I keep crackers by the bed for the morning sickness, but wait till Ned takes his morning shower before munching them and getting up. I don't mention the baby when he talks about where to go for our summer holiday – *I'll be seven months pregnant. I won't be in any shape to hike in the Carolinas!* – or make a fuss when he pours me a glass of wine at dinner. It nearly kills me to keep quiet when I want to immerse myself in what's happening to me, but I manage it, waiting for Ned to be ready.

It's exactly the same as when I was pregnant with Agness, history repeating itself. I just have to hope that when this baby is born, Ned falls in love all over again.

Except he never gets the chance.

'I'm sorry,' the sonographer says. 'The baby didn't make it. There's no heartbeat.'

I stare up at the monitor. 'Oh,' I say.

'It looks like it died a little while ago, at around nine weeks. I really am so sorry, Kate.'

'But there was a heartbeat last time,' I say stupidly. 'I saw it. I *heard* it.'

She gently wipes the gel off my stomach. 'I know. It's nothing you did, Kate. Sometimes this just happens, especially with older mothers. It's nature's way of taking care of something that wasn't quite right. There's absolutely nothing you could have done to prevent it. Doctor Walbert will come and see you in a few minutes to explain what happens now.'

She switches the monitor off and quietly leaves the room. I lie there in the semi-darkness, my hand fluttering over my still-rounded stomach. I can't quite take it in. I just came in for a routine nuchal scan, so they could check for Down's. I'd prepared myself for the one-in-a-hundred chance, at my age, that the baby might have something wrong with it; steeled myself to make a choice if I turned out to be that one. It never occurred to me the baby might have died. I made it through the dangerous first trimester. I heard the heartbeat. I still *feel* pregnant. Morning sickness, peeing all the time, swollen breasts. Nothing to suggest my poor baby quietly left me without me even noticing.

Doctor Walbert returns and kindly explains my options. I can wait and let nature take its course, which might happen in days or weeks; I can try to induce the missed miscarriage chemically; or I can have a D&C tomorrow to remove the 'products of pregnancy'.

'I don't want to wait,' I say. 'I need this to be over.'

'The D&C, then,' she says.

When I get home and tell Ned, he doesn't trouble to hide his relief. 'I'm sorry for you,' he says, 'but I can't be sorry for me. I'd be lying if I said otherwise.'

'You're not the least bit sad?' I ask curiously. 'We made this baby out of love, and now it's died. You don't feel anything at all?'

'I'm sorry. I love you, Kate. I'd do anything for you. Maybe I'd have loved this baby too, for you. But I can't feel sorry it's gone. For your sake, I wish I could, but I can't.'

How can I blame him for being honest? He's as entitled

not to want another child as I am to want one. Everything he'd said before was true: a baby would have transformed our lives, but while I welcomed that, it was a transformation he hadn't sought or wanted. He warned me that my age would count against me, and he was right. I'm too old for a baby. My eggs are hard-boiled, past their sell-by date, and my body has now made that plain.

He comes with me when I go to hospital for the D&C, and drives me carefully home. He's solicitous, attentive, loving. I can't fault him in any way.

And yet every time I look at him, all I can think of is that Ned didn't want this baby. And now it's gone.

Ned

I can't believe I didn't think of Julia before. In the past two days, I've called everyone in Kate's address book and gone through her whole email history. Julia wasn't in either of them; it's been so long since Kate mentioned her, I'd forgotten she existed. But it totally makes sense, now the cops have told me she's in Rome. If Kate's having some sort of emotional meltdown, it stands to reason she'd go off to that bloody hippy dyke. The bitch has never liked me, not since the day we met.

I open the fridge and take out a beer, surprisingly calm as I wait for someone to answer the phone. Now I know where Kate is, we can get things sorted out. Clearly I mishandled the whole baby drama. It obviously upset her more than I realized, and she's having some sort of hormonal breakdown. It's only been a couple of months, after all. I'll apologize, make it clear I'm not going to hold this running-away nonsense against her, and we can all move on.

To her credit, Julia doesn't hang up when I tell her it's

me. She doesn't even sound rattled as she goes off to get Kate. Cool as a cucumber, that one.

'Kate?' I say as I hear the phone being picked up again. 'Kate?'

'Yes,' she says.

I wait for her to continue, but she doesn't say another word. I realize I haven't really thought through what to say. It's only been five days since she left, but it might as well have been five years. Fifty. I don't know where to begin.

'I knew you'd be with Julia,' I say eventually, to break the ice. 'As soon as the cop said Rome, I realized where you must've gone.'

'The police?'

'Well, I had to call them,' I say reasonably.

'Yes. Of course. How did they know I was here?'

Her voice is calm, matter-of-fact. I crack open my beer on the edge of the kitchen counter with one hand, noting with a degree of satisfaction the deep groove the bottle-top leaves in Kate's expensive granite. 'Oh, it doesn't take much, these days,' I say, matching her tone. 'They can pull up everything about you at the touch of a button. You used your credit card at Heathrow—'

'Of course. My ticket.'

'You threw us for a while,' I add lightly. 'Using a card in your maiden name. Kept us all guessing for a bit.'

'It's the only one not maxed out,' Kate says.

I move to the other end of the kitchen, peering out of the window at the rain. 'I don't know why I didn't think of Julia before. I called everyone else in your address book.'

'It's a new one,' Kate says. 'I didn't get round to transferring all the numbers.'

She goes quiet again. I watch two raindrops chase each

other down the pane. You'd think she could make this a bit easier on me. I don't know what to say to her. All this talking about feelings is the kind of stuff women do so much better.

'You're all right, then?' I manage finally.

'Yes, I'm fine.' Another pause. 'Well, not fine, of course. Or I wouldn't be here. But I'm OK otherwise, I think. You?'

'Oh, fine, yes. All things considered.'

We're like strangers discussing the weather.

I take another long pull of beer. I've been so worried about Kate that I haven't had time to get angry. But now, when for the first time in days I know she's safe – not dead in a ditch, not raped or murdered – and I start to think of what she's put me through, angry doesn't begin to cover it. Without warning, I'm consumed with a rage so intense it snatches the oxygen out of the room.

'*Christ, Kate!*' I shout. 'What in hell possessed you? You just vanished! Without a word! D'you know how worried I've been?'

Silence.

I slam the bottle on the counter. 'Couldn't you have called, at least?' I demand. 'Left a bloody message? Jesus, Kate. I thought you'd been kidnapped or murdered!'

I take another beer out of the fridge and open it the same way I did the first. I finish half of it in one gulp, forcing my temper back under control. Still Kate says nothing, though I can tell from the sound of her breathing that she's still there.

'The police wanted to know if you'd been depressed,' I say tightly. 'I suppose they thought you might have killed yourself. Then they asked if there was another man.' I laugh harshly. 'You should have seen the bastard's face when he let that one drop. Loved every minute of it. Your little game has turned me into a bloody laughing stock. Whatever you're playing at, I hope it's made you happy.'

'Of course it hasn't made me happy,' Kate says finally. 'This isn't some kind of perverse game, whatever you might think. I didn't set out to upset you. This isn't really about *you* . . .'

'You're my *wife*! You left me! How can that *not* be about me?'

She sighs. 'The world doesn't revolve around you, Ned. I realize you're upset, but—'

'What about Agness?' I interrupt furiously. 'She's been worried sick. How could you do this to her?'

'I told you, I didn't *do* this to anyone. I've only been gone five days, and I'm sure the children have managed. They're not babies.'

Babies. The word reverberates between us. I spent most of last night going over and over in my head why she left. I don't know where I could have gone wrong. I took her to the hospital for the D&C and stayed with her till she came round. I drove her home, made her soup, bit my tongue when she snapped at me over nothing. I treated her with bloody kid gloves for weeks. I kept out of her way as much as I could, and didn't mention the baby in case it upset her. I didn't even say a word when she didn't want to have sex. Frankly, I don't know what else I could've done to make her happy, but clearly I screwed up somewhere along the line. Things evidently aren't going to get back to normal until I make an apology. I just wish I knew what the fuck it was *for*.

I grit my teeth. 'About that. The – you know. The baby.'

'Don't,' Kate says quickly.

'Tell me. Is that what this is all about?'

'It's not that simple . . .'

I cough nervously. 'Because I get it. The hormone thing. I mean, it was only, what, a month or two ago . . .'

'Ten weeks,' she says stonily.

'Well, there you are, then,' I offer awkwardly. 'Hormones all over the place. It's my fault. I realize I should've been a bit more supportive—'

'*Supportive*? Ned, you said you were *glad* our child had died!'

Why do women always have to *talk* about things? Why can't they just get through them and keep their mouths shut?

I shift uncomfortably, switching the phone to my other ear. 'Come on, Kate. I didn't exactly say that. And it's not like something happened to Agness or Guy . . .'

'What are you saying? That it didn't matter? *It wasn't a real baby?*'

'Christ, you don't have to yell. I said I'm sorry. I don't know what else you want from me.'

'No. You never do,' she says bitterly.

I finish the second bottle of beer. God knows I didn't want another kid, but despite what Kate thinks, I didn't wish it dead either. I'd never tell her this, it'd only make everything worse, but I'd actually started to come round to the idea of a new baby. Got a bit teary-eyed myself when I realized it wasn't going to happen after all. I was looking for the insurance papers in Kate's office one afternoon the week after it all went wrong, and I found this tiny Babygro she'd hidden away in a drawer. The length of my forearm. I can remember holding Agness that way when she was born, her head in the palm of my hand, her tiny feet in the crook of my elbow. Never forgotten it.

'Fine,' I sigh. 'Fine. We can talk about it tomorrow when you get back.'

'I don't think I'm ready to do that yet, Ned.'

I freeze. It hadn't occurred to me she might not come back.

'Well, when *will* you feel "ready"?'

'Ned, this isn't just about the miscarriage. I've been feeling unhappy for a long time – I didn't realize how unhappy until now. Work, Eleanor, the way the kids are around me. Something has to change. I need a bit more time to think about what I want before I come home.'

'You can't just stick me with the kids!' I exclaim. 'How am I supposed to manage?'

'The same way I do, I should imagine.'

She sounds different. Steely, and not in her usual hard-arsed business way. It's like everything's suddenly up for grabs.

'Oh, very funny,' I snap. '*You* only cope because you have me at home, remember? And what about your bloody mother? Am I supposed to look after her, too? I have a job too, you know. How am I going to get everything done and write as well?'

'It's only for a few more days. Please, Ned. Don't make this any more difficult than it has to be.' She hesitates. 'Can I speak to the children?'

'How many more days?'

'I don't know. I didn't plan any of this, Ned. It just . . . happened. I don't expect you to understand. I'll be back soon. Can you just trust me?'

'So I'm supposed to just sit here and wait till you decide you're ready to come home?' I demand, hurt and confused. 'Fine, if that's the way you want to play it. I'm certainly not going to come out there and beg you to come back. Just don't expect me to still be here waiting when you finally come to your senses.'

I slam down the phone, which promptly falls off the wall and smashes on the tiled floor.

'Nice going, Dad,' Agness yells, storming into the kitchen. 'She's never going to come back now!'

Kate

For a moment, as I stare up at the ceiling and watch thin strips of sunshine spill through the shutters and play across the whitewashed walls, I don't remember where I am. And then, as it does every morning, it all comes rushing back on a wave of guilt.

Sawyer 2 leaps onto my stomach to demand his breakfast, and with a sigh I flip back the covers and get out of bed. It's Monday: a week to the day since I left. I can't believe I'm still here. I hadn't realized until Ned asked me two days ago when I was coming back that I wasn't yet ready to. I'd assumed that sooner or later he'd find me and then I'd go home; I was almost as surprised as he was when I said I was staying. It wasn't that he didn't understand about the baby, or that he still wanted to brush it all under the rug. It wasn't even the infuriating dig about my hormones. It was the fact that he assumed I would just come back, without ever really understanding – or *caring* – why I'd left.

I still can't believe he put the phone down without letting me speak to the children. I've left dozens of messages on their mobiles since Saturday, but neither of them has called me back. I just want a chance to try to explain that it's not *them* I've left. But why should they listen? I'm the one who's behaved unforgivably, after all.

Forcing the dark thoughts away, I dress quickly in a thin cotton skirt patterned with vivid blue irises and a skimpy white vest while Sawyer 2 watches impatiently from the top of the dresser. Last week I went into the village and bought some cheap basics to last me in case I stayed beyond the weekend. I told myself I could always use them at home. Buying a six-pack of knickers didn't mean I was *staying*. Now, I realize, I never had any intention of going back on Friday.

Perching on the end of the high bed, I lace up the pair of knock-off high-tops. Not very me at all, these pink sneakers; which is precisely the point, of course. If I could climb out of my own skin, I would.

I open the bedroom door and go down the outside staircase to the kitchen, trying not to trip as Sawyer 2 twists in and out of my legs. It's still early. A shallow mist lingers in the garden like dry ice, cloaking the blueberry bushes and mint and cladding the pine trees in sweeping grey skirts. The air smells cool and crisp and fresh, even though we're just a couple of miles from the shrill clamour of the clogged, polluted city streets.

I feed the kitten and make myself a quick mug of instant coffee, thankful Julia isn't yet up to witness my heresy. Bolting down a slice of toast and sweet plum jam, I grab an old-fashioned string shopping bag from behind the back door and scribble a quick list. We need fresh milk from the *latteria*, bread from the bakery, and some salad and fruit from the grocer's. As far as I can make out, Julia seems to live on a diet of coffee and cigarettes.

Her bone-shaking Fiat is parked in the courtyard outside, but I prefer to walk. I like using the time and the cool morning air to clear my head.

In the village, I linger over my errands, taking time to pick and choose the ripest tomatoes, the crustiest loaf, instead of flinging everything into a supermarket trolley as fast as possible, the way I'd normally shop. So much of my life has been spent on fast-forward, rushing to save time. Now, all I want to do is spend it.

I end up at the *latteria*. Inside the dairy shop it's cool and dark. Smiling at the aproned woman behind the old-fashioned till, I take a pint of milk out of the chilled cabinet. She wraps the carton in a brown paper bag and hands it to me as I fumble for some euros. '*Lie è turista?*'

My Italian is a little rusty, but I recognize the word. '*Turista, sì.*'

'*Tedesca?*'

'German? No, English. *Inglese.*'

She smiles and hands me my change. '*Quanto tempo rimane?*'

I shrug incomprehension and smile back. I understand the question; I just can't give her an answer. I can't tell anyone how long I'm staying until I work that out for myself.

Weighed down by my shopping, I stroll slowly through the centre of the village to the bar-gelateria on the corner and order a cappuccino, a habit I've developed over the last few days. The skinny old man behind the counter smiles and nods wordlessly in greeting, as he does each morning now. It's only a little after nine, but the café is already busy: the aluminium tables on the pavement outside are filling up with old men playing dominoes and middle-aged women in flower-print dresses. The men are silent; the women talk loudly over each other, pausing only to cluck at a baby passing by in a pushchair, or glare at a girl daring to show an inch too much skin.

Gently blowing the foam off my cappuccino, I sip it and watch the world go by. I'm sure that concealed beneath the pastoral village charm are the same marital strains and financial worries you find in homes across the world. But for now I let myself be lulled by the illusion that life is gentler, kinder here. I can almost imagine living here for ever.

With a small sigh, I finish my coffee and go inside to pay. A teenage boy is the only waiter on duty. As I approach the bar, he backs out of the kitchen with a heavy tray of espressos and full glasses of water. With the intuition of mothers the world over, I see the accident coming before it even happens. Dropping my shopping on the floor, I dive forward and catch the tray, twisting up and sideways so it doesn't hit the bar or the wall, then deposit it promptly on the counter. It's not the boy's fault; he's just trying to do too much too fast. They need more waiters when it's this busy.

The old man rushes out from the kitchen and starts yelling in voluble Italian at the boy, who flushes and ducks his head, the tips of his ears – which is all I can see of him beneath his thatch of schoolboy curls – scarlet with embarrassment.

'Good catch, *cara*.'

I turn, trying to quell the sudden flutter of butterflies in my stomach. I knew I'd run into Alessio sooner or later, but I'm still thrown. He hasn't changed. He's still ridiculously good-looking, but, unlike so many Italian lizards, carries it off with a quiet confidence that doesn't tip over into smug. He wears his expensive khaki linen suit with ease, his open-necked pale blue shirt a perfect contrast to his amber eyes and the caramel of his skin. In London, he'd stand out like a peacock in a yard full of sparrows.

I wipe my palms surreptitiously on my cotton skirt. Alessio has always had a dizzying effect on me, from the moment I first saw him. It was one thing to react like this when I was twenty-one, but I'm forty next month. I have two children now. I'm *married*, for heaven's sake!

He kisses my cheeks, his smile telling me he knows the effect he's having on me. The last time we met, he was gently wiping the tears from beneath my eyes after having politely, charmingly and firmly dumped me. I seem to remember my last words to him were a pathetic plea for one more chance and the declaration that without it, my life was over.

I position myself firmly as a confident woman of the world. 'Julia said you'd moved to the village,' I say. 'Do you like living here?'

'It seemed easier to be with the family when the children were born.' He nods towards the old man behind the bar. 'This place belongs to Uncle Maurizio. His wife helps Cinzia with the children.'

'I heard you'd got married. Congratulations.'

He waves his hand. 'It was a long time ago.'

'Me too. Fifteen years last week, in fact.'

Alessio reaches into his inside pocket and pulls out a packet of Italian cigarettes. 'Rome is not a place to experience alone,' he observes, tapping the box against the back of his hand. 'Where is your husband?'

I hesitate, wondering how much Julia has told him. 'Working. He's very busy.'

He cups a tanned hand around the cigarette and lights it. I follow the movement with my eyes. I know smoking is bad for you, of course, and bad for those around you, but he makes it look so damn sexy.

'Too busy to take his lovely wife to the Eternal City?'

'Someone had to stay with the children.'

'Of course.' He exhales a stream of smoke. 'So, *cara*, what do you do, all alone in Rome?'

Cara. Beloved.

I give myself a brisk shake. 'As I'm on my own I can spend as long as I like looking at the Sistine Chapel, and no one laughs at me for throwing coins in the Trevi Fountain.'

'Your husband is not a lover of art and history?'

I bristle at the mocking tone in his voice when he talks about Ned.

'Perhaps,' he adds casually, 'you'd care to have lunch with me later?'

'I don't think so,' I say primly.

He laughs. 'Kate, I'm asking you to have lunch with me, not to run away together. My uncle tells me that every morning you sit and drink your cappuccino alone, with such a sad look in your eyes. And you have such a beautiful smile.' His tawny gaze holds mine. 'I remember it.'

My skin tingles. I know flirting is practically reflexive with Italian men, but there's no denying it feels good to be on the receiving end of such attention; particularly from a man as handsome as this.

I'm startled by a small boy suddenly careening into the back of my knees. Alessio catches him and holds out a hand to steady me as a pretty woman in pink kitten-heels follows her son into the cool interior of the bar.

'Kate,' he says, quickly dropping his hand from my waist, his expression a study in schoolboy guilt, 'this is Cinzia, my wife. Cinzia, this is Kate, a friend of Julia's from England.'

Cinzia smiles tightly at me, dark eyes flashing with barely suppressed irritation. I'd put her in her late twenties. Wasp-waisted and voluptuous, she looks like a young Sophia Loren. On my best day, I couldn't hope to compete.

'*Fabio, di' ciao a Kate,*' Alessio prompts his son.

'It's OK,' I smile. The little boy is the most gorgeous child I've ever seen, with skin the colour of caramel and a rumpled halo of dark brown curls. If we'd had a son, I wonder if he'd have been as handsome as this. '*Ciao, Fabio.*'

'Perhaps you'd like to join us for a cappuccino?' Alessio says as I pick up my shopping bags.

'I can't. I have to be somewhere. Another time?'

We both know I'm lying on both counts.

'Of course. If there is anything I can do for you while you're here, please let me know. *Ci vediamo, Kate.*'

He carries the little boy out of the bar, and his wife slips her arm possessively through his as they leave. Wistfully, I watch him go. It's not that I still have any feelings for him: I can see already how little we actually have to say to each other, and I don't envy Cinzia her task keeping him in line. But how different my life might have been if I'd married Alessio. No high-powered job, no stressful commute and complicated juggling act to keep work, marriage and family satisfied. Just a handsome man to love and a beautiful child to care for.

Not that that kind of marriage would ever suit me, of course. I could never live Eleanor's life. Helpless, passive.

Suddenly I make up my mind. I run outside and catch up with Alessio as he stops to unlock a car parked halfway down the street, Fabio's arms still wrapped tightly around his neck.

'Alessio,' I pant, ignoring Cinzia's glare. 'Actually, there *is* something you can do for me after all.'

Agness

'Dad is starting to really piss me off,' I tell Harry crossly. 'I mean, I'm totally on his side and everything. But all he's done since he spoke to Mum a week ago is sit on the stupid sofa watching *Survivorman* on the Discovery Channel. Which is, like, totally ironic, since he's basically camping out in the living room.' I drop my backpack on the floor and fling myself onto the bed beside him. 'If this carries on much longer, we'll have to move the piano and put in a portaloo. Seriously, he hasn't shaved or showered or *any*-thing. He looks like a tramp. If Liesl saw him, she'd *totally* want to marry him again.'

Harry backs up against the headboard to give me room, and wraps his skinny white arms tighter round his knees. I lie back beside him and stare up at the black painted ceiling. Everything in Harry's room is black: the walls, the blinds, the carpet. It's kind of cosy, really.

'My life is *beyond* embarrassing,' I sigh. 'I mean, my own *mother* running off and leaving me. How sad is that?

If she'd gone somewhere cool, it wouldn't be so bad, but Italy's not exactly original. How come no one ever goes to find themselves in, like, Bangladesh or Haiti?'

'*Eat, Pray, Love*,' Harry mumbles.

'Whatevs. You got any ciggies?'

'Menthol.'

'Give me one.'

Harry reaches under the bed and hands me a packet of cigarettes. I pull one out and light it. 'Mum keeps leaving all these messages on my phone. I haven't called her back. I'm not mad at her or anything,' I add quickly. 'I, like, don't blame her for going, really, though I wish she'd taken me with her. I'm just not ready to talk to her yet, you know?'

Harry picks at the scab on his elbow and looks up at me through his heavy black fringe. I recognize this for the enthusiastic sign of encouragement it is.

I grope around on the floor for an empty Coke can and tap my ash into it. 'You'd think my father would be there for me in a crisis,' I say crossly. 'I've been abandoned! I need *support*. I need *attention*. I need extra pocket money so I can be kind to myself. But all Dad does is sit on the sofa and look pathetic. He can't even cook dinner. I've had pizza for the last three nights running. Does he *want* me to end up with scurvy?'

Harry scratches his nose. 'Maybe he's, like, upset?'

'If he's that bothered about Mum leaving, why doesn't he go and get her back? He knows where she is.' I roll onto my side, propping myself on my elbow. 'Gran's totally useless, too. She doesn't even know how to work the microwave, never mind the dishwasher. It's like, I'm the only one doing anything around the place since Mum and Dad split up.'

'Your mum and dad have split up?'

'How do I know?' I say tartly. 'No one tells me *anything*. Dad says she'll only be gone a week or two, but who knows? They treat me like a total moron. It's like that whole thing with the baby.' I roll my eyes. 'Suddenly Mum can't stand the smell of eggs and she's got this weird craving for pickles and Marmite for breakfast every morning. Like, *hello*? You don't have to be a genius to know what *that* means. But no one says a word to me. I'm always the last to find out. For all I know, they could both be axe-murderers. Nothing would surprise me.'

Harry takes a puff of my cigarette then hands it back, and I draw in another lungful of smoke. It freaked me out, Mum getting pregnant. If they have to do it at their age, that's bad enough, but they don't have to *flaunt* it. She might as well take out an ad in the freaking paper. What would my friends say if she turned up at school with this huge great pregnant stomach? *Beyond* embarrassing.

I wasn't that thrilled at the thought of a new brother or sister, either. I don't want to be a bitch or anything, but where was *I* supposed to figure in all this? Bad enough Guy being her favourite, but how can I compete with a cute and cuddly baby? I'm not a big fan of things that puke and dribble and shit from every orifice, but grown-ups seem to think differently. Mum only has to spot a pram in the supermarket and she turns into a gibbering mass of hormones.

So, OK, I might not have *wanted* it, exactly, but I was actually quite sad when she lost it; though of course, since nobody *told* me about it, the first I knew was when she came back from the hospital all white and tragic after they did whatever it is doctors do when a baby dies inside you. Scrape it out, I suppose. Gross. It's always sad when something dies. I'm totally against the death penalty, except when someone really deserves it for, like, blowing up a whole plane of people or starving horses to death or something.

Didn't take a genius to figure Dad was way more upset than he let on. A few days after Mum came home from the hospital, I saw him sitting in the study and he was holding this tiny Babygro in his lap and just staring at it with this totally weird look on his face, like he was going to start bawling. It nearly set me off, just watching him.

But he wouldn't tell Mum he cared, of course. He just acted like it was no biggie, as if she'd had her wisdom teeth out or something. No wonder she left. Honestly, *men*.

'No one talks to anyone in your family,' Harry says unexpectedly.

It's not like Harry to volunteer his opinion, never mind toss off meaningful psychological insights like he's Jeremy Kyle or something. But he's right. Mum and Dad have got so many secrets, it's like living with MI5. Then there's Guy, with all that stuff going on at his school. When you come down to it, the only one with nothing to hide is me.

'I've got to go in a minute,' I say, dropping the cigarette butt into the Coke can. 'Dad'll freak if I'm late. See you tomorrow?'

Harry nods. As I unfold myself from the bed, my sweatshirt snags on the underside of his bookshelf. I twist round, trying to free myself, but can't quite reach where I'm caught. 'Harry, d'you mind?'

His hands hover inches away from my body, like there's a force field or something around me. 'Get a move on, Harry,' I say crossly. 'I'm not bent over like Quasimodo for my health, you know.'

He reaches tentatively behind me. His wrist accidentally brushes my nipple, and instantly it leaps to attention, standing out like a big pink cherry on top of an ice-cream sundae. The feeling is warm and tingly, like when you get a swig of wine and it burns down your throat. Clearly Harry feels something too, because he's breathing like he's just run a marathon and his face looks redder than I've ever seen it.

My heart hammers in my chest as we stare at each other, frozen into position like some weird cartoon. Neither of us breathes. And then, very slowly, I reach towards his jeans.

It's harder than I expected. It feels like there's an actual *bone* in there, not just, you know, blood and stuff.

I don't *mean* to squeeze it.

Harry moans and falls back against the bedhead. For a moment, I think I've actually killed him.

'Oh God, I'm sorry,' I say, panicked. 'Are you OK?'

Weakly he nods.

'I didn't mean to—'

'It's OK.'

In the excitement, my sweatshirt has somehow come free. I get off the bed and stare at my Converses, fiddling with the strings of my hoodie.

'Harry,' I say, looking up after a long pause. 'Harry, have you ever . . . *you* know. With anyone?'

Red to the tips of his ears, he shakes his head.

'Me neither.'

We both ponder this.

'I think I might be less nervous if I do it with you the first time,' I say finally. 'I don't think it'd feel so weird with you.'

He nods energetically.

I pull up my hood. 'I really have got to go now. I don't want Dad calling the police on me too.'

'I like your mum,' Harry says. 'She's all right.'

When I get home, Dad's asleep on the sofa as usual, the hands-free phone on the cushion next to his head, like he's still waiting for it to ring. I feel kind of sorry for him, but not *quite* as sorry as I did a few days ago. I mean, he doesn't have to just give up and wait for Mum to decide what she wants to do. He could take matters into his own hands and be a bit more proactive. If I'd been him, I wouldn't have bothered phoning Mum, I'd have got on the next plane to Rome and staged a sit-in outside Aunt Julia's house till she agreed to come back with me.

I sigh as I go back to the kitchen. Typical Dad. If he ever *had* any get-up-and-go, it had got up and gone long before I was born.

I scowl at the state of the place. It looks like squatters have moved in: dirty plates everywhere, rubbish on the floor next to the overflowing bin, grounds from the coffee percolator clogging up the sink. The milk's been left out and has separated, and a hard, dried-out lump of cheddar is still sitting on the counter where someone's left it. God, I miss Mum.

With another sigh, I feed Sawyer and then open the dishwasher and start to empty it, pausing now and then to scrape dried food off a plate with my fingernail. Clearly no one else is going to deal with the mess in here, so unless I want to go out and buy paper plates, I'm going to have to get on with it myself.

It takes me over an hour to get the place halfway decent,

and my back is killing me by the time I finish, but as I straighten up and survey the clean, uncluttered surface, I feel kind of proud of myself. It's not perfect, but it's, like, *way* better than it was.

I'm in the utility room, knee-deep in stinky socks and skid marks, trying to figure out how to work the washing machine, when Dad stumbles into the kitchen. He looks like a wino with his stubble and crumpled clothes and hair sticking up in all directions. I watch him open the fridge, take out a beer and pop it on the edge of the counter, ignoring the spurt of foam that sprays across my clean work surface. Before I can say anything, he grabs a box of cornflakes and shoves a handful in his mouth, scattering crumbs all over my newly swept kitchen floor, and staggers back towards the sitting room.

OK. I am *so* over all this.

I storm after him into the sitting room. 'Where is everybody?' I demand.

'Guy's at Liesl's. I think Eleanor's upstairs . . .'

'Gran!' I yell up the stairs. '*Gran!*'

'What's going on?' Dad says fretfully.

I wait till Gran comes down, making a right meal of the stairs for our benefit. I've had enough of her freeloading, too. She can boil an egg, for fuck's sake. Her hands aren't broken.

'This can't go on!' I shout at the pair of them. 'We've got, like, nothing to eat! I'm fed up with pizza and takeaways! And no one's done the laundry for *weeks*! This place is a total pit, and I'm sick of being the only one to clean up! This entire family is falling apart, and you're doing nothing to stop it, Dad! I've had enough! We need Mum to come back!'

'Your mother doesn't want to come back,' Dad says.

I stamp my foot. I love my dad, of course I do, but I'm *totally* getting why Mum left.

'Then *you*,' I cry, 'have to go and *get* her!'

Eleanor

'Your mother doesn't want to come back,' Edward says feebly.

'Then *you*,' Agness shrieks, 'have to go and *get* her!'

I've never heard such arrant nonsense. Does nobody understand what this is about?

I slam my cane against the floor. 'Absolutely not!'

'But Gran—'

'The *last* thing Edward should do is chase after her,' I snap.

'Dear God. It's been sixteen years. Could you *please* call me Ned,' he mutters.

I ignore the interruption. I don't believe in diminutives; his mother christened him Edward for a reason. 'Katherine is behaving like a spoilt child, and she needs to be treated like one,' I say, shooing the cat from the sofa and sitting down. 'We've got no choice but to put up with this silliness until she comes to her senses, since we can hardly drag her home by her hair. But the more fuss and bother we make, the harder it'll be for her to swallow her pride and come home.' I smooth the nubby heather tweed of my skirt with satisfaction. 'We simply have to ignore her tantrums and let her stew in her own juice for a while. She'll soon have had enough once she realizes it's getting her nowhere. We won't need to wait long.'

Edward pulls unattractively on his lower lip. 'You think so?'

'I don't like all this any more than you do,' I say crisply. 'She's leading us all a merry dance, and no mistake. But if you go rushing off after her like a bull in a china shop, she may never come home at all.'

'Don't listen to her, Dad,' Agness says rudely. 'I'm telling you, Mum's not going to come home on her own. She wants you to *persuade* her.'

'Edward, are you going to let your daughter talk to me like that?'

'Agness, that's no way to speak to your grandmother,' he says weakly.

Agness puts her hands on her hips and glares. I hate to admit it, but there are times when she reminds me of myself. 'Neither of you are getting it! Mum *wants* you to rush off after her. That's the whole point! If you don't, she'll think we don't care!'

'Maybe she's right, Eleanor,' he says doubtfully.

'She's right about one thing,' I sniff. 'This is certainly about getting your attention. But unlike you, young lady, I have actually raised a child before. You never give in to these sorts of antics or you live to regret it.'

'So what should I do, then?' Edward asks.

I regard my son-in-law with distaste. The man has completely fallen apart. He hasn't shaved or changed his clothes in a week, and he stinks like a polecat. Of course it's all been a worry and a shock, yes-yes, but there's no need to let the side down like this. Agness has far more spine than her father, I'm glad to say. Follows the female line. I can't abide weak men. My James was many things, but never weak.

'I've told you already,' I say tartly. 'Ignore her. Nothing puts out a fire like lack of oxygen. Trust me. Once Katherine sees this silliness isn't getting her anywhere, she'll be back with her tail between her legs.'

'She *so* won't,' Agness mutters.

'Agness—'

'Look, Dad, even if Mum comes home tomorrow, we still need to go shopping *now*. We're out of everything, even loo roll. We can't keep raiding the garage shop. We need to go shopping *properly*, the way Mum does.'

Edward shoves a bundle of brown envelopes into the Welsh dresser. 'Can't it wait?'

'No, it can't! I told you, I'm sick of takeaways for dinner every night!' Agness yells. 'They're full of MSG and high-fructose corn syrup. I can *feel* the carcinogens taking over.'

'Who are the Carcinogens?' I demand.

'*Dad*—'

'Yes, all right,' Edward says irritably. 'Eleanor, would you mind picking up a few bits?'

I hesitate. I have no intention of running around after this man the way my daughter has foolishly done all these years, but I'm aware my position here is tenuous. Edward and I both know I'm well enough to go home. My ankle has healed sufficiently for me even to manage stairs with the aid of my cane. But Edward hasn't yet asked me to leave, and I haven't volunteered. Chaotic and sloppy though the household is without Katherine, I'd still rather be here than tripping over Lego at my younger daughter's dreary council flat, or rattling around in my own cold, empty house on my own.

'I can't drive,' I point out reasonably. 'Not with my bad ankle.'

Edward rubs the palms of his hands back and forth over his stubbled jaw. 'Christ. OK, OK. The three of us can go. I wouldn't have a clue what to buy on my own.'

'Not until you've showered,' Agness says pertly. 'There's no way I'm going out with you looking like *that*.'

When Edward comes back downstairs, his face is raw and chapped, and the buttons on his shirt are done up wrongly, but he is at least clean for the first time in a week.

He drives to a brand new out-of-town supermarket I've never seen before, and the two of them wander the aisles with the confused air of inmates on day-release. Grocery shopping is clearly a new experience for the pair of them. I must say, even I'm rather overwhelmed by the scale of choice on offer in a shop this size. I usually stick to the little Tesco Express at the end of my road. I can't see the need for jeans and books and DVDs to be sold alongside the bread and Marmite. All this excess just encourages spending beyond your means. Make out a shopping list and stick to it, and you'll never break your budget. Ice-cream makers have no business in a British kitchen.

I put a small tin of salmon in the shopping cart, and Agness immediately takes it out and replaces it with a multipack of tinned tuna. I purse my lips at her extravagance. She seems to think we're feeding the French Foreign Legion. As soon as her back's turned, I remove a suitcase-sized packet of Kellogg's cornflakes and throw in a small own-brand variety pack. One family couldn't possibly eat that much cereal before it all went stale. False economy, in my book.

'We need to plan out some meals for the week,' Agness says as Edward disappears to find some beer. 'You know, like Mum does.'

'What about starting with a nice Shepherd's Pie for tonight?'

She pulls a face. 'Like, carb central. Can't we have spinach salad or something?'

'You can't eat spinach *raw*! It'll give you salmonella.'

'Not if you wash it properly. You don't have to boil everything to death these days, Gran. We've got rid of the plague, or hadn't you heard?'

'No need to be cheeky, young lady. What about steak and kidney pie, then? Or liver and bacon? Plenty of protein in that.'

'*Offal?*'

I push the trolley past the rows of absurd pasta shapes and fancy oils and vinegars and dressings as Agness dawdles beside them. Salad cream has always been good enough for me. 'Pork chops. Can't go wrong with a nice pork chop.'

'Guy won't eat pork.'

'Why on earth not?' I say waspishly. 'He's not Jewish, is he?'

'*Gran!*'

The trolley is overflowing by the time Edward joins us at the checkout, though I'm not sure we have the makings of a single decent meal. Far too many pointless things in it like pesto and pine nuts, whatever those may be. You can't make a proper dinner out of *nuts*. What's wrong with a jar of pickled herrings or some corned beef, I'd like to know? All this exotic nonsense. It's no wonder the bill is over three hundred pounds. Clearly Katherine has been spoiling this family half to death.

Edward pulls a plastic card out of his wallet and swipes it through the machine. It beeps, and he tries another couple of times before putting it back and taking out a second card, which is also declined.

'*Dad*,' Agness hisses. 'This is *embarrassing*.'

Edward turns helplessly to me. 'Kate usually transfers money to our joint account when she gets paid.'

'So use yours,' I retort.

'There's nothing in mine,' Edward mutters, flushing.

'Nothing in yours *or* the joint account?'

'Kate usually handles all the money,' he says defensively.

'What about your credit cards?'

He looks sheepish. 'Up to the limit.'

'Excuse me, sir,' the checkout girl says nastily. 'Is there a problem?'

'I'll pay this time,' I say, rummaging around in my handbag. 'But you need to sort this out when we get home, Edward. If you don't have access to Katherine's account, you'll have to organize your own finances for a while. You must be able to keep things going until she comes back. It's not as if it'll be for long. I've told you. She'll be home in a week.'

If I say it often enough, perhaps I'll even believe it.

Kate

I watch Julia stop by a small green door set into a much larger one a full two storeys high. If I follow her now, everything's going to change.

She turns. 'Are you coming?'

Ned knows where I am, I tell myself firmly. He can reach me if he wants to. I miss the children more than I'd have thought possible, but the truth is, they're better off without me. I'm not surprised they won't answer my calls. What kind of mother am I if I can't even hold on to my baby?

It wasn't your fault. You couldn't help it.

Then why do I feel so guilty?

I cross the narrow side street, which is just off the Spanish Steps, and follow Julia through the small door, feeling a little like Alice in Wonderland trailing after the White Rabbit. It's a sensation that's reinforced when I unexpectedly find myself in a cool, shadowed courtyard dotted with lemon and lime trees, right in the heart of Rome's most expensive shopping district. Apartments overlook us on all four sides, but the courtyard itself is open to the bright blue sky.

I crane my neck. 'Which floor is he on?'

'Sixth. He's got a lovely little roof terrace with the most amazing view across the city.'

'Are you sure I can afford this?'

'I told you. Luca doesn't want much rent if you don't mind watering the plants and taking care of his parrot,' Julia says. 'He only ever lets this apartment to friends. It's not really about the money – he just wants someone to keep an eye on the place when he's away over the summer.'

'Let's hope I get good tips at work,' I say drily.

'You don't have to do this,' Julia says. 'I told you, you can stay with me as long as you like.'

'I know. But I'd rather stand on my own two feet.'

Waitressing may not pay much, but I can't keep putting things on my credit card. Alessio was as good as his word: he persuaded his Uncle Maurizio to give me a job at the bar, and I should be able to earn enough to pay a peppercorn rent and put food on the table. That's all I need for now.

Since Ned finally called a week ago, I've been on pins waiting for him to turn up on the doorstep. I'd be surprised if he showed that much initiative, but there's no knowing what a lack of clean underpants might drive a man to.

But he hasn't come. Nor has he called again. I have to start to get used to the idea of a life without him, and finding a place of my own is the first step.

'Let's hope you can still stand on your own two feet when you've climbed six flights of stairs,' Julia says as we start up a staircase on the far side of the courtyard.

'No lift, I suppose?'

She grins. Grasping the iron banister, I follow her up the worn stone steps, wishing I hadn't quit my aerobics classes. By the time we reach the top floor, I'm red-faced and out of breath.

Julia presses the buzzer as I lean against the wall panting, my hands on my knees.

The door opens, and I curse the law of nature that ensures a woman inevitably runs into a handsome man when she looks her absolute *worst*. I'd put Luca in his mid-forties, but he has the rangy, snake-hipped body of a teenager, with lean legs in faded jeans, a perfectly cut navy blazer, and a tight white T-shirt that shows off a well-defined six-pack.

'You always were a sucker for a pretty face,' Julia whispers, grinning.

'I'm sorry I can't stay,' Luca says, kissing Julia on the cheek and bowing courteously at me. 'Someone is waiting. If you have any questions, please, call me.' He kisses Julia again. '*Baci, cara.*'

Apart from the fact that I need oxygen to climb the stairs, the apartment is perfect. Its single bedroom is light and airy, if a little masculine, with billowing navy curtains at its shuttered windows and a wrought-iron four-poster bed draped in crisp white muslin and made up with white linen sheets. A wooden fan – a rarity in Rome – turns gently overhead. The antique freestanding wardrobe is small, taking perhaps seven hangers front to rear instead of sideways, but there's a large chest of drawers on the other side of the room, and anyway, I don't have many clothes.

The sitting room has a more feminine imprint. Crammed with antique furniture that has clearly seen better days, there are two pale green sofas facing each other across a low coffee table, a pretty escritoire off to one side, and, scattered around the walls, several mismatching chairs in various shades of gold and ochre. Three or four small side tables are covered with silver-framed photographs. I suspect Luca's mother furnished the room with family cast-offs. A wife would have insisted on new curtains.

The kitchen and bathroom are basic, equipped with appliances that probably predate the Roman Empire, but the stunning roof terrace, with its breathtaking views across the city, more than makes up for it. Scarlet geraniums spill out of pots at each corner, and a bright yellow awning protects against the heat of the day. It's like a different world up here among the chimney pots, far from the chaos and noise of the traffic below. Worth the climb.

'You don't need to worry about paying for electricity or water,' Julia says as we shade our eyes and gaze across the city rooftops. 'It's included in the rent. There's no phone or cable, but you've got your mobile, and I can always lend you a few books if you get bored. Luca won't need it again until October, so for the next six months, it's all yours.'

'I won't need it anywhere near that long,' I say quickly, not sure I believe myself. 'Where's the infamous parrot?'

'In the bathroom behind the shower curtain. Luca says to move the cage when you want to take a shower, but otherwise keep her there or she squawks and annoys the neighbours. He hates her, but his dead grandmother left her to him, so he can't get rid of her.'

'And it's OK if I bring Sawyer 2?'

The little ginger kitten and I seem to have adopted each other in the past few weeks. Every night, he curls up on top of the bedspread in the crook of my knees, his vibrant purr lulling me to sleep. I'd hate to leave him behind.

'As long as you keep him away from the parrot, I'm sure it'll be fine.'

I tilt my head to the sun. 'It's perfect,' I sigh happily.

I move in the next day, staggering up six flights of stairs with Sawyer 2 and my few bits and pieces. The kitten inspects the apartment thoroughly and then curls up in the centre of my new bed, grooming himself.

'Don't feel too at home,' I warn him. 'This isn't going to be for long.'

Sawyer 2 gives me a sceptical look, then goes back to washing his ears.

It takes me a day or two to get back into the swing of things, but waitressing is like cycling or skiing: you never really forget. All those summers putting myself through university the hard way stand me in good stead. I'm soon balancing half a dozen plates along my arm and twirling heavy trays of glasses above my head as if I've been waiting tables for years – indeed, as a wife and the mother of two teenagers, I suppose I have.

I love leaving work behind the moment I walk out of the bar. No responsibility or deadlines; no managing delicate egos or insubordinate employees. I simply turn up and do the job for which I'm paid.

For the first few days, I'm too tired when I get home to do anything but make myself a quick salad and fall into bed, but as I get used to being on my feet all day, that changes. It's at night that Rome truly comes alive. Some evenings I walk along the banks of the Tiber, or through the winding streets of Trastevere and the historic *centro storico*, stopping for a drink or *gelato* when I get tired. On other nights, I find a table at a trattoria in a hidden piazza and simply sit and watch the world go by over an exquisite puttanesca or zucchini ravioli and a glass or two of earthy red wine. To my surprise, I find I quite like my own company. It's like getting to know an old friend I thought never to see again.

On my first day off, I go to the Galleria Borghese, one of the museums I never got the chance to explore when I was living here last time. I take my time, reading about each artwork in a thick guidebook and studying it carefully before moving on to the next.

I pause by the life-sized marble sculpture of Bernini's *Apollo and Daphne*, arrested by its magnificent beauty. According to my book, two gods, Apollo and Eros, argued, and so Eros wounded Apollo with a golden arrow which made him fall in love with a beautiful nymph called Daphne. Apollo chased and captured her, whereupon her father turned her into a laurel tree. Heartbroken, Apollo cut off some of her branches and leaves to make a wreath, and proclaimed the laurel a sacred tree.

I close my book with a satisfied sigh. Now *there* was passion.

I'm not a sentimental teenager. I know marriage settles into a routine; it's the nature of the beast. Part of the price you pay for security. I don't expect hearts and flowers or a pounding heart every time my husband walks into the room, but most couples have at least the *memory* of passion to keep them going when enthusiasm and interest wane. It's two weeks now since Ned and I spoke, and he still hasn't tried to contact me. Perhaps he's taking me at my word and giving me the space and time I've asked for. But I can't help being disappointed that he hasn't made the extravagant gesture I've looked for throughout my marriage: the gesture that would tell me we *did* have passion between us after all.

I blink back a sudden rush of tears. All Ned has to do to win me is get on a plane. No dragons to slay or vengeful gods to defeat. The worst he'd have to face is losing his luggage.

For the first time, I wonder if Ned's actually happier without me.

Ned

'This is a fucking nightmare,' I mutter, throwing a sheaf of red bills onto the kitchen counter. 'Every day there are more bills, and I've got no bloody money to pay them.'

'Kate managed,' Eleanor sniffs, buttering two slices of Nimble. I wish she'd buy some bloody normal bread when she goes shopping; this plastic crap sticks in my gullet. 'It's just a question of keeping on top of things.'

'It's a question of having *no fucking money*,' I retort.

'You must have something put by,' Eleanor says.

'We don't float on a lake of ready cash,' I snarl. 'By the time we've paid the mortgages, two sets of school fees, council tax, the car loan and all the rest of it, there's barely enough left over to put food on the table. We're in the middle of a recession, or hadn't you noticed?'

'But you must have *some* savings?' she insists. 'Something for a rainy day?'

I open the fridge and grab a beer. Paying off my

gambling debts last year cleaned us out. Our savings these days amount to what we can find down the back of the sofa.

'It's not just me,' I mutter defensively. 'They say most people are just one pay cheque away from bankruptcy. We're lucky we've lasted this long.'

'But you said Katherine's still getting paid.'

'For now. Her boss said she's owed eleven weeks' leave. All those years of refusing to take a proper holiday,' I add bitterly. 'He agreed to hold her job open till she's used it up and said he'd tell everyone she's taking a sabbatical. But if she's not back by then, she'll be out on her ear.'

'Eleven weeks! She'll be back long before that!'

'I bloody hope so. But if I can't access her account and physically get at the money, it doesn't make any bloody difference whether she's paid or not.'

Eleanor takes a bite of her fish-paste sandwich. 'I don't know why she doesn't just have her salary paid into the joint account in the first place.'

I redden. Kate cleared my debts, but she demanded her pound of flesh in return. Cut up all my credit cards, separated out our accounts. Even insisted on paying me an 'allowance', like I was one of the bloody kids!

'Well, she doesn't,' I snap. 'Which means I can't pay a single one of these damn bills. We've got a small overdraft facility, but the mortgage payment has just driven us right through that. God knows what'll happen if she's not back by the start of next month. What the hell am I supposed to do?'

'Write a few more stories,' she says crisply.

'It's not that easy.'

'It certainly is. You've a good brain in that head of yours, Edward. Put it to good use. It's not as if she's going to be gone long—'

'Would you stop saying that, Eleanor! Kate hasn't gone away for a spa weekend with the girls! She's left me! Who knows if she's ever coming back?' I take an angry pull of beer. 'In the meantime, I have to hold everything together somehow and find a way to keep all our heads above water!'

'Well, as I said, Katherine seems to have managed it all these years.'

'What's that supposed to mean?'

'I think it's about time you faced facts, Edward,' Eleanor says curtly. 'My daughter is the one who puts a roof over your head and food on the table. Not many men would be happy to live off their wives the way you do. I don't suppose your income even covers the electricity bill. That's supposing you actually *have* a job, of course; I haven't seen you sit down at your desk the whole time I've been here.' She dabs at the corners of her mouth. 'I could understand it if you picked up the slack at home, but let's be honest. You didn't do much when the children were small, as I recall, and now they're teenagers, I'm finding it a little difficult to understand what it is you actually *do* all day.'

It takes all my self-control not to hit her.

'I'm sorry to be the one to say it,' she adds, not sounding sorry at all. 'But it's about time someone did. Look how quickly you've fallen apart without her. You don't know the first thing about running this house. You can't tell me the name of your insurance company, much less call a plumber. Katherine did it all. I never thought I'd say it, but I'm starting to see why she left.'

'Kate did it all? Oh, that's rich, coming from you.'

'I beg your pardon?'

'Come on, Eleanor. If we're going to tell it like it is, let's really dish some dirt.' I fold my arms and regard her coolly. 'You haven't lifted a finger your entire life. You let your husband take care of everything, and when he died, Kate had no choice but to take over. You haven't been a mother to her. You're nothing more than a *parasite*.'

For a blissful moment, she's speechless. 'Well!' she splutters finally. 'Talk about the pot calling the kettle black!'

'Birds of a feather,' I say shortly.

'How *dare* you presume to know what my marriage was like?'

'Right back at you.'

'You have no idea what it was like living with James! I didn't *let* my husband take care of everything. In my day, wives didn't have a choice!'

'Give me a break. If you didn't like it, you could've left.'

'My generation doesn't just quit when the going gets tough.'

'Whatever. Frankly, Eleanor, I couldn't give a damn about you or your marriage. It's Kate I care about. You let that man treat her like shit her entire life. Nothing she ever did was good enough for him. The harder she worked, the more the bastard ignored her. She never had a fucking chance.'

'I'd appreciate it if you didn't use that kind of language in—'

I push my face into hers, feeling a flare of satisfaction as she backs away. 'If she's a control freak now, it's *you* she has to thank,' I say savagely. 'You heartless bitch. *You* were the one who taught her the only person she could rely on was herself.'

'Well, it's just as well, given the kind of man she married,' Eleanor retorts, quickly recovering herself. 'When are you going to grow up and act like a *proper* husband? It's all very well blaming me, but I can't help the way I was raised. Women of my generation were brought up to defer to their men. But you?' Her eyes rake me with contempt. 'You're supposed to be the man of the house. What's *your* excuse?'

It's my turn to be skewered by the truth.

My anger drains away as abruptly as it arrived. 'D'you think I don't know what a useless husband I am?' I say wearily. 'I've never been good enough for Kate, and we both know it.'

'Katherine loves you,' she says, taking me by surprise.

I stare at her. 'Well, much good it's done her. According to you, I've let her down since the day we married.'

'I've let her down since the day she was born.'

She drops into a chair, suddenly looking a decade older than her sixty-odd years. 'This is my fault as much as yours,' she says quietly. 'I never stood up for her when she was a child. I was *glad* James took it out on her instead of me.'

'What was his problem, for God's sake? Why couldn't he just be proud of her?'

She hesitates. 'It's complicated. He wanted to hurt me. He knew the best way to do that was hurt the person I loved most in the world. Oh, I know you think her sister was my favourite.' She shrugs. 'So does Katherine. Communication was never our family's strongest suit.'

'Well, Kate didn't leave because of you,' I sigh. 'I'm the one who screwed up. I left everything to her, and she's obviously had enough.'

'She didn't give you much choice. She never gives *any*one much choice.'

'She can't help it.'

'Well, of course she can't,' Eleanor says tartly. 'James and I did that to her. You were right. Nothing she did was ever good enough. She always had to try harder. She doesn't know how to switch it off.'

'What on earth was she doing, marrying me? Was I some sort of science project? A fixer-upper?'

'You needed her. No one else ever had. I told her it was a mistake. I knew something like this would happen if she married you. I suppose it's not your fault,' she adds grudgingly. 'She just needed someone a bit tougher. Someone who'd stand up to her and push back.'

'She likes being in control,' I say bleakly. 'It's the way she wants it. You of all people should understand what it's like to live with someone like that.'

There's a brief flicker in her steel eyes. If I didn't know better, I'd say it was pity.

'If it's the way she wants it,' Eleanor says quietly, 'then why has she left?'

Kate

My mobile rings just as I leave the Pantheon, where I've spent my second Monday off rapt in front of Raphael's tomb. It's not a number I recognize, but it has a local area code. With a flutter of butterflies, I wonder if it's Alessio, and then rebuke myself firmly for thinking that way. *He's married. Off-limits.*

Warily, I answer the phone.

'Kate?' a man's voice says. 'Is that you?'

It takes me a moment to place the velvety soft Irish brogue. 'Keir?'

'Hey. Just thought I'd call and see how you're doing. Still in Rome after all?'

'How did you get this number?' I demand.

'You gave it to me,' he says, sounding surprised.

I sit on a stone bench by the vast fountain in the centre of the piazza, out of the way of the tourists milling around the ancient circular temple. My phone beeps irritatingly, telling me there's another call waiting, but for once I ignore it.

'Sorry,' I tell Keir, softening my tone. 'You just got me off guard, that's all. How are you? How's Molly?'

'She's fine – shit. Look, where are you?'

'Just leaving the Pantheon. Why?'

'Reception on this line is crap. If you're at the Pantheon, you're only just round the corner from me. I've been looking at ruins all afternoon, and I could really use a break. Why don't we meet up for lunch? If you're free, of course.'

I hesitate. I barely know him, or Molly.

'We had such a good time with you the other day.'

'It *was* nice,' I admit.

'D'you know the Hostaria Antica just behind Piazza Navona? Great place, does cool Tuscan food. You can't miss it. See you there in five.'

'Wait. Keir—'

He's gone. I try to call him back, but his phone goes straight to voicemail; all these tall stone buildings seem to play havoc with phone reception. I can't just leave him and Molly sitting at the restaurant. Agness says I'm far too hung-up on what people think, but it would be such bad manners to stand them up. Besides, it's not as if I have anything better to do. My plans for the rest of the day involve a home-made caprese salad eaten alone on my terrace, and a tour of the Mamertine Prison where Saint Peter and Saint Paul are said to have been imprisoned. It's survived two thousand years; it'll still be there tomorrow.

It might be nice to have some company at lunch for a change. I like Keir and Molly, even if they are a bit young. I'm fairly sure they're not serial killers, and if they are, I don't suppose they're going to abduct or murder me in the middle of a crowded restaurant. It's time I started being a bit more sociable again. Apart from Julia and my limited exchanges with Uncle Maurizio, I haven't spoken to a soul in four weeks, and I've scarcely even seen Julia since I moved into Luca's apartment. She has her own life, after all. She can't constantly babysit me.

Much as I'm enjoying my freedom, I'm still lonely. I may not like being at the beck and call of Ned and the children, but there was always someone around when I got home, and if our conversations revolved around the need for clean socks or who last fed the cat, at least I had company. I was part of something. Julia can take off whenever she wants, do whatever she wishes, because no one actually *cares*.

What makes you think anyone cares about you? *If it wasn't for the lack of those clean socks, they wouldn't even notice you'd gone.*

It takes me a little while to find the right restaurant in the labyrinth of streets around the bustling Piazza Navona. By the time I spot the foxy gleam of Keir's hair at a clashing burgundy-clothed table outside the restaurant, my cheeks are pink, I'm panting slightly, and I have blisters on both my big toes from my new leather flip-flops.

He stands up with old-fashioned courtesy as I hurry over.

'Sorry I'm late.'

'Don't worry about it. Only just got here myself.'

I slide into a chair, carefully wrapping the leather strap of my handbag around the seat-back so a Vespa-mounted pickpocket can't grab it and zoom away. 'No Molly yet?'

'She's not here. She went back to uni last week.'

'Oh. Yes, of course,' I say, taken aback. 'She did mention she had to go back.'

'Sorry if you thought . . .'

'It doesn't matter,' I say quickly. 'It's lovely to see *you*, anyway.'

He smiles, but he doesn't quite meet my eye, and there's a slight flush on his high cheekbones. *I didn't give him my number*, I realize suddenly. He must have called his own phone from mine when he programmed his number into it the day we met. It occurs to me he might be short of money and doesn't know anyone else to ask. I have a feeling archeology teachers don't make much, especially when they're on sabbatical.

'Shame you couldn't make *Carmina Burana*,' he says, recovering himself. 'Molly hasn't stopped raving about it. The whole thing was a serious one-off.'

'I had a lot going on,' I say lightly.

'I figured. I hoped you'd call, but when you didn't . . .' He shrugs. 'Anyway. You're here now.'

His amber gaze is peculiarly intense. I find I'm the first to look away. I shake the heavy linen napkin across my lap, wishing I'd worn a longer skirt.

'I haven't eaten here for years,' I say brightly, scanning the menu. 'Anything you'd recommend?'

'*Mangeremo la ribollita, due da cominciare, ed allora una coppia di bistecche*,' Keir tells the waiter at my shoulder. '*E una bottiglia di vino rosso della casa, per favore.*'

'Did you just order *for* me?' I ask incredulously as the waiter nods and disappears.

'You asked me what I recommended,' he says reasonably. 'I recommend vegetable soup and steak. They serve it on a very hot plate with olive oil and rosemary. You'll love it.'

I don't know whether to be insulted or amused by his youthful arrogance. I've almost forgotten what it's like to have the confidence to make a decision without examining its ramifications from every angle. These days, I second-guess myself about everything. Was I right to give way to that client, despite the fact that I fear his decision will damage his brand? Should I take Guy out of his school because he hates it, even though I know it's the best education he could have? Ski at Whistler or Klosters? Buy a Kindle or iPad? Sometimes it feels like too much even to decide between peas or beans for dinner.

Keir puts his hand on his heart in mock apology. 'I'm devastated. Would you have preferred it if I'd told you first and then *you'd* ordered it?'

I laugh and let it go. He wasn't making a point. There's no baggage, no history here.

'So how come you're still in town?' Keir asks as the waiter returns with our wine.

Briefly I consider telling him the truth: *Four weeks ago, I walked out of my life and I don't know if I have a home to go to any more.*

'I didn't want to go home,' I say simply.

'What did those at home want?'

'I didn't ask them.'

He takes a sip of wine. 'Interesting. You don't seem the sort of woman to abandon your family without good reason.'

'What sort of woman do I seem?' I ask curiously.

'The sort *with* a good reason.'

Our soup arrives. We each pick up our spoon and busy ourselves with the food. He was right: it *is* delicious.

'Aren't you going to ask me what my reason is?' I ask after a moment.

'Do I really need to know?'

'No.' I tear off a small piece of bread, embarrassed. Of course this boy doesn't care about my life. He's just being polite, making small talk. 'No, of course you don't.'

'It's not that I don't want to know about *you*,' Keir says. 'But why you left your family has nothing to do with who you are, not really. I don't care about the past. I'm only interested in *now*.'

He's so very young. Only youth thinks the past, the ties that bind, don't matter.

'How old are you?'

'Twenty-eight. How old are you?'

I suppose I asked for that. 'Thirty-nine. Well, forty in two weeks.'

'Does it make any difference? Now we know how old we both are?'

I'm suddenly tired: tired and confused. I don't know what he wants. If he needs money, I'd rather he simply asked for it.

'Look, Keir,' I sigh, putting my napkin on the table. 'It's lovely to see you, of course, but I'll be honest with you. I'm not really sure what I'm doing here. If you and your girl-friend are in some kind of—'

'Girlfriend?'

'Molly. If you need money . . .'

'Molly's my sister, not my girlfriend.' He stares at me intently, as if this changes everything.

'Keir,' I start.

He shoves back his chair. I sigh. Clearly he's going to walk and I'm going to get stuck with the bill. Wonderful.

The last thing I expect is for him to kiss me.

Ned

'Sorry it's not better news, old son,' Simmons says. 'Wish I could help, mate. I really do.'

I knock back my Scotch. Cheap and nasty, like Simmons himself. 'Forget it, Jeremy. It was just a thought.'

'Any other time. You know how much we like your stuff.' The editor reaches across his desk to take back the half-empty bottle and locks it in a drawer. 'I'll be frank: it's been a bad year for the paper. Christ, it's been a bad year all round. Lot of belt-tightening going on. Never know who's going to be next.'

He hauls his fat belly out from behind the desk and nods towards the newsroom on the other side of the glass. 'Fucking vicious out there,' he says, digging his hands into his pockets and playing with his balls. 'Six months ago, they let half the staffers go and hired the rest back on contract. No holiday, no pension. Closed down Books and Health altogether. Only reason we haven't lost anyone on Sports is because they're mostly stringers anyway. Not that we're using them; we're taking most of what we print off the wires.'

'Yeah. I get it. Well, no harm in asking . . .'

'Remember Bill Munro?' Simmons interrupts. 'On the financial desk? Repossessed. Bailiffs came round and kicked him out on the street. Wife, three kids, another one on the way. If anyone should've seen the crash coming, you'd think it would have been him.'

'It's been a tough time all round. Look, if you hear anything . . .'

'Will do.'

I shake his fat, sweaty paw, forcing a smile. Slimy bastard. He's waited years for this. He never got over me beating him to Sports Journalist of the Year the only time he ever got nominated.

As I cross the newsroom, a familiar voice calls my name. 'Ned! I thought it was you.'

A tall skinny guy with a distinct resemblance to Mr Bean waves across his desk. It takes me a second to place him. 'Martin! I thought you'd fucked off to Spain years ago! You're never still here?'

'Jackie threw me out.' He grimaces. 'Bitch waited till I'd finished paying off the mortgage, and then took me for the lot. House, pension, the works. Next thing I know, she's moved her bloody tennis coach in. Couldn't afford to quit the job and take early retirement after all. I was lucky to keep the clothes I stood up in.'

'You poor bastard,' I sympathize.

He grabs his jacket off the back of his chair. 'Don't suppose you'd fancy a drink?'

We stroll round the corner to the Green Man, one of the few hostelries left in town where a man can still get a

TESS STIMSON

decent pint. None of your gnat's-piss American beer with a slice of lemon shoved in the neck. The barman turns a blind eye to a few discreet smokes, too, as long as you don't stint the rounds and put a few in the bin.

'So how's it going?' Martin asks as we pull out a couple of stools at a scarred table in the corner. 'Still enjoying a life of leisure thanks to that lovely wife of yours?'

I blow the head off my beer. 'Not so much, as it happens. Kate upped and left a month ago.'

He whistles. 'Mate, I'm sorry.'

'Yeah, well. These things happen.'

'Tell me about it.' He hunches over the table. 'Shit, I thought you and Kate were golden. Love's young dream. Don't tell me you were dipping your wick where it didn't belong?'

'Chance'd be a fine thing.'

'So what the fuck happened?'

'You tell me.' I drain half my pint in a single gulp. 'Ran off without a word. Didn't even say goodbye to the kids. We thought she was dead in a ditch somewhere. Police had me fitted up as the next Crippen; seriously, mate, I thought I was going to be banged up for life. Next thing I know, she turns up in Rome.'

'Rome? You're shitting me.'

'Wish I was.'

'Another bloke, was it?'

'Kate? She's a hard-nosed bitch sometimes, but she's not a slapper.' I pause. 'Sorry, mate. No offence. Didn't mean to imply . . .'

He waves his hand. 'Forget it. Jackie always was a slag.'

I finish my pint. 'Kate's never been that interested in sex, to be honest. I was lucky if I got it once a month. You could lock her in a room with the Chippendales and she'd pick up a book.'

'You're not worried about her out there with all those Latin lovers, then?'

I snort. 'Only one I'm worried about is the dyke she's staying with.'

Martin stubs out his cigarette and picks up our empty glasses for another round. 'You know, mate, you want to get things sorted. Take it from me: get your retaliation in first.'

'Cheers, mate. Next round's mine.'

'I'm serious, Ned,' Martin says when he returns with our refills. 'Get yourself a brief before she does. Once these bitches get the lawyers involved, it's all over. If she's buggered off to Rome, you should make your move now. Empty the joint account and change the locks, I would.'

'Account's already bloody empty. Why d'you think I'm kissing Simmons's arse?'

'Even more reason. You want her swanning back home with some bloody Romeo and kicking you out of your own house?'

'Look, I appreciate the concern, but it's not going to happen. We're not getting divorced, mate. You know what women are like. She's just taking some time out to get her head together.'

'That's what Jackie said,' Martin mutters darkly.

I stare into my beer. Kate's been gone over a month. It's weeks since I spoke to her, and she still hasn't come home. I thought she'd stay another few days or so to make her point, then come back home and we'd say no more about it. But she hasn't even called to check in since then. *I'm* not going to be the one to chase her and beg her to come back.

Eleanor was right: the more I run after her, the worse I'll make it. If she's going to come home, she'll do it in her own sweet time, and nothing I can do will make any difference.

Only it looks more and more like she's *not*.

I love my wife. I want her back, and not just because the house can't run without her. I *miss* her. More than I'd have thought possible, given the way things were between us before she left. Maybe I wasn't a perfect husband, but did I really deserve this? Couldn't she at least have talked to me first, instead of leaving without a word?

'Look, mate,' Martin says with forced cheerfulness. 'Divorce isn't the end of the world. Jackie got the house and the kids, but I got my life back. I'm a free man again! Plenty more fish in the sea. I can take my pick. I tell you, Jackie leaving was the best thing that ever happened to me.'

Martin's not even fifty, but he looks a decade older. His nose is red and veiny, and he's started to cultivate a comb-over. The hem of his cheap shiny jacket is coming down, and there are old sweat stains under the arms. He looks like what he is: a sad, washed-up loser who can barely hold down a job on the local rag.

'Yeah,' I echo. 'Who needs 'em, right?'

'Be a bit easier if she hadn't left me brassic, of course,' he sighs. 'Girls like to be shown a good time. Doesn't go down well if you ask them to go Dutch.'

He digs around in his pocket for a pen, then scribbles a name on a coaster and shoves it across. 'Learn from my mistakes. Get yourself sorted, pronto.'

I pick up the coaster. 'Nicholas Lyon? Who's he? Your lawyer?'

'No,' he says. '*Hers.*'

*

I leave Martin nursing his fifth pint and head back to the car. Today was a total wash-out. Simmons would cut off his own arm rather than throw me a bone. Martin promised to give me some investigative work on a football match-fixing scam he's been working on, but even if it comes off, which I seriously doubt, it'll be a day or two's work at most.

I toss the coaster in the glove compartment. It would serve Kate right if I did screw her for every penny. She's the one earning the big bucks; she's the one who left the family home. What the fuck are *we* supposed to live on? How am I supposed to pay the mortgage and feed the kids?

Then there's the trifling matter of the eighty grand I owe the bookies.

I start the car. If I don't make some kind of down-payment on what I owe, I'm going to end up with both my legs broken. I haven't heard a dicky-bird from the bastards for weeks, but it's only a matter of time before they send me a message. Dog shit through the letterbox, a key down the side of the car. Then it'll get serious. Last time, they threatened to hurt Kate. With her out of the picture, I need to make sure they don't turn their attention to Agness.

The fuel indicator light comes on as I turn on to the motorway and I cross my fingers I've got enough to get home. I don't have a fucking bean left on me. Our AA coverage has lapsed, too. Last thing I need is to be stranded on the hard shoulder of the M3.

I'm running on fumes by the time I make it back. I'll have to tap Eleanor for more cash just to fill up, which'll mean eating another shit sandwich. We may have called a truce the other day, but she's got me over a barrel, and we both know it. Without her money, I'd be screwed.

Agness pounces the minute I'm through the door.

'Dad, you didn't pay my school fees,' she accuses. She waves a letter at me. 'They were due at the start of term. This letter is, like, really serious.'

'Jesus. Would you let me get through the fucking door?'

'Language, Edward,' Eleanor sniffs.

I fling my coat over the back of a chair. 'Get me a beer, would you, Agness.'

'What about my school fees?'

'I'll get to it. You shouldn't have been opening my post, anyway.'

'It wasn't addressed to you. It was addressed to Mum, and she's not here.'

'Christ, Agness,' I sigh, opening the fridge myself. I shift cartons of juice and boxes of eggs. 'Where the fuck is my beer?'

'We've run out,' Eleanor says crisply.

'Well, why didn't you go shopping, then?'

'I'm not sure I should be driving yet . . .'

'Gran, it's been over a month. It was only a sprain,' Agness interrupts. 'And Mum's car's an automatic – you should be fine.'

I glance warily at my daughter. She's been a bit of a revelation recently, exhibiting a side none of us knew existed. Making shopping lists, sorting through bills, organizing the lot of us. She reminds me alarmingly of Kate. If I didn't know better, I'd think she was actually *enjoying* this crisis.

'Dad,' she says now, 'you really need to pay this. They'll expel me if you don't.'

'I'll get to it,' I say irritably.

'You said that last time.'

'For God's sake, Agness! I said I'd get to it! What d'you want me to do?'

'I want you to sort it out, Dad!' Agness yells. 'I want you to take charge!'

I stare at the door as it slams behind her. Agness and I have always had a special bond. She's adored me since she was a baby; Kate used to get upset at the way Agness preferred to sit on my lap and always insisted I was the one to tuck her into bed at night. It got worse as she grew older, with Agness following me around the house and climbing all over me if Kate so much as tried to hold my hand. During her teens, her preference has been so marked, it has sometimes reduced Kate to tears. The two of them were barely speaking in the weeks leading up to Kate leaving. Outwardly, I sympathized with my wife, but secretly, I loved the attention.

But there's no adoration in Agness's eyes now. Suddenly I feel about two inches tall. A wave of fury rips through me. *This is Kate's fault.* Yeah, I'm not a perfect husband. I dumped too much on her, I screwed up over the baby, I took her for granted. And Christ knows I fucked up big-time over the gambling. But I didn't deserve this.

They want me to take charge? Fine. On their own heads be it.

Kate

Apart from the fact that he's practically half my age, Keir's not my type at all. Julia's right: I'm a sucker for a pretty face. Alessio, with his melting chocolate eyes and caramel skin, or Luca, my landlord, the snake-hipped *Vogue* model, are much more my kind of man. Even Ned, a long time ago. There was a time when my husband could make me tingle with just a look. I'd forgotten that.

Keir does have a certain aesthetic appeal. A strange Celtic beauty, all blue-white pallor and ruddy leonine hair. Fey, my mother would call him. Not quite of this world. Certainly not the kind of man to get your pulse racing. He's curiously bloodless to look at, like a Greek statue. I can't begin to imagine what he might be like in bed, and it feels strangely indecent to try.

Then he kisses me full on the mouth at the restaurant table, in front of everyone, and everything I thought I knew about myself is turned on its head. For the first time, I understand that a bolt of lightning is not just a romantic novelist's cliché. If Alessio's kisses once made me tingle, Keir's touch is like being thrown across the room by a thousand-volt shock.

When he releases me, I collapse in the chair like a puppet whose strings have been cut. I can't quite catch my breath. My hands are shaking. My whole body is throbbing with a need so intense it's actually painful.

Keir throws several euro notes onto the table and takes me by the elbow. For a moment I don't respond, too stunned to move.

'You had no idea?' Keir asks disbelievingly, his amber eyes searching my face. 'You really didn't know?'

I shake my head.

'I thought you realized,' he says. 'I thought you knew.'

I stumble to my feet. 'This is ridiculous,' I whisper.

Keir picks up my bag and, still possessively holding my elbow, guides me out of the restaurant and across the cobbled square.

'I have to go home—'

'That *is* ridiculous,' Keir says.

I glance around the piazza. I can't quite get my bearings; I feel as if I've been spun in a circle. I'm dizzy and disoriented. I know my flat isn't far from here, but I have no idea in which direction to strike out.

Keir stops by a parking bay filled with dozens of Vespas, and I watch as he opens the rear locker of the nearest one.

'What's this?' I ask stupidly as he hands me a pale gold helmet.

'A basket of flowers.'

I push it back at him, pulling myself together with an effort. 'I know what it is, Keir. But I don't need it. I can walk from here.'

'You're not going on the back of this scooter unless you wear it. And we can't walk, not with you wearing those silly shoes. It's at least five miles.'

It takes me a moment to realize what he means.

I laugh. 'I can't possibly go back with you!'

'Why not?' Keir asks. He sounds genuinely puzzled.

'Well, for a start, I'm *married*. I don't go off with strange men.'

'I wouldn't call me strange, exactly. Would you?'

'You know what I mean. And yes, I would, actually. Call you strange, I mean. Anyway, you're practically half my age, it'd be almost—'

'I'm twenty-eight. And you're forty in two weeks,' he says impatiently. 'Can I stipulate to the age difference, counsellor, or do we have to go through it all again?'

'Keir, seriously. You can't possibly imagine anything's going to happen between us?'

'Are you asking me or telling me?'

'I'm telling you, obviously.'

'The thing is,' Keir says, 'I think it already has.'

A shiver runs down my spine. Staring into his strange gold eyes, I feel the world tilt. It takes a moment for me to recover myself.

'Come on, Keir. This is just—'

'Ridiculous. Yes, so you've said.'

He reminds me of Agness: young people always have an answer for everything. They don't understand that the world isn't black and white.

'I'm very flattered, obviously,' I try again, 'but you must see it could never work.'

'Must I?'

I laugh in frustration. 'Keir, please.'

'Oh, all right. If it's really bothering you that much, we can talk about it when we get there. Now can you please put that helmet on, before we get arrested?'

This is hopeless. He's like a small child insisting it should be Christmas every day. I don't want to stand here in the street debating this nonsense; it's too exhausting. It would be simpler to humour him and tactfully disentangle myself later.

Walk away. Why should you care if you hurt his feelings?

No one likes being rejected. I remember what it was like. I can let him down gently without denting his pride.

Come on, you're enjoying the attention. Why shouldn't you? It's been a long time.

I wait patiently as Keir adjusts the helmet strap under my chin. He eases the Vespa from among the massed ranks of scooters and I clamber on behind him, struggling not to flash my knickers beneath my short skirt. It's twenty years since I got on the back of one of these. Putting as much space between our bodies as I can, I grip the back of the seat behind me, the way I've seen Italian girls do with such insouciance, and nearly tumble onto the cobbles as Keir rounds the first corner. Gasping, I swallow my pride and fling my arms round him, clinging on to his waist for dear life.

Unexpectedly, I want to giggle. Risking life and limb on a souped-up sewing-machine in a skirt that shows my underwear, going off with a man I barely know, a man half my age who's already kissed me and made his intentions clear: it's all so far from the kind of thing I'd normally contemplate. I thrill with pleasure as Keir zips through the traffic. Isn't that why I'm here, after all? To break a few rules? It's not as if I'm actually going to *do* anything.

The May sunshine warms my bare shoulders as we head out of Rome and up into the encircling hills. Classical architecture gives way to clusters of low-fronted shops and grimy high-rise apartment buildings. My thighs ache and my nipples are as hard as pebbles against Keir's back. I press my cheek into his bony shoulder blade, smiling to myself. I'd kill Agness if she got on the back of some boy's bike, but now I remember the appeal.

By the time Keir pulls into a narrow, rubbish-strewn alleyway between two rundown tower blocks, I'm stiff and sore and flushed with excitement. I slide off the back of the Vespa, fumbling with the helmet strap. Keir puts it away in its locker, takes my hand and leads the way to the nearest apartment building without a word.

Inside, the hallway smells of dirt and urine. A single bulb hangs from a bare wire, and the tiled floor is cracked and filthy. It's not exactly what I expected.

'Belongs to a friend,' Keir says briefly. 'It's better upstairs.'

My excitement drains away. *Upstairs.* Where there are bedrooms.

I need to put a stop to this now, before it gets out of hand, but I don't quite know how to. When the lift doors shut behind us, enclosing us alone in the tiny space, I can almost hear the crackle of electricity pass between us. I'm horrified to realize how much I want him to kiss me again.

His apartment is on the top floor. Nervously, I follow him into a dark, shuttered living room, making out the silhouette of a high-backed settle and a marble-topped sideboard in the gloom. Through a folding door, I glimpse an unmade bed and clothes scattered on the floor. I'm relieved and unexpectedly touched. *This wasn't planned, then.*

I turn my back firmly on the bedroom, ready to marshal my excuses, but to my surprise Keir doesn't even glance in its direction. Instead, he strides over to the window and throws open the shutters, flooding the room with sunlight, before unlocking a pair of French windows.

I follow him out onto the terrace. The view is breath-snatching. I can see all the way across Rome, from the dome of St Peter's to the Colosseum and the Forum itself. I pick out the seven hills tucked inside the ruined Servian wall: the Aventine and Esquiline with their monuments and parks, the Capitoline topped by Rome's modern city hall, the archaeological treasure trove of the Palatine Hill where Keir spends so much of his time. It's like seeing history spread at your feet. I can almost hear the armies gathering on the Field of Mars, Nero fiddling while his city burns.

'How did you find this place?' I ask, leaning on the warm stone parapet.

He shrugs. 'Friend of a friend. Got it for peanuts. Most people don't get further than the hall downstairs. I didn't move in till after Molly left – she wouldn't even come up to look at it.'

'I can't say I blame her. It's not the most salubrious building I've ever walked into.'

'I'd like to kiss you again,' Keir says abruptly.

I tense. 'You didn't ask permission last time.'

'This is different. If we're going to take this further, I'm not doing all the running. It's got to be a two-way street.'

'Take what further?'

'Don't be disingenuous, Kate,' he says evenly. 'I'm not going to seduce you. There won't be a convenient get-out if and when you decide to go back to your husband. You go into this with your eyes wide open, or you don't go into it at all.'

Heat rushes into my cheeks. 'What makes you think I want to go into anything with you?' I splutter, my sophisticated veneer splintering. 'I've told you, this whole thing is ridiculous! I'd never even have come here if you hadn't practically *dragged* me!'

'*That*,' Keir says, 'is precisely the kind of hypocrisy I'm talking about.'

I open my mouth to retort . . . and close it again. He's right, of course. I came willingly, knowing the score. I can hardly pretend to be an ingénue at my age. How does a boy like this have so much self-assurance?

'Come on, Kate,' he says softly. 'I don't want to play games. This isn't high school. We're both adults. I don't want anything from you that you don't want to give. Can you at least respect what's happening here enough to be honest?'

'What *is* happening here?' I whisper.

His hand hovers by my cheek. 'It's not love yet,' he says. 'But it's more than lust. Is that enough for you?'

I press his fingers to my lips. I'm ready for the electricity this time, and I give myself up to it, my body vibrating with excitement. But Keir disengages himself and gently holds me at arm's length when I reach for him again.

'Is it what you really want?' he asks seriously.

'Is this a youth thing?' I ask. 'Analysing regrets before you have them?'

'I don't want to be a revenge fuck, Kate. This has nothing to do with your husband. For as long as it lasts, this is about you and me.'

I don't want to think about this, I just want to do it. But

Keir gives me no choice. I force myself to acknowledge that, if we kiss again, it won't stop there. We'll end up in bed together; we'll have sex. I will commit adultery. I've never cheated on anyone in my life, much less been unfaithful to the man I promised to love till death do us part. For all his faults, I'm certain Ned has never been unfaithful to me either. If I sleep with Keir, I'll be crossing the Rubicon, changing the nature of my marriage for ever. And I'll be doing it fully awake, with my eyes wide open. There will be nowhere to hide afterwards.

I don't hesitate.

'I love my husband,' I say. 'But you're right. This isn't about him.'

My heart is curiously light. For once, I don't second-guess myself. I can't, thanks to Keir's insistence on honesty. No false regrets or faux guilt. I want this. *I want him.*

The bedroom is latticed with sunshine. Keir goes to stand beside the bed and waits for me, already barefoot in his jeans and T-shirt.

'Come here,' he says.

The marble floor is cool on my bare feet as I slip out of my leather flip-flops and go to him.

I stop a pace away, and without moving any closer, Keir reaches out and gently slides the straps of my camisole down my shoulders, so that the cinnamon-coloured silk slithers to my waist.

Keir drops to his knees, his tongue tracing whorls down my stomach to my navel. 'I like that you don't wear perfume,' he murmurs. 'I like the smell of you. Soap and water and something sweet, something like honey. I wonder if you'll taste like you smell.' He eases my skirt over my hips, pressing his face lightly to the fine pink mesh of my knickers. Briefly I wish they matched my blue bra; a moment later, all I can think is that I want him to take them off.

How does he know what to say? How does he have such confidence, more than most men twice his age?

I thread my fingers through his long hair. Keir catches my hand, and brushes his lips against the inside of my wrist, kissing his way to the inner crook of my elbow. I don't know if it's what he's saying or how he's touching me, but I'm so hot with need I feel feverish. I arch my back, pressing my sex against him as he unfurls my other hand and kisses his way up my left arm.

'Keir,' I gasp. 'Keir, please.'

'We've got all afternoon,' he says easily.

He rises to his feet and yanks his T-shirt over his head. His chest is lean but toned, the planes of his stomach surprisingly defined. Gold-red hairs dust his upper torso. I fumble with his belt buckle, and Keir shucks off his jeans and underwear. I can't look at his cock yet.

Keir cups the back of my head and pulls me towards him, his cock nudging my belly-button as his lips come down hard on mine. Gently he dances us backwards, until the back of my knees touch the edge of the mattress. Slowly he eases me back onto the crumpled sheets and spreads my knees with his own. His lips brush my collarbone, my throat, my shoulder with a feather-light touch, and I squirm with pleasure as he scoops my breasts from my bra and thumbs my nipples. Clawing at his back, I arch my pelvis towards his, my sex aching for his cock.

'I love your body,' he whispers, slithering down the bed. His tongue darts beneath my knickers, flicking across my clitoris, his fingers still kneading my nipples.

'Please,' I gasp again. 'Please!'

He tugs at my knickers, and I lift my bottom so that he can get them off. His amber eyes have darkened to the colour of molasses as he raises his body above mine, his cock poised at my entrance.

'Slowly,' he says, as I moan and spasm beneath him. 'Slowly, Kate. This is just the first round.'

He enters me, and as his cock fills me up and the energy radiates outwards and I start to come, I feel a brief rush of pure rage at what I've been missing all these years.

And after that, all I feel is Keir.

Ned

Christ Almighty, I feel like I've wandered into a Vinnie Jones movie. Any minute now Ray Winstone's going to pop up with a sawn-off and tell me I ain't doing myself no favours monkeying wiv fings I don't understand.

My source, Gav, has picked possibly the dodgiest pub in Salisbury for our meet. It's a real spit-and-sawdust place: several of the windows are boarded up, the tables are bolted to the floor, and the scarred wooden stools look like they've done more hard time than the local toughs propping up the bar. Even the barmaid looks like she's been ridden hard and put away wet.

I pull out an envelope from inside my jacket. This little fucker better not be stringing me along, or I'm out five hundred quid. Martin said I could forget about reimbursement from the tight-arses at the *Globe* unless we make the front page.

'Put that away!' Gav yelps, glancing frantically round the pub. 'Jesus. You want to get me legs broken for me?'

Hastily I shove the envelope back into my pocket. Gav looks like he's going to bolt any second, so I move this along before he changes his mind. 'I need that name, Gav.'

He chews anxiously at a hangnail. 'Yeah, well. I'm not sure this is such a good idea, Ned. They'll kill me if they find out I've talked to you.'

'They won't hear a dicky-bird from me. C'mon, Gav. We go way back. You can trust me, you know that. I've never let you down before, have I?'

'This is different. You've no idea how big this thing is, Ned. Take it from me, Morrison's not a bloke you want to cross.'

'Gav,' I say reasonably. 'I'm afraid our little rendezvous here hasn't gone unnoticed. Whether you talk now or not, you're a marked man. My editor's not going to let this story go, and there'll be plenty to point the finger when it breaks. If I were you, I'd get out of town for a bit till things blow over. That's going to be a lot easier with half a ton in your back pocket.'

He looks like he's going to throw up.

'Look, Gav. All I need is a name. I've got most of the story already.' I smile persuasively. 'Let me make this easy on you. I'll tell you what I know, and you can just sing along to the words, OK?'

After a long pause, he nods reluctantly.

I count off on my fingers. 'I know Drew Morrison's behind the match-fixing scam, and I know the names of at least six of the players in on it. Cliff City have thrown three of the last four matches they've lost, am I right? Ditto Derby Celtic. And Morrison's making a bloody king's ransom betting on the results.'

'If you know all that, what d'you need me for?' Gav mutters.

'Because I need *proof*,' I say, leaning forward. 'I want a list of matches they're going to throw, and the names of the bookies in on the scam.'

'You think they tell me that?' Gav exclaims. 'Only two people ever know what Morrison's planning, and one of them's God. If I knew who was going to bleedin' win, d'you think I'd be taking five hundred nicker off you? I'd be making me own bloody fortune, wouldn't I?'

Yes, I realize suddenly. You would, wouldn't you?

My legs are actually shaking as I leave Drew Morrison's boxing gym two days later. Jesus H. Christ. Gav wasn't kidding. Morrison's not the kind of man you want to give a reason to hold a grudge.

I unlock my car, climb in and lean my head back against the headrest. Christ. *Christ*. I don't think I've ever been so scared in my entire life. The man actually exudes menace. My hands are trembling, and I can't stop shivering. I can't believe what I've just done. If things had gone the other way, they'd have been picking bits of me up from the side of the A3 for miles.

Finally, when my heart has slowed to a semblance of its normal rhythm, I open my eyes and pull Martin's number up on my phone. 'Mate? Look, this story. It's a bloody wash-out. No one's saying anything. I'm not sure there even *is* a story, to be honest.'

'Shit, really? I thought you said your source was solid.'

'Pissing in the wind. Didn't know a bloody thing.' I jam the phone awkwardly between my ear and shoulder and pull the car away from the kerb, still a bit shaky. 'I'm starting to wonder if someone's giving you the runaround on this one, mate. I've put out dozens of feelers and come up with fuck bloody all. If Morrison *has* got some sort of scam going, he's managed to put the frighteners on an awful lot of people. I don't think even he's got that much clout. I reckon someone's yanking your chain.'

'Blast. That leaves a huge bloody hole in Saturday's paper.' He sighs gustily. 'Oh well. If the story doesn't stand up, it doesn't stand up. Least you got a few days' work out of it.'

'Yeah. I owe you for that, mate.'

'No probs. Thanks for trying. Send me your invoice and I'll pass it along to Accounts. Anything else comes up, I'll give you a bell.'

'Appreciate it, Martin.'

I toss the phone onto the passenger seat. I feel a bit bad leaving Martin swinging like this, but one scoop isn't going to make or break his sorry-arse career. Or mine, come to that. The most I'd have got out of this story, even if we'd made the front page, would've been another week's free-lance work, and maybe my byline at the bottom of page seven if I was lucky.

Whereas by killing the story altogether, I'll be set for life.

I could bloody kiss Gav. The little darling. In the end he didn't just give me any name, he gave me an in with Drew Morrison's lieutenant, his right-hand man. It's like getting a hotline to God. I didn't have a hope of getting the man to turn on Morrison, of course. But thanks to Gav's unwitting stroke of genius, that was no longer the plan.

Make me own bloody fortune. Why didn't I think of it before? I must be more of a pillock than Gav himself, and that's saying something. The answer to all my prayers, and it was staring me in the face. Mind you, I nearly didn't go through with it. When I walked into Morrison's gym for the 'interview' his number two had arranged, I thought I was going to shit myself for real. But it turns out Morrison's a reasonable man. As soon as I explained that this story could be made to go away for ever in return for a little quid pro quo, he quickly saw my point of view.

For the first time in two days, I start to relax. My face splits into a grin. *I pulled it off*. The biggest fucking gamble of my life, and I bloody pulled it off!

With an effort, I force myself to keep calm. The trick now is not to get greedy. If I walk into Ladbrokes and put fifty grand on a second-division footie match, it's bound to raise a few eyebrows. I'll spread it around at half a dozen different bookies over three or four matches. Given my reputation, I could put money on two raindrops racing down a pane and no one would turn a hair, as long as I don't get carried away. And as soon as I make enough money to pay off what I owe, I'm done. I've learned my bloody lesson.

Take charge, Agness said. I think this could be said to fit under that heading.

Now all I have to sort out is Kate.

Kate

I miss the children so much it hurts. I'm happy with my new life here in Rome, and with Keir, of course, but the visceral ache to see Guy and Agness never goes away.

Keir rolls over in bed and pushes himself up on one elbow, his russet hair flopping into his eyes. 'Hey. Why're you up so early?'

I turn back from the window. 'It's not every day you turn forty.'

Keir pushes back his hair and sits up against the pillows. I can't imagine how I ever thought he was bloodless or unattractive. He's the sexiest man I've ever met. Long, firmly muscled legs, broad shoulders, flat, well-defined abs covered in a smattering of golden hair that disappears in a V beneath the sheet. His jaw is square and well-defined, and he has a Cary Grant dimple in his chin. Whenever he kisses me with that full, sexy mouth, I feel like a Hollywood screen siren in a black-and-white movie.

Maybe all the amazing sex we've had over the past three weeks has something to do with my change of heart.

'You're missing the kids,' Keir says.

Or maybe it's that. His ability to read my mind. It's not that difficult; yet after fifteen years of marriage, Ned still doesn't know my favourite colour, never mind what I'm thinking.

'Agness made me breakfast in bed last year,' I say wistfully. 'I think it was the last time she was nice to me. Although,' I add, 'given the fact that the toast was burnt, the eggs were raw, and she put salt in my coffee instead of sugar, perhaps *nice* isn't quite the right word.'

'I was going to make you breakfast in bed,' Keir smiles.

'It's OK,' I say hastily. 'I'm not really a breakfast person.'

Not entirely true. I'm very much a breakfast person when on holiday in, say, the Maldives and the breakfast in question is a delicious buffet of fresh pineapple and mangoes, complemented by warm croissants and rich, freshly brewed coffee. On skiing holidays, I've been known to devour a full skillet of hash browns and bacon and sausages and cheese. But most days, I don't have time for more than a hot cup of Nescafé as I dash out of the door. And though lack of time isn't my problem these days, breakfast – actually, cooking in general – isn't really Keir's strong suit.

The morning after our first night together (or rather the afternoon after, if we're being strictly accurate) Keir made lunch. I watched him rush from the sink to the ancient electric stove and back to the sink again in something of a panic, and realized that cooking wasn't an activity he did on a regular basis. The pasta boiled over, the sauce curdled – no easy feat, given that it was just tinned tomatoes and fresh basil – and he managed to set fire to a tea-towel. Twice. Clearly the culinary arts don't come as naturally to him as those of the bedroom. Which made it all the more touching that he was trying so hard to impress me.

Normally I'd have watched him flail for five minutes and then taken over. It was what I did, I remembered suddenly, when Ned tried to cook for me the first time, a month or so after we'd started dating. Pasta again (clearly a bachelor staple): spaghetti Bolognese this time. But unlike Ned, and despite his evident lack of practice, Keir didn't have the desperate look in his eye of a man just waiting to be rescued. And more to the point, and for reasons I haven't yet fathomed, my desire to rescue him – to rescue anyone – has been left behind at home, along with my sense of responsibility.

Nonetheless, despite Keir's willingness to channel his inner Jamie Oliver for my sake, I have no desire to be poisoned. We eat out a lot.

Keir climbs out of bed, not troubling to wrap a sheet around his nakedness. I find it hard to take my eyes off his morning semi-erection.

'D'you want to call the kids?' he says, wrapping his arms around me from behind.

His erection digs into the small of my back, and I can't help but tense. I've never liked morning sex. Even at weekends, I always feel there's so much I should be doing. I hate the starkness of daylight, the way it shows up every flaw, turning soft hollows and shadowed curves into something harsh and pornographic. My mouth feels cottony, and without a shower, I feel sweaty and unclean.

I pull away. 'They know it's my birthday. They don't need me to remind them.'

'So just call and tell them you're missing them.'

'If they wanted to talk to me, they'd have called. I don't want to push them and drive them even further away, if that's possible. I can't abandon them and then expect to speak to them whenever I feel like it.'

He doesn't tell me I didn't abandon them. I like that he doesn't try to placate me; that he allows me my feelings without trying to correct them or corral them into something more manageable, easier to live with.

He pulls on a pair of faded jeans without bothering to seek out underwear. I resist the maternal urge to question his hygiene.

'Kate, you're their mother,' he says, rearranging himself and buttoning his fly. 'OK, maybe they're mad at you, but they'll be missing you too. Sooner or later you'll have to give it another try, so why not suck it up and pick up the phone now?'

'You sound like an American high-school teenager.'

'I *was* an American high-school teenager,' Keir says.

'Were you?' I say, surprised. 'I didn't know that. I know nothing about you, really, do I?'

'Two years in Boston, from when I was fourteen. My father worked for an Irish bank, and we all went with him. What else d'you want to know?'

'I don't even know you well enough to know what to ask.'

'You know I love you,' Keir says easily.

Goose bumps rise on my arms. It's the first time he's told me this, other than in bed. I have a sense that we're getting into dangerous territory. He knows that I'm married, that I plan to stay married. This is just a hiatus, I told him the first time we slept together, not permitting myself to look

194

any deeper; a holiday fling. I've made it clear it can't be otherwise, just as Keir has made it clear that he won't be constrained by my restraint. If he wants to love me, he says, he will.

I tell myself he's just a boy; that he doesn't know what love means.

'Anyway, I can't call the children now,' I say sensibly, steering the conversation back into safer waters. 'It's six o'clock in the morning in England.'

He pulls me towards him, his hand sliding between the folds of my satin dressing gown. I'm instantly wet for him, my foolish hang-ups about morning sex already fading like dew in the sun.

'How *will* we fill the time?' he says.

Later, as I watch Keir pull his jeans back on and tug a soft grey college sweatshirt over his head, I marvel that I can have reached the age of forty – forty! – and still know myself so little. It's as if I've been living with a stranger all these years, and it's taken this boy to show me who I am.

I *like* morning sex: it's more erotic, hungrier, than sex at night. I find men in jeans sexier than the expensive suits I thought I preferred. I like Keir's modern, minimalist furniture and bare hardwood floors, when I've always chosen soft, thick carpeting and antiques. I like leaving the house without planning where I'm going. I like the real, redwood colour of my hair. I also like not having to make all the decisions. I don't want to be the boss all the time, even if that means living with someone else's mistakes.

Now that I've had time to stop and think, I've come to realize something I've quietly known for a few months:

that I don't want to run Forde's or take over from Paul. Let his protégé do it. I don't want to keep climbing the greasy pole, pulling knives out of my back to plunge into someone else's. I don't want, have *never* wanted, success: it's just that I've always been so terrified of the consequences of failure.

I've also been able to admit to myself that I wish I'd spent more time at home when the children were young and not been quite so afraid of motherhood. I wish I'd followed my dream and taught art. I wish I hadn't taken charge of Ned quite so completely and turned him into a third child.

Keir pockets his keys and tosses me my phone, making me jump. 'I'm going to pick up a couple of cappuccinos. Call the kids. I'll be back in ten.'

I stare at the phone in my hand as the door slams behind him. *They're better off without you. You couldn't even keep your own baby alive.*

It wasn't my fault!

If it wasn't your fault, why do you still feel so guilty?

Guy, I decide. He'll understand if either of them will.

I pull up his number, my hand shaking. This is ridiculous. How can I be afraid to call my own children? I've already left them both dozens of messages, all unreturned. But sooner or later, surely one of them will pick up? If Guy doesn't answer now, I'll try again and again until he agrees to talk to me.

It doesn't occur to me until the number is ringing that I have no idea what I will say. I don't know whether to be disappointed or relieved when his phone goes straight to voicemail.

'Did you leave a message?' Keir asks, when I tell him.

'There didn't seem much point. He'll see the missed call.'

'He will,' Keir says as I feel tears threaten. 'Come on. It's your birthday. Get your glad rags on.'

I push the children to the back of my mind, absurdly grateful that Keir is here. 'Where are we going?'

'I told you I had it covered, didn't I?' he says. 'Trust me.'

When I see Keir collect his worn canvas messenger bag and helmet from the hall closet, I take the hint and change out of my skimpy sundress and put on a T-shirt and sensible pair of navy capris, along with my fake Converses. I don't intend to make the short-skirt-on-a-Vespa mistake again.

I climb onto the scooter behind Keir and slip my arms around his waist. Despite the early hour, the sun is already hot on my back as he picks out a route that takes us north of the city, deep into the Umbrian countryside. The views are spectacular as we wind our way high up into the hills, the Tyrrhenian Sea a hazy, sparkling blue in the distance. I tighten my thighs around Keir's, my body aching pleasantly from our lovemaking. Just two months ago, I could never have imagined I might be spending my fortieth birthday like this.

Ninety minutes later, the road starts to climb steeply up a hill covered in olive trees and gorse, and I crane my head over Keir's shoulder, trying to work out where we're going. To our right, a deep, narrow gorge falls away to a river, and above us, a medieval fortress town dominates the landscape. Moments later, I spot a pock-marked metal signpost. I hug Keir with delight. I've wanted to visit Narni, the town that inspired C.S. Lewis's Narnia stories, for as long as I can remember.

We cross the ravine via an unnervingly crumbling aqueduct and enter the town through an immense and very weathered stone gate. Instantly we're transported into a different world. It's like a film set, with its cobbled streets and winding alleys, brooding medieval buildings and impressive churches. I half expect Gandalf and a couple of hobbits to materialize.

Keir parks the Vespa in the main square, and I dismount stiffly, rolling my shoulders so that my spine pops. Taking off my helmet, I run my hands through my damp hair, which is plastered unflatteringly to my head. Beads of sweat trickle between my breasts, and I have to pluck my T-shirt away from my skin. I can't believe how hot it is. I expected it to be cooler up here in the mountains, but there's absolutely no breeze.

I perch on the edge of a stone fountain in the centre of the square and dip my hands in the cool water, wishing I could just climb in. If I don't get something to drink soon, I'm going to start feeling dizzy.

As if by magic, a bottle of chilled water appears in front of my eyes. 'Thought you could use this,' Keir says, handing it to me.

I unscrew the cap and take a grateful sip. Keir does the same with his own, shading his eyes as he gazes around the square.

'We might want to start with the cathedral,' he says, putting the sweating bottle into his backpack. 'It should be much cooler in there.'

We make our way up the long flight of shallow stone steps, indented with the tread of countless thousands of feet. Keir's right: the air inside the church is at least fifteen degrees cooler, and suffused with the musty scent of incense, candles and age. As we make our way slowly down the shadowy main nave, I start to revive, glancing at the magnificent frescoes and mosaics with interest. Beautiful in themselves, they are even more extraordinary when you think how many centuries – how many wars – they have endured.

In a small side chapel, we stop in front of a glass coffin containing the three-hundred-year-old remains of a mummified nun. The pristine white wimple framing her desiccated face is fresh and crisp; her withered hands are folded peacefully on her chest.

'There's no way she's worn that outfit for three centuries,' Keir whispers. 'Who d'you reckon gets the short straw and has to change it?'

I shush him, laughing. That's just the kind of thing Agness would say. Guy, like me, would find it all a little macabre.

We spend the next couple of hours exploring the town, dipping in and out of palazzos and chapels, doubling and then trebling back on ourselves in the maze of tightly knit streets, at one point going underground to visit the ancient church of San Domenico, which is also home to a prison from the time of the Inquisition. The narrow, cramped room is covered with graffiti inscribed over past centuries by doomed souls. I shiver as we leave. It's impossible to visit anywhere in Italy and not be impressed, and a little unsettled, by the enduring power of the Catholic Church.

The shadows are lengthening by the time we return to the secular twenty-first century world and sit down at a table in a tiny secluded square surrounded on all sides by ancient stone buildings covered with wisteria and jasmine. A waitress appears through a small archway in the building behind us and takes our order. As she leaves, Keir digs around in his backpack and then hands me a small wrapped gift.

I open it: it's a smoky, faceted stone heart on a black silk cord. 'Oh, Keir! It's beautiful!'

'It's a Labradorite,' Keir says. 'The colour changes depending on the light. It made me think of you.'

I lift my hair and turn, so that he can fasten it around my neck. 'I love it,' I say.

I love you. The words are on the tip of my tongue, but I bite them back. This is just a fling, I remind myself. Feelings aren't part of the deal. Even if he wasn't far too young for me, my life is too complicated. It wouldn't be fair to him.

The waitress returns with our starters: a caprese salad for me, and terrine of squid and potato for Keir. 'Are you staying at the hotel?' she asks, indicating the building behind her.

'It's a hotel?' Keir asks. 'Kate, what d'you think? We could stay over instead of going back tonight.'

'I can't,' I tell Keir. 'I have work in the morning.'

Maurizio has come to rely on me. I can't let him down. For the past few weeks, he's been going home early for lunch and an extended siesta, leaving me in charge. I've rewritten the menus to focus more on the house specials, and organized the rest of the bar staff on to a more efficient roster, so that we all get a fair share of the busy periods and good tips. I've also spent some time working out a way to increase our evening covers, which is where we're losing the most money. I don't want to ruin my reputation by simply not turning up.

'Kate, relax. You're not the CEO of a multinational here. The whole point about this kind of job is that you don't have to take it seriously.'

'I can't leave Maurizio in the lurch. It wouldn't be fair, not after all he's done for me.'

'Kate,' he says lightly, 'it doesn't all depend on you.'

I'm doing it again, I realize wearily. I abandoned my husband, my family and my job because it was all too much, and here I am, taking responsibility for everything all over again. I've replaced one man with another; swapped one job for a different one. If I want so much to be free, why am I already weighing myself down with the same burdens?

Keir reaches across the table, his expression softening. 'It's OK. Enough spontaneity for one day. We'll go back after dinner.'

'No, you're right. We don't have to—'

'Kate. It's cool.' He raises his glass. 'Happy birthday.'

I touch my glass to his, shaking the cold hand from my heart. It *has* been a happy birthday; perhaps my happiest since I was twenty-one. It's the first time someone has taken charge of the day and made plans for me, made me feel special. Ned always left it to me to pick the restaurant, book the weekend away. Last Christmas, he even told me to choose and buy my own present – and then left me to wrap it, too, because he forgot to get any paper.

But when did you give him a chance to plan anything? If he tried to be spontaneous with you, you cut him off at the knees.

He never tried! It was always down to me! Always!

Really? Or is that your selective memory speaking?

I suddenly remember our first Christmas together. Ned surprised me with tickets to Paris on Eurostar; I was heavily pregnant with Agness and couldn't fly. He'd arranged for Guy, not yet two, to spend the weekend with Liesl, and had even spoken to my secretary to make sure it was OK for me to take the Friday off.

I told him I couldn't go. I had an important presentation

I was working on; I couldn't afford to let my concentration slip, especially now, when I was pregnant.

I touch the crystal heart at my neck, swamped by an ineffable sadness. Perhaps Ned behaves like a child because I treat him like one. I took charge the very first day we met, as Ned struggled to cope with Guy in the supermarket, because Ned clearly needed me to. But that was a long time ago. Sixteen years. Looking back at our marriage now, did I ever give him a chance to prove himself? Or did I go on taking charge, never giving him space to breathe?

I know the answer already. Ned let me down because it's the only thing I leave him room for.

Ned

Nicholas Lyon looks like a fancy divorce lawyer straight out of central casting. Double cuffs, red braces, mono-grammed gold cufflinks, the works. Big corner office with a huge mahogany desk and a panoramic view across the Thames. Plush carpets. Croissants and fresh-brewed coffee. I hope Martin hasn't given me a bum steer on this guy. Christ knows how much it's costing me just to set foot inside the door.

The lawyer extends his hand over the desk. His grasp is firm and cool, and he meets my eyes steadily as we shake. Got to give him points for that. Despite the pinstripe and braces, there's something about him that's solid and down-to-earth. The far wall is covered with his kids' artwork, and his desk is crowded with silver-framed photos of his family on a variety of bucket-and-spade holidays. The wife looks vaguely familiar; it takes me a moment to place her as Malinche Lyon, the only cookery presenter who, in my book, can give the pneumatic Nigella a run for her money.

'I've got the basic details here from our phone conversation,' Lyon says, opening the slim manila folder in front of him and unscrewing a gold fountain pen. 'But I'd like to go through it again with you now, if you wouldn't mind.'

Bet he would, at three-fifty an hour. 'Shoot,' I say.

'You and your wife, Katherine, have been married for fifteen years?'

'Kate. It was our fifteenth anniversary last month. We lived together for about six months before that.'

He makes a note in his file. 'And there are two children: a boy aged seventeen, and a girl of fourteen?'

'Yeah. Guy's from my first marriage, but he's lived with me since the divorce. He was one when Kate and I met. Agness was born about a year later. She'll be fifteen in a couple of weeks' time.'

'And how old is your wife?'

'Forty. Today, actually,' I add.

Bloody ironic: it's the first time I've ever remembered her birthday without prompting since we got married. I even bought her a present in case she came home in time: a fancy leather wallet from that posh company the Prime Minister's wife runs. Cost about the same as a small car, but I figured I might as well push the boat out, especially now I can afford it. I've got quite a bit of ground to make up here, after all. Kate gets upset if I don't buy her something for Christmas and birthdays, but it's not because I don't care. I just never know what to get. That's the problem, Kate always says. I *should* know.

I've never understood why things like presents, anniversaries, Valentine cards matter so much to women. But I suppose that's not the point. They matter to Kate, so I guess she figures they should matter to me.

Briskly, the lawyer runs through the rest of the basics: what property we own, which schools the kids go to, what Kate and I do for a living, blah blah. He asks about our respective salaries, his expression not flickering when he learns my wife earns about six times more than I do. I'm relieved he doesn't dig any deeper into our finances for the time being. It's not illegal to place a bet, of course, which is all anyone would be able to prove, but I don't particularly want to explain why I'm suddenly in clover if I don't have to.

'You said your wife left you the second week in April,' Lyon says, looking up. 'I realize it's painful, but can you tell me anything more about that?'

'Not much to add,' I say, shrugging to show I don't care. 'She just got on a plane and flew to Rome. Didn't say a word to anyone, just went.'

'How did you find out where she was?'

'The cops tracked her down. They thought I'd buried her under the patio till they traced her through her credit card.'

'Have you spoken to her since?'

'Once. There didn't seem much point pushing it,' I add. 'If she wants to come home, she knows where I am.'

'Did she give you the impression that she *would* return?'

'She said she needed a bit more time to "get her head to-gether",' I snort, scribbling quotation marks in the air with my fingers. 'But how long am I supposed to wait? I haven't heard from her in weeks now. Meanwhile, the kids and I are struggling to cope, the bills are piling up—'

'Mr Forrest, I do understand,' Lyon says. His expression is sincere and sympathetic. 'I just want to be sure we aren't being a little premature here. Your wife has only been gone eight weeks, and you say she does plan to return.' He hesi-tates. 'Unless there is a third party involved?'

'I've never even looked at another woman, and Kate knows it!'

'I was talking,' Nicholas Lyon says gently, 'about your *wife.*'

The idea has occurred to me; of course it's bloody *occurred* to me. Even if it hadn't, everyone from the cops down seems keen to point it out. I almost wish Kate *had* run off with another bloke: at least that way I'd have someone to blame. I just can't see it, that's all. It's just not her.

'Look, Kate's not like that,' I say, uncomfortably aware that I must sound like every cuckold in history. 'I know what you're thinking, but she's always been into her work, her *career*. She doesn't have a lot of time for one man, never mind two.'

He puts his pen down and leans forward on his clasped hands. 'Mr Forrest . . .'

'Ned, please.'

'Ned, then. If no one else is involved on either side, do you have any idea why she *did* leave?'

Yeah. She lost a baby, and I was a total fuck-up about it. She thinks the kids and I take her for granted, and she's right. Her mother's a passive-aggressive, blood-sucking bitch. She's pissed off with that young tosser moving in on her territory at work. She's married to a loser who earns peanuts and can't even hang on to that without blowing it on the nags. She's a chronic overachiever who probably blames herself for any and all of the above.

I wave my hand to indicate his family photos. 'How many kids do you have?'

'Five,' he says, slightly thrown by the question. 'Three girls, two boys. Why?'

'How would you feel if *your* wife upped and left without a word?'

He sighs. 'Ned, I can see why you're upset. But are you sure that aggressively pursuing a divorce is really what you want to do?'

'I've got grounds, right?'

'We can always find grounds. Unreasonable behaviour, for one. Desertion perhaps. But that isn't what I meant.'

'Martin said you were a ball-breaker,' I comment. 'You certainly broke his.'

His expression doesn't waver. 'Naturally, I pursue my clients' interests with vigour when required. But I have to tell you, Ned, that that usually means settling these affairs without ending up in court. Litigation is costly and draining, both emotionally and financially. It's a weapon of last resort. '

I hear what he's saying. But things have gone too far. I'm too angry and too hurt. She's humiliated me in front of everyone, and I've had enough of sitting around and taking it like a patsy.

'She left me,' I say doggedly. 'I need to take charge.'

For a long moment, Lyon says nothing. Finally, he picks up his pen again and draws a pad of foolscap towards him. 'I find,' he says neutrally, 'that a legal shot across the bows can have a very sobering effect on occasion. It focuses the mind. You'd be surprised,' he adds, looking up suddenly and catching me by surprise, 'how many times people realize, once they see everything down in black and white, that divorce is not what they want after all.'

Kate

Most of the time, I forget Keir's twelve years younger than me. He has such a serious air about him, even when he's reading the paper or relaxing. Unlike so many men, he doesn't seem to have that competitive, childishly macho need to prove himself all the time. He debates without taking it personally; he's able to say he's wrong, even when he's right. The magazines next to his bed are *Time* and the *New Yorker*. His fridge contains basil and tarragon as well as beer; he's well-read, thoughtful, and knows the difference between Oman and Amman, Milton and Melville. Most of the time, it slips my mind he's nearer my son's age than my own.

Most of the time.

I cling on as Keir swerves to the side of the road and waits for his friends on the other two Vespas to catch up with us.

'It's gotta be somewhere around here,' Keir says, peering at his palm-pilot.

The other two boys lean over to study the map on the tiny screen. Behind them, their girlfriends shake out long, shiny hair – neither of them is wearing a helmet – and touch up their lipstick.

'Roberto did say Via Pigneto, right?' asks one of the boys.

I don't know why I keep thinking of them as boys. They're probably the same age as Keir.

'Near a restaurant called Primo,' Keir confirms. 'We've probably missed it again.'

I smother a sigh. We've been up and down this stretch of road at least four times in the past half-hour, and it's nearly midnight. I don't know why we couldn't just stay at the bar we were in, or at any of the other three bars we've been to tonight, for that matter. I suppose I shouldn't be surprised. As I recall, the number of bars you hit in an evening is inversely proportional to how old you are.

After another five minutes of debate between the boys, we all pull back out onto the road and try again, Keir taking the lead. At the next junction, he turns right and threads his way down a street so narrow that any car bigger than a Fiat 500 would probably take the front doors on both sides of the road with it.

'Via Pigneto!' he yells suddenly, slewing the Vespa in a tight left turn.

The street we've been searching for is sleazy and ill-lit. The walls of the seedy apartment buildings are covered with obscene graffiti, and foot-high heaps of rubbish are piled at intervals along the kerb. As we pass, two men furtively exchange something in a darkened doorway, and under a flickering orange street light, a couple of skimpily dressed prostitutes jut out their scrawny hips and catcall in Italian.

I tighten my grip on Keir's waist as he slows to pick his way around deep potholes filled with rainwater. I dread to think what the party itself is going to be like.

The road dead-ends in a run-down piazza surrounded by boarded-up shops. We pull over outside a bar whose owner is putting chairs on tables inside. A thick chain and padlock dangle from the door, ready to be fastened.

'We're definitely in the right place,' Keir says without irony, checking his palm-pilot against the peeling street sign on the wall above us. 'Via Pigneto. That's the one.'

'I thought it was near a restaurant?' I say. 'We haven't passed any.'

'Maybe it's closed down. Let me ask the guy inside. Someone's got to know it.'

I climb off the scooter and quickly follow Keir. There's no way I'm standing outside on my own, even with his friends hovering nearby.

The barman glances up as we walk in. His head is shaved; spacers drag his earlobes to chin level, and his muscular forearms are sheathed in tattoo sleeves. I suspect many of his customers look the same; no wonder he regards us, in our pressed chinos and expensive heels, with wary surprise.

Keir asks for directions in Italian, but the barman responds in perfect, if heavily accented, English. 'You are in the wrong side of Via Pigneto. It is divided by the railway bridge. Cross to the other side, and you will find Primo on the left after twenty metres.'

'Got it,' Keir says. 'Thanks.'

'Be careful,' the man warns. 'This is not a good area. The bridge is closed, and you cannot drive across, you must walk. It is very narrow and dark. There are bad people who hide there. Many drugs. Be careful,' he says again.

'Keir,' I whisper nervously as we step back outside. 'Are you sure this is such a good idea?'

'It'll be fine,' he says easily.

It takes age and experience to know that it *won't* always be fine. Mothers worry for a reason. They know danger lurks in the dark. Some hitch-hikers *are* murderers and rapists. Some boys *will* spike your orange juice with vodka; just one ecstasy tablet can be too much. We've learned the hard way that ropes give way, parachutes fail to open, ice breaks.

Babies die before they're even born.

I remind myself that the optimism of youth is one of the things I love about Keir. I've wasted far too much time worrying about things that have never happened, missing out on too much that's good.

We park and lock the Vespas (I can't help wondering if they'll be there when we get back) and walk down Pimp Alley and over the bridge. None of the others seems in the least bit bothered by the drug deals or the couple having noisy, urgent sex against the railway parapet, though Keir lets me hold his hand tightly all the way, for which I'm grateful.

And of course nothing does happen. We find the restaurant and locate the apartment two doors down where the party is taking place. No one even glances our way.

The apartment is crowded, the music discordant and loud – 'industrial metal', Keir tells me – and the other guests are just kids like Keir and his friends. Graduate students and teachers, mostly. No one is shooting up or trading baggies. A few couples are entwined in corners, but most are standing around in the kitchen and on the outside terrace, drinking cheap wine from plastic cups, smoking cigarettes and chatting.

I remember parties like this: noisy, smoky, fuelled by BYOB plonk and existentialist conversation. They weren't that much fun when I was twenty.

I sip wine that could strip the lining from my oesophagus and smile till my face hurts. I don't understand the references to various hip websites and must-have apps, and I don't know any of the people they're talking about. My buzz from a couple of martinis earlier in the evening has gone, and I'm starting to get a full-on headache. More than anything, I wish I could sit down. My feet are killing me in these heels.

I watch Keir chatting animatedly with a couple of teachers and realize I'm seeing a subtly different side to him: he's more comfortable, less intense, amongst his peers. I wonder if this has to do with the fact that he and I are in a relationship, or because he feels he has to behave differently with me because of my age.

'You want to leave?' Keir asks during a lull in the conversation.

'Why don't we go back to Julia's?' I suggest, too tired to dissemble. 'Her place is only five minutes away from here. It'll be a lot quicker than going back into town.'

'Lend me a toothbrush?'

'You can share mine.'

The Vespa is still where we left it. I climb on behind him and almost fall asleep on the way home. Keir leaves it in the courtyard behind the cottage, and we tiptoe up the stone steps to the room I stayed in when I first arrived. Julia never locks it, and I thank God once again for her laid-back, hippie approach to security. Gratefully, I kick off the sadistic shoes and pull my dress over my head. I'm too tired even to think about going down to the outhouse to brush my teeth. Keir shucks off his clothes and climbs into the narrow single bed beside me, and we wriggle around for a moment, all elbows and knees, trying to fit together. In the end, we spoon, my knees pressed into the rough whitewashed walls, his arm slung heavily over my haunch. I remember doing this often when I was a student, and wonder how on earth I ever got any sleep. One of the greatest pleasures of growing older is being able to afford a king-size, pillow-top bed.

I wake early, pins and needles shooting through my shoulders. I lie motionless, trying not to wake Keir, growing more and more uncomfortable.

'On a count of three,' Keir mumbles, without opening his eyes, 'we do a ninety-degree turn to the right.'

I laugh. 'I'm sorry. Did I wake you?'

'It's cool. I can't think of a better way to start the day.'

His erection is hard in the small of my back. 'In this bed?' I say. 'Are you kidding?'

'Kidding? I'd do it with you in a hammock.'

His hand slides along my hip, and despite my tiredness and stiffness and the pins and needles, I feel myself grow wet. I turn in his arms, inhaling the warm, soap-and-sweat scent of him. A shaft of sunlight slides between the shutters and catches the molten red-gold stubble on his chin. He bends his head to my nipple, and I moan softly as a spiral of lust ripples between my legs.

There's a sudden knock at the door, and we both freeze.

'Kate?' Julia calls. 'Are you awake?'

Quickly, I pull the white bedspread up to our chins, and we straighten ourselves like a pair of wooden dolls. 'Come in.'

'I saw the scooter outside and figured it must be – oh! Keir!'

He bends his arm behind his head and smiles lazily, enjoying her discomfort. 'Hey.'

Julia looks everywhere but at the pair of us. 'I didn't mean to disturb you. I'll see you later. Whenever. There's coffee in the kitchen if you want it.'

'We should get up,' I giggle as the door shuts behind her. 'I need to get back home to feed Sawyer 2.'

'He can eat the freaking parrot.'

He turns on to his side, tracing a line between my breasts, down over the soft mound of my stomach, into the warm, silky wetness between my thighs.

'Keir. Seriously,' I say weakly.

'Seriously,' he whispers, slithering down the bed.

His mouth follows the path his fingers have just drawn. A fish leaps in my sex, and I arch beneath his touch. His tongue flicks across my clitoris, and I tangle my fingers in his hair, feeling my body flood with lust.

Keir pulls back and raises himself over me, his cock nudging against me. I hook my legs around his waist, pulling him into me as my orgasm breaks. Moments later, Keir comes, and we collapse in a tangle of sheets and sweat and limbs.

Later, after we've showered together in the bath house, we dress in our crumpled clothes and tumble into the kitchen, laughing and kissing, unmistakably a couple who have just had sex.

'What's that?' I say suddenly, staring at the envelope on the kitchen table.

Julia takes the coffee pot off the stove. 'It came for you yesterday. I was going to bring it over this morning, but you beat me to it.'

'Kate?' Keir says, instantly concerned.

I pick up the envelope. *Fisher Lyon Raymond*, it says in the corner.

And beneath: *Divorce and Family Law Solicitors.*

IN THE PRINCIPAL REGISTRY
FAMILY DIVISION

BETWEEN

EDWARD MICHAEL FORREST
Petitioner

-and-

KATHERINE JANE DRAYTON FORREST
Respondent

The Petition of Edward Michael Forrest shows that:

1. On the 8th day of April 1997, the Petitioner Edward Michael Forrest was lawfully married to Katherine Jane Drayton Forrest (herein-after called "the Respondent") at the Catholic Church of Our Lady of Succour in the District of Salisbury in the county of Wiltshire.

2. The Petitioner and the Respondent last lived together as husband and wife at The Oast House, Uppingham Lane, Little Wishford, Wiltshire.

3. The Petitioner is a Journalist and still resides at the marital home in Little Wishford, and the Respondent is a Client Service Director and is believed to reside at Via Appia Antica 270, Rome, Italy.

4. There are two children of the family now living, namely:-

   Guy Charles Hawthorne Forrest born on 17th January 1995 to the Petitioner and his former wife, Liesl Imogen Forrest; and Agness Juliet Forrest born on 30th December 1997.

5. No other child now living has been born to the Petitioner during the marriage

6. There are or have been no proceedings in any court in England and Wales or elsewhere with reference to the marriage or between the Petitioner and the Respondent with reference to any property of either or both of them.

7. There are or have been no proceedings in the Child Support Agency with reference to the maintenance of any child of the family.

8. There are no proceedings continuing in any country outside of England and Wales which relate to the marriage or are capable of affecting its validity or subsistence.

9. The said marriage has broken down irretrievably.

10. The Respondent has deserted the Petitioner and behaved in such a way that the Petitioner cannot reasonably be expected to live with the Respondent.

11. Particulars

1. The Respondent who is a Client Service Director for a well-known advertising agency is completely absorbed by her work and has, throughout the marriage, devoted the majority of time to it, even to the extent of cutting short family holidays and working at weekends. Additionally, she would volunteer for additional assignments, increasing her workload to the extent that there has been virtually no family life. Even when the Respondent was at home, she spent a good deal of time in her office and was not at all involved with the children, or the family, except on sporadic occasions.

2. The Petitioner, therefore, has had to take responsibility for the children throughout and has had to make a social life for himself apart from the Respondent who was not there to share it most of the time and who, when she came home from work, did not want to go out in the evenings.

3. The Respondent has been particularly obsessed by her work for the last eighteen months, fearing that internal power struggles within her company would lead to the loss of her employment. These fears induced volatile mood swings which made for an uneasy atmosphere in the home which had its effect upon the children.

4. During the last eighteen months the sexual life between the parties has been extremely sporadic and sexual relations between the parties took place on fewer than six occasions in the last 12 months of the marriage.

5. On the morning of April 11th the Respondent left the marital home to go to work in her usual fashion. She did not return home that night, and made no attempt to inform the Petitioner as to her whereabouts. Since this was not unusual, the Petitioner was not initially concerned. However, after three days when the Respondent had still not returned nor responded to numerous telephone and electronic mail messages from both the Respondent and her employer, the Petitioner believed he had no option but to inform the police. The Petitioner was subjected to rigorous and humiliating questioning over two days before it was established by the police on April 15th that the Respondent had, of her own free will, flown to Rome, Italy, withdrawing a substantial sum from the marital account before doing so.

6. On April 16th, the Petitioner had a telephone conversation with the Respondent, during which she informed him that she did not intend to return to him or to the marital home.

7. Since that date, the Respondent has made no further contact with the Petitioner, or with either of the children of the family.

Ned

Nicholas Lyon was right. Seeing everything on paper in black and white certainly focuses the mind. He's managed to get it all on just two pages. The story of my marriage: from hopeful beginning to bitter end.

On the 8th day of April 1997, the Petitioner Edward Michael Forrest was lawfully married to Katherine Jane Drayton

I remember being so frigging nervous that morning that I covered my chops with toothpaste instead of shaving foam. I'd scraped one side of my face raw before I clued in to the minty smell.

Right up until the moment I saw Kate walk down the aisle, her Jessica Rabbit curves accentuated by that smoking cream fish-tailed dress, I was terrified she was going to come to her senses and change her mind. But as soon as she saw me turn towards her in front of the altar, her gaze locked on to mine like a heat-seeking missile and held it all the way. She was all on her own: no bridesmaids because she didn't want to make a fuss, and no proud father to give her away either: the bastard had refused to come to the wedding because she'd agreed to a Catholic service to keep my old mum happy. Papists, he called us. Like it was still the bloody Middle Ages.

It was just Kate and me, the two of us against the world, standing together in front of the altar. I thought I was the luckiest man on the planet.

I kept on thinking that, even after she got the job at Forde's and started working all the hours God sent. When she fell for Agness just a couple of months after we got married, it was a bit of a shock, obviously, but we soon got past that: I don't suppose Kate even remembers now how upset I was at first. It would've been nice to have had another baby, but it didn't happen, and I was OK with that too. I'd have walked barefoot over broken glass for my daughter.

Maybe I did put a bit of pressure on Kate, looking back. Guy was a good kid, but Kate had effectively gone from having no children to two in barely a year. Perhaps pushing for a third so soon was asking too much. But it's not like I wasn't prepared to do my bit. I was the one staying at home with them, after all.

The Petitioner . . . had to take responsibility for the children throughout

OK, so I wasn't that brilliant at juggling work and the kids. I've got to hand it to Eleanor: I'd never have held it all together if she hadn't helped out back then. It wasn't just looking after Guy and Agness that was the problem, either. I thought the freelance lifestyle would be a breeze, but I missed the buzz of the newsroom more than I'd expected. It got me down. I hated sitting at home all day staring at the computer screen, with only a trip to the kitchen for another coffee to break the monotony. I was jealous of Kate going off to the office every day. Each night she had to work late felt like a slap in the face.

> The Petitioner . . . had to make a social life for himself apart from the Respondent who was not there to share it . . . and who . . . when she came home from work, did not want to go out in the evenings.

Christ. I sound like a total fucking dick. She's working her arse off to pay the bills and coming home too knackered to speak, and I'm whining because I have to go down the pub on my own every night. Kate's lawyer will piss his pants laughing when he reads this.

I rub my hands wearily over my face. Kate's a workaholic, yes, but it's not her fault my career went down the crapper. It was just easier to blame her than look in the mirror. I should have told Kate how I felt and got off my arse and gone back to the newsroom. Instead, I let the resentment build up and fester and then took it out on her for making a success of her own career.

It wasn't all bad, though, was it? We had some good times. Look at last Christmas Eve, when the four of us got out Twister and ended up making a family pretzel. We were all crying with laughter by the end of it. Or that time a couple of years ago when we were snowed in and sat down in front of the fire to watch the entire first three series of *Lost* from start to finish. There have been some great family moments in there. Sporadic? Maybe – but isn't that just par for the course? No one's life is a montage of rom-com shots. You just have to hope the good stuff outweighs the shit when you get to the end.

OK, I knew Kate wasn't happy, but I honestly had no idea it was so bad she'd end up running away from us all. Well, running away from *me*. I can't blame the kids. I was the one who screwed things up. The words jump out of the page at me. *No other child now living*. Losing the baby in February was the straw that broke the camel's back, but the truth is that our marriage had been unravelling for a long time – years – before that happened. And I did nothing to stop it.

We can all be Monday morning quarterbacks, as they say in the US; it's easy to spot the mistakes now, when it's all there in front of you in black and white. All I can say is it wasn't so bloody obvious at the time.

The said marriage has broken down irretrievably.
 . . . informed him that she did not intend to return to him or to the marital home.

I throw the paper down. I can't bear to read any more. What the fuck was I *thinking*, serving this shit on her? The lawyer has made it all sound like Kate's fault, because that's his job. But when it comes down to it, what've I really got to bitch about? What was so 'unreasonable' about her behaviour? She worked too hard? She was fucking terrified she was going to lose her job and everything would blow up in her face? It's not like I ever pulled my weight on that score. If she stopped earning, we were all screwed. Jesus. I was a fucking bum. A *leech*. Yeah, OK, she left me. Deserted me, as Lyon puts it. If I'd been Kate, I'd have walked out years ago.

Going to the lawyer was a huge mistake. If Kate's been wavering, if there was a chance she did still plan to come home, I've just slammed the door in her face. I should never have taken things this far. Lyon knew that, I realize suddenly. He tried to stop me. It wasn't Kate he ever intended to shake up by putting it all on paper. It was *me*.

'Dad?'

Maybe it's not too late. I could phone her, explain I never meant things to go this far. We can call off the lawyers and put things back the way they were. It's not as if she did something unforgiveable, like have an affair or run away with another man. I don't think I could ever get past that. But I understand why she left. I can forgive her if she'll just give me a second chance—

'*Dad!*'

I jump. Guy is hovering in the doorway to my office. He looks like shit, I notice. His clothes are filthy, and he obviously hasn't taken a shower in days.

'Dad, can I talk to you?'

'Does it have to be now?'

He stares at the floor and mutinously chews his lip. I never know what to say to Guy. Kate was always so much better with him than me.

'Come on, then,' I sigh. 'Out with it.'

He looks up. The expression in his eyes is that of a frightened, feral animal, and I suddenly feel a sweep of pity for the poor bastard. Losing Kate's been hard on him, too. I've been so worried about Agness and money and all the rest of it, my son's kind of got lost in the mix. But before he can spit it out, we're interrupted by the sound of my mobile. I hold up a hand to tell him to wait, and check the number. Shit. I've been waiting for the bank to call all morning.

'Sorry, Guy,' I say, shrugging apologetically. 'I've got to take this.'

He leaves without a word. If it was important, he'll come back.

'Don,' I say easily into the phone. 'Where are we at?'

By the time I end the call, I'm a free man. For the first time in my life, I don't have a single debt to my name: I've paid off the bookies, my credit cards, even the bloody mortgage. I've made two hundred grand in a matter of weeks and I'm walking away without a scratch. I should feel on top of the world.

Funny how none of it seems to matter any more.

Guy

Dessler's an asshole, but he's smart. He keeps his head down and his nose clean. Never gets caught with blood on his hands. Death by a thousand keystrokes, that's more Dessler's style.

He's the one behind this freaking sick page: *www.Guy ForrestShouldKillHimself.com*. It's already had over a thousand hits, and it's only been up two days.

Fucking trolls. What kind of sad bastard gets off posting shit like this?

Chewing my free thumbnail, I move the cursor down the page. The red text stands out like blood against the black background.

> *You fuckin homo you don't disserve 2 live I hope they hold u down and shove hot rods up ur ass.*
>
> *Kill yourself or we'll do it for you.*

Guy Forrest should be carved up with rusty scythes and his remains poured into a cement mixer.

Why don't you just fucking do yourself now and help the planet by dying, you loser?

They'd never write this stuff if they had to put their real names to it. Miserable fucking cowards.

It's not just this website, either. They keep trolling my Facebook page, writing all kinds of sick stuff. It's like they've got nothing to do but post their slime. I've got used to the texts, but this is taking things to the next level. I mean, *every*one can read this stuff. People who don't even know me scent blood in the water and jump on the band-wagon. Mob mentality. I know it's all crap and I shouldn't give a shit what these morons say, but it gets to you, you know?

I slam my laptop shut. Who gives a fuck? Trolls only post to get a reaction, everyone knows that. If you don't feed them, they soon give up and look elsewhere.

There's a tentative knock at the door. A beat, then Agness cracks it and puts her head round. 'Can I come in?'

I shrug, though right now I could use the company.

'How's it going?'

'How d'you think?'

'Ignore them,' Agness says. She wanders over to my shelves and starts fiddling with my computer shit. 'They'll soon get bored.'

'Yeah? And what would you know?'

'I know none of this crap matters out in the real world,' she says tartly. 'Don't let it get to you. Those losers'll end up stacking shelves in Tesco while you're off inventing a cure for cancer or something. You'll probably end up running the country, and then you can cut all their benefits for being tossers.'

I take the salvaged hard drive out of her hand and put it back on the shelf. 'Was there something you actually wanted, or did you just come to bug the shit out of me?'

'He's done it,' she says, slumping next to me on the bed. 'Dad. He's filed for divorce.'

Now she has my attention. 'No shit,' I exclaim. 'Did he tell you that?'

'I saw a copy of the papers on his desk.'

'Fucking moron. What'd he go and do that for?'

'I think it's my fault,' she says guiltily. 'I told him to take charge and do something. I meant he should go to Italy and persuade her to come back, not get a *divorce*!'

I reach for a tin on the shelf behind me and take out a packet of Rizlas and some weed. 'Relax. It'll never happen.'

'He's posted them already! They're going to get divorced and we'll have to sell the house and you'll probably have to go and live with Liesl, and I'll be stuck on my own with Dad or living on the streets with druggies and winos and rapists! We'll never see each other again!'

'Would you stop,' I sigh, crumbling the weed into the Rizla paper and rolling the joint between my fingers. 'No one's going anywhere.'

'Stop saying that! Mum's been gone, like, three months already. What's to stop Dad getting divorced if he wants? And then what'll happen to us?'

'He's just mad, is all. Once he calms down, they'll sort it all out.'

I lick the edge of the Rizla and roll it together. I'm about to light it, but Agness suddenly looks like she's about to burst into tears. I put the joint down and ease my arm around her, and she buries her face in my shoulder like she used to do when she was little. I suddenly feel way grown-up and protective. She's held it all together so well since Kate left, I forget she's just a kid. She's really matured this last three months. It's hard to believe what a brat she used to be. For the first time in years, it feels like we're friends.

'I don't think Mum's ever coming back,' Agness mumbles, her voice small. 'Guy, what's going to happen to us?'

'Shhhh. It's going to be OK,' I say. I rub her back gently. 'She just needs some space, that's all. She'll come back when she's ready.'

Agness lifts her white face to look at me. 'D'you think it's our fault she left?'

I hesitate. I don't want to make her feel worse, but I don't want to lie to her either. 'A bit,' I say finally. 'But mostly I think it had to do with Dad.'

'I don't blame her for going,' Agness says, surprising me. 'I was a total bitch, and so was Gran. Dad didn't even know she existed most of the time. You're the only one who was ever nice to her.'

I give Agness's shoulders a final squeeze and let go to light the spliff. 'Forget it. She knows you didn't mean it.'

'Can I have some of that?'

'As if. Didn't anyone tell you it's bad for you?'

'According to Liesl, it's medicinal.'

'According to Liesl, acorns have souls.'

'Spoilsport,' she says, but she's smiling. 'Fancy pizza tonight? Gran's at bridge, and I don't feel like cooking.'

'Sure.'

My mobile buzzes and automatically I pick it up and click on my inbox. I don't give a shit if it's from Dessler and his morons. Agness is right: give it a year or so and none of this will matter. In the meantime, they can throw all the verbal they like. Sticks and stones . . .

But when I see the video, I have trouble trying to make sense of what I'm seeing. I know what it is: I just don't want to believe it.

Dessler's voice bounces off the tiled walls: *Did you get it all? Cool, that'll do.*

The bastards filmed it. They fucking *filmed* it, and now it's gone viral.

They're careful to keep the camera-phone away from the mirrors so it's impossible to see their faces, but there's no mistaking it's me on the receiving end. My head bangs against the edge of the bathroom sink, snot and tears mingling with blood from where I've bitten through my bottom lip. I don't even remember doing that. It's like a horror flick, except it's real, and it happened to me.

And now everybody knows it.

Agness, watching over my shoulder, snatches the phone from my hand and throws it across the room as if it's a grenade, her face grey. *She's only fourteen.* She shouldn't have had to see that.

'You've got to tell Dad,' she whispers.

'No!'

'You have to!' she insists. 'Guy! You have to go to the police!'

'You think I want the whole fucking world to know about this?'

'They already do!'

I cringe against the wall, covering my face with hands. 'What am I going to do? Agness. What am I going to do?'

'You've got to go and talk to Dad. He'll know what to do.'

I look up helplessly. 'This can't be fixed. I'm screwed.'

'You don't know that,' she says stubbornly. 'You have to try.'

www.GuyForrestShouldKillHimself.com. For the first time since all this started, I seriously consider it. I just want all this to be over. It's too hard. Too much fucking work.

Agness starts to cry. Quietly, without drama. I look at her pinched, ashen face and a cold, hard knot of resignation settles in my stomach. I can't do that to her. Not after all she's had to cope with already.

She comes downstairs with me and sits on the bottom step, waving her hands in little shooing motions towards Dad's study.

I suck down a breath and knock on the open door. 'Dad?'

His back's to me, and I have to say his name several times before he jumps and swings round in his chair. 'Dad, can I talk to you?'

'Does it have to be now?' he says tersely.

I choke on the words. I know it's not my fault, what happened, but all of a sudden I'm not sure Dad's going to see it that way. *Are you sure you didn't do anything to provoke them? What sort of signals are you giving off?*

Are you gay?

I can feel his attention slipping away before his phone even rings.

'Sorry, Guy. I've got to take this,' he says, turning away.

In a way, I'm almost relieved. There's only one option left.

'Sorry, Ags,' I whisper as I pass her on the stairs.

Kate

'What did you expect?' Julia asks, not unsympathetically. 'You left him, Kate. You can't expect him to wait for you to come back for ever.'

'He never even discussed it with me,' I protest. 'I'm gone a few weeks, and just like that he files for *divorce*?'

'Three months. And did you talk it over with him before you decided to leave?'

The awkward silence that follows this uncomfortable truth is interrupted by the arrival of our waiter. We both lean back in our chairs, glad of the diversion, as he places a plate of *insalata tricolore* in front of each of us. I reach for my glass of fizzy water. It's blisteringly hot today, even for mid-July. Beneath the shade of the restaurant's yellow canopy, it must be close to forty degrees. A shimmering heat rises from the baking cobbles, and in the centre of the piazza dozens of tourists have taken off their shoes and are standing in the fountain in a futile attempt to cool down. Overhead, tiny pipes spray a fine mist of water over the tables, as if we're hot-house flowers in a greenhouse. I pluck my damp T-shirt away from my skin. It's like being wrapped in a hot, wet duvet.

I pick up my fork and then put it down again. 'It's just so *final*,' I say. 'Julia, I swear, I never wanted this.'

'Nor does Ned, not really. He's hurt, and he's angry.'

'He *hates* me.'

'No, he doesn't. He's just upset.'

'*Upset?* Julia, you saw what he's told his lawyers about me. "Obsessed with my work. No time for the children. Volatile mood swings . . ." For God's sake!'

She forks up a mouthful of avocado. 'Come on. It's just the way it works. He's gone to the lawyers with his laundry list of complaints, and they've whipped it up into a petition for unreasonable behaviour. That's their job. Apart from using desertion as grounds, they've got nothing. They've made it all sound far worse than it is. They pit you against each other, then stand back and cash in.'

'He's told them how many times we had *sex*!' I cry.

'It'll get a lot worse than this if you contest it and it goes to court.'

I take a small bite of tomato and try to swallow. Since the papers arrived I seem to have a permanent lump in my throat. Of course I knew Ned and I couldn't continue in limbo for ever, but even I am surprised by the shock and grief that's overtaken me in the days since I received the letter from his lawyer. Surely the death of a marriage is one of the saddest things in the world.

I have a sudden image of Ned turning at the altar to watch me walk down the aisle, his face alight with innocent trust and hope for the future. No one ever gets married thinking they won't make it. I was so afraid that morning as Julia helped me into my silk fish-tailed wedding dress: scared beyond reason that Ned wouldn't turn up, would jilt me at the eleventh hour in front of everyone, like Miss Havisham. I hadn't even wanted any bridesmaids, so convinced was I that the more fuss I made, the more abject would be my eventual humiliation.

I've never told Ned that, I realize sadly. I was always too afraid to let him know how much I loved him; I learned the hard way from Eleanor that whoever loves least – or at least appears to – has the upper hand.

For the first time, I feel the full weight of all our blunted dreams. During the past three months, I've rewritten my own history, casting him in my memories as the safe choice, the dull choice; an escape from my father, and from the destructive passion of men like Alessio. Maybe that's partly true; but I *did* love Ned once, very much. How ironic that I've been unable to acknowledge it until now, when the last of the love we shared has gone.

'*Are* you going to contest this?' Julia asks carefully.

'I can't go back to him.'

'Are you sure?'

My eyes prick. 'I had to leave, Julia. I couldn't stay in that marriage any longer. I felt like I was being walled up alive. But this breaks . . . it breaks . . . my heart.'

'I know, darling.'

'Everything in that petition is true. I know the lawyers present the facts in the worst possible light, but I *was* more committed to my work than to my marriage. I thought I was doing the right thing, but at the end of the day I'm as responsible as Ned for letting things between us die. It's no wonder he gave up on me so quickly. What incentive did I give him to wait?'

'He had a choice,' Julia says robustly. 'He could have come out and laid siege.'

'I thought he would,' I admit. Suddenly sick to my stomach, I push my food away. 'I didn't mean this as a test, but I suppose in a way it was.'

The waiter collects Julia's empty plate and my untouched salad, balancing them on his forearm as he sets two steaming bowls of *spaghetti alle vongole* in front of us. My stomach heaves.

'Listen to me,' I say, forcing a smile. 'I sound pathetic. I don't want to be with him, but he's not allowed not to want me?'

'And Keir?' she asks gently.

I crumble a piece of bread between my fingers. I don't know why this is suddenly so difficult. Until a few days ago, when the letter arrived, I've been happier than I've felt in years. It's not just the sex – it's the way Keir *sees* me. It's the fact that he's often lost for words because he's listening to what I'm telling him rather than thinking about what he's going to say next. It's the graduate art school brochure left beside my bed. It's the pair of flip-flops he produces from his backpack just at the point I think my heels are going to kill me. It's the gap between his front teeth, the way he holds his cigarette between his third and fourth fingers, the indescribably beautiful expression on his face when he comes.

'I love him,' I say simply. 'I know it makes things so much more complicated, but I do.'

She spreads her hands. 'Then why the tears over Ned?'

'I don't know. Because of the *waste*, I suppose. Ned and I got it so wrong. It could have been so different.' I lick my forefinger and dab at the crumbs I've made. 'It was a shock when I got that petition. I don't know why it should've been, but you're right: I can't expect Ned to wait around for ever. We might as well get this over so we can both move on with our lives.'

Julia doesn't reply. I watch the top of her bent head as she studiously pushes a clam around the plate as if her life depends on it.

'What?' I say.

'It's none of my business . . .'

'*Julia*.'

She puts down her fork with a clatter. 'OK. You really want to know what I think?'

I nod warily, not at all certain that I do.

'I think Keir's distracting you from what's really going on. Maybe you do actually love him, though I can think of another L-word that would be more appropriate. Either way,' she adds, 'either way, *he's* the reason you're not fighting to save your marriage, and that worries me.'

'Keir has nothing to do with this. My marriage was over long before we even met.'

'Are you sure?' she asks softly. 'Or is it just easier to tell yourself that, so that Ned has to make the decision for you?'

With impeccable timing, our waiter reappears and refills our glasses of water, giving us both time to regroup.

'I don't know how it happened, or what I did to deserve it,' I say finally, 'but Keir is the best thing that has ever happened to me. I'm sorry if that sounds clichéd, but it's true. Maybe you're right; maybe it'll all end in tears. But this isn't some kind of holiday romance. I would've fallen in love with him whenever we met. He makes me feel . . . I don't know . . .'

'Sexy? Appreciated?'

'What's wrong with that?' I ask, nettled.

'Nothing. But you don't need to screw a teenager to feel that way.'

I gasp as if I've been slapped. 'I know you mean well,' I say, holding on to my temper with difficulty. 'But you don't understand. I love Keir because when I'm with him I can simply be *me*.'

She slams her glass on the table. 'You're not *you* with Keir! Of *course* you like the way you are with him. You don't have any responsibilities. It's not *real*.' She sighs in exasperation. 'Wise up, Kate. No one likes getting older. We all wonder how we ended up where we are. But whether you like it or not, part of you *is* being a wife and mother. We'd all like to be twenty-one again, and not just for the great skin. But think back. It all seemed pretty stressful at the time, didn't it? No knowing what we wanted to do with our lives, wondering if we'd ever fall in love. Frankly, I'm bloody glad to be forty, if you want the truth.'

'It's different for you. You have your freedom. You get to be yourself every day. You don't know what it's like—'

'You think my life is perfect?' Julia demands. 'I'm permanently broke, I'm lonely, and I'll never have a child. Chances are I'll grow old alone. I'd like to run away from *my* life to *yours*.'

Unexpectedly, I laugh. 'I've always wanted curly hair,' I say.

Julia stares at me for a long moment and then smiles tiredly. 'And I'd have given anything for mine to be straight.'

We look sadly at each other. 'No one said it would be easy, did they?' I say.

'You really love Keir, don't you?'

'I do,' I say simply.

The moment is broken by my phone ringing. I pull it out, glance at the number and feel myself going pale. 'It's Ned.'

'Talk of the devil.'

I take a deep breath to steady myself, and answer it.

'Is Guy with you?' Ned says without preamble.

Instantly, I'm alert. 'Why, what's happened?'

'I don't know.' He sounds fraught, worried. 'He's left. We thought he might have come to see you.'

'When did he leave?'

'Yesterday. I can't be sure when. Maybe even the night before.'

'He's been gone *two days* and you didn't notice?'

'Kate, he's seventeen. I don't keep him on reins any more.'

My stomach lurches. 'If he was on his way here, he should've arrived by now.'

'Christ,' Ned says, and I can hear the fear in his voice. '*Christ.*'

It's not like Guy to disappear without saying a word. He's normally so reliable.

'What is it?' I demand sharply. 'Ned, what's going on? What is it you're not telling me?'

He hesitates. 'Look, there's been some trouble at Guy's school. Some of the other lads have been bullying him, and I'll be honest, it got pretty nasty.'

'What do you mean? What kind of bullying?'

'I'll explain another time. Right now, I'm just worried about finding him before things get totally out of hand.'

'Call the police,' I say crisply. 'Tell them he's missing. Tell them it's been more than twenty-four hours. Tell them anything you have to to get them to take you seriously.

I'm leaving for the airport now. I'll be home in a few hours.'

'You don't have to come back. I can handle this.'

'Don't be ridiculous. He's my son.'

I put the phone back in my bag and stand up. I always have my passport and wallet with me out of habit; I don't need anything else.

'Go,' Julia says anxiously. 'Go, I'll deal with this.' She gives me a hug.

'I'll call you,' I say.

I hitch my bag over my shoulder and dash across the piazza, ruthlessly cutting into the line at the nearest taxi rank. 'It's an emergency,' I pant as I yank open the door of the first yellow cab. I bark instructions to the airport and collapse against the sticky vinyl seat. Even in the midst of my fear and worry, the irony of the situation doesn't escape me: I'm leaving Rome as precipitately as I arrived, with only the clothes I stand up in.

And once again I have no idea when, or even if, I'll be back.

Ned

It's starting to feel like a bloody French farce. And I've never liked the fucking French.

'*Another* family member missing, Mr Forrest?' Plod says drolly. 'It's a bit like an Agatha Christie novel, isn't it? *Ten Little Indians*, or whatever the PC brigade call it now. Would you like us to bring in Mr Poirot?'

'This isn't a joke,' I say furiously. 'My son is missing!'

'So was your wife,' the cop says blandly. 'Until she wasn't, of course.'

It had to be the same sanctimonious bastard, didn't it?

I lean over the counter and get right in his face. 'Are you going to take me seriously, or do I have to go over your head?'

He sighs gustily and pulls the computer keyboard towards him. 'Name?'

'Guy Forrest.'

'When did you last see him?'

'Wednesday night. Nearly two days ago.'

'Two *days*?' he says sharply. 'How old is your son, Mr Forrest?'

'Seventeen.'

'Seventeen.' He gives me a long, measured look and pointedly pushes the keyboard away. 'Look, Mr Forrest. I'm sure he's just gone out with his mates and forgotten to tell you. They do that at this age, you know—'

'What's it going to take? I'm telling you my son is *missing*. Not off with his mates, not out getting bladdered, not shacked up with some bird getting laid. He may be seventeen, but he's just a *kid*.' I slam my palm on the counter. 'Now, are you going to do your job and find him, or do I have to start making a real stink around here?'

'Mr Forrest. Please. Do you have any reason to believe your son has actually come to any harm?'

'Look, I told you—'

'Has he been threatened?'

I've paid the bookies off, with interest; thanks to the football scam, I'm suddenly back in the black. They've got no reason to go after Guy. 'Not as far as I'm aware, but—'

'Is he a danger to himself or to others?'

'No! Of course not!'

'And as far as you know, he left home of his own free will?'

'He left on his own, but not because he *wanted* to,' Agness interrupts, appearing suddenly at my side. 'He didn't have a choice!'

'Agness, go and sit back down.'

'What d'you mean, young lady?' Plod asks.

'It doesn't matter,' I snap. I don't want that filth on Guy's phone seeing the light of day. 'Agness, sit down and let me deal with this.'

'Show him the video!' Agness cries, ignoring me completely. 'Go on. Show him!'

'Agness, I said, *I can handle this*.'

'What video?' the cop asks curiously.

'There's no point trying to hide it, Dad,' Agness sighs. 'It's all over YouTube. You might as well show him. Maybe then they'll start to take us seriously.'

I realize she's right. No point worrying about Guy's privacy now. We just need to find him. Reluctantly, I hand my son's phone to the cop and watch his expression change from sceptical to grim as he watches the short clip.

'Where did this come from?' the cop demands after he's watched it through twice.

'Someone sent it to Guy's phone,' Agness says tearfully. 'It's gone viral. I don't know who actually shot it, but anyone could've forwarded it to him.'

'Did your brother discuss this . . . incident with you?'

She bites her lip. 'Guy doesn't really talk to anyone. I knew he was being bullied a bit at school, but he said he could handle it. He didn't want anyone else to get involved. He knew it'd just make it worse.' She turns to me. 'I didn't know it was this bad, Dad, I swear.'

'It's not your fault,' I say firmly.

I must be the shittiest parent on the planet. Why didn't I know about any of this? I had no bloody idea Guy was being bullied. And this is way beyond the usual schoolboy head-down-the-lav stuff. This is criminal sexual assault. Possibly even rape. Poor fucking bastard. Why the hell didn't he come to me?

I suddenly remember him standing in the doorway of my office two days ago. He *did* come to me, and I gave him the brush-off. Christ. If I'd only known.

All of a sudden, everyone is taking this very seriously. The Laughing Policeman disappears, and five minutes later a far more senior officer escorts me into an interview room while a female uniform minds Agness. For the next two hours, I'm bombarded with a thousand questions – what are the names of Guy's friends, where does he like to hang out, does he have a girlfriend? Boyfriend? – exactly as I was when Kate disappeared. I suppose at least this time no one thinks I've buried him under the floorboards.

In a way, though, I feel even worse. As the interview progresses, it becomes clear I don't know the first thing about my own son. I can't name a single one of his friends, I haven't a clue what he does outside school, or even if he's passed his driving test. I haven't thought to bring a photo of him with me to the station. In the end, we have no choice but to fetch Agness. She handles all the questions I can't answer, and has even brought his most recent school picture to give the cops. Once again, I feel surplus to bloody requirements.

'Guy's particulars will be circulated on the Police National Computer,' the senior cop says finally. 'Any police officer nationally, or internationally, for that matter, will be able to contact us to find out more in-depth details should the need arise.'

I put my hand on his arm as he goes to leave. 'Tell me the truth. No bullshit. What are the odds we'll find him?'

He glances at Agness, who rolls her eyes at his delicacy, as well she might, given her involvement up to now. 'With young runaways, it's always more difficult,' he says carefully. 'They tend not to have credit cards we can trace, and obviously your son didn't take his phone with him, so we can't triangulate his position from that. But we'll do our best, Mr Forrest. I promise you that.'

'He's not a runaway,' I say. 'Not the way you mean. He'd never have left if he hadn't been driven to it. I hope you're going to catch the bastards who did this to him. If anything happens to him, they're the ones responsible.'

'Dessler's the one you want to talk to,' Agness interrupts. 'He's behind this, I know it.'

'Who the hell is Dessler?' I demand.

'Some homophobe at Guy's school. He's always beating up on him—'

'What did you say?'

'Guy's gay, Dad,' Agness sighs. '*Hello?*'

Gay? My son's *gay*? This is the first I've bloody heard of it!

'Are you *sure*?' I ask doubtfully. I mean, my own son. Surely I'd have known?

'Like, get with the programme, Dad,' Agness mutters.

I'm not sure how I feel about this, to be honest. I've got nothing against poofs. Each to his own, and all that. As long as they stick to the privacy of their own bedrooms. I've got no time for the raging queers who parade down the high street in studs and black leather hot pants, shoving it in our faces. But if Guy's gay, fine. Makes no difference, really. It might explain why he's always had more of a rapport with Kate than with me, though.

The cop scribbles something down in his notes. 'We'll talk to the school on Monday. If this boy Dessler *is* behind this, we'll be wanting to have a serious talk with that young man.'

It's early evening by the time Agness and I leave the station and drive home. I put down the car windows, resting my arm on the ledge as a balmy summer breeze drifts through the vehicle. At least Guy won't freeze to death if he ends up sleeping on a park bench, I think grimly.

'I wish Mum was here,' Agness says quietly.

I pull her against me, my free hand on the steering wheel. 'I know,' I say.

I haven't told her Kate might be coming home. There are no guarantees, after all. She's left us to sink or swim on our own for the past three months, so who's to say if she'll come back now? I'm not sure I even *want* her to. We've coped perfectly well on our own without her. I don't need her swooping in to rescue us at the eleventh hour. We can handle this just fine between us.

But as I pull the car into the driveway, a taxi is just leaving. And standing by the kitchen door, looking taller and slimmer and younger than I remember, is Kate.

Agness throws herself into her mother's arms like a small child. 'You're back! You're back!'

Kate buries her face in her daughter's hair, holding her tight for a long moment. 'Hey, sweetheart, let me look at you,' she says finally, disentangling herself and holding Agness at arm's length. 'Your hair's grown longer. It's very pretty.'

'Harry says he likes it this way,' Agness says, glowing with pleasure.

'And you're so tall! I almost wouldn't have recognized you!'

'It hasn't been that long,' I say irritably.

Kate glances across anxiously. 'Any news?'

'No.'

I unlock the kitchen door and go inside, not bothering to wait for Kate to go first.

She follows and dumps her bag on the kitchen table. 'Have you called the police?'

'That's where we've just been.' Pointedly, I move her handbag onto the table by the door our *guests* use. 'Agness, can you tell Eleanor we're back? She had a bit of a headache, but I'm sure she'll want an update.'

Kate follows me round the kitchen. 'But what did they say? Did you tell them he's been missing two days? Are they going to—'

'Kate,' I say levelly, turning to face her. 'You abandoned this family three months ago without even saying goodbye. You didn't even bother to call and tell us you were OK. You just *left*. We didn't know if you were alive or dead. For three months, we've had to manage on our own without you. What makes you think you can just march in now and pick up where you left off?'

'He's my *son*. I'm worried about him . . .'

'He was your son three months ago, too. You gave up your right to be worried about Guy when you walked out and left him.'

Her face pales under her tan. '*You* called *me*,' she protests. 'You must have wanted me to come back?'

'I thought you had a right to know, that's all. As you say, he's your son.'

'Ned . . .'

'Katherine!' Eleanor stops dead at the sight of her daughter. 'Where did you come from?'

'Surprise!' Agness carols behind her.

'Didn't you tell anyone I was coming home?'

I shrug.

'Would you like some tea?' Eleanor says politely. I have to hand it to the old bitch: she knows how to stick the knife in. In five words, she's managed to convey just how much everything's changed in the last three months: Kate isn't in charge any more. She doesn't have the right to put on the kettle and make her own tea. She's a *guest* here; no more, no less.

From the expression on her face, Kate hasn't missed it either. 'That would be lovely,' she says carefully.

'Where are your bags?' Agness demands.

'I haven't got any,' Kate says awkwardly. 'I was out having lunch with Julia when Dad called me, and I went straight to the airport.'

'But you're staying, right?'

'We have to find Guy, don't we?' Kate says, giving her daughter a quick hug. Agness doesn't notice she hasn't answered the question, but Eleanor throws me a sharp look.

I go to the fridge for a beer, needing the distraction. I thought I wanted Kate to come home on any terms, but now that she's here, all the old anger and bitterness have come flooding back. I literally can't bear the sight of her.

Is it possible to love someone more than you thought possible, and hate them at the same time?

'Is it OK if I go up and find a sweater or something?' Kate asks, rubbing her bare arms.

I don't reply, and she takes my silence as a yes. From the corner of my eye, I watch her go up the stairs, her pale blue skirt – new, I take it – swishing around her brown knees. She's wearing heels, too: spindly silvery ones. Kate never used to wear heels during the day.

Agness runs after her mother like a puppy. She doesn't even glance in my direction. For three months, I've held this family together on my own. Kate's been in the house three minutes and I'm out in the cold.

'Katherine's her mother,' Eleanor says, watching me.

'Not for the past three months she hasn't been.'

'I know you're angry,' she says, 'but now isn't the time.'

'Kate can't just come swanning back in here expecting everything to be the same! Who the hell does she think she is? She fucking walked out on us, Eleanor! She's lucky we let her in the bloody door!'

'I'm sure she doesn't expect everything to be the same. But what would you like her to do, Ned? Her son is *missing*. Did you expect her to wait for an engraved invitation?'

'No, of course not . . .'

'Your priority is finding Guy. Whatever you two need to sort out comes afterwards.'

Eleanor's right, damn her. And frankly, I could use some breathing space to get my head together. Seeing Kate again has unsettled me more than I'd expected. Clearly she hasn't been pining for me, I think bitterly. Underneath the obvious worry about Guy, she looks better than I've seen her in years. I can't put my finger on it. It's more than the tan and the new haircut and the sexy clothes. She seems more confident somehow. More like she used to be when we first met.

'Ned,' Kate says, coming back into the kitchen. 'Where are all my clothes?'

'I needed the room,' I say coolly.

She blanches. 'You didn't throw them out?'

'Keep your hair on. They're in a trunk in the loft. They may be a bit creased, but you can always iron them.'

I meet her gaze head on, shocked to discover that I suddenly have an erection that could stop traffic. I can tell she's bursting to say something, but she keeps a lid on it. Fine by me.

'Where would you like me to stay tonight?' she asks stiffly.

'Here, of course!' Agness laughs. 'Right, Dad?'

'Of course,' I say easily. 'I'm sure you must be suffering from jet lag, so I suggest you use Guy's room. I'd hate to disturb you.'

'That's very thoughtful of you.'

I incline my head, praying she doesn't notice the tent pole in my trousers.

'I'll cook us all dinner tonight,' Agness offers eagerly. 'I'm really good in the kitchen now, Mum. I do this really cool zucchini and sausage stew. I got the recipe off the Internet. It's delicious, isn't it, Dad?'

'Sounds great,' Kate says brightly.

'Let me get you one of my fleeces,' Agness says, already halfway up the stairs. 'You must be freezing. Dad can bring all your stuff down from the loft later.'

'I'll put some fresh sheets on Guy's bed,' Eleanor says with a shudder. 'Teenage boys. You don't want to catch anything.'

'You don't have to do that . . .'

'Of course I do,' Eleanor says. She touches her daughter's arm briefly. Coming from her, it's the equivalent of a full-blown hug. 'It's good to have you home, Katherine.'

Eleanor too, I think bitterly as she follows Agness upstairs. Fucking turncoats, the lot of them.

Kate turns to me. 'I know this is difficult,' she begins. 'But—'

'You can stay here till we find Guy. That's the only reason you're here, right?'

She hesitates and then nods. 'I *am* sorry, Ned. I never meant—'

'This doesn't change anything, Kate.'

Her tone is suddenly as cold as mine. 'I wouldn't expect it to.'

'Good. Just so long as we understand each other.'

'Yes,' Kate says, her expression unreadable. 'Yes, I think for the first time, we do.'

Kate

I didn't expect Ned to welcome me back with open arms. The divorce petition made it pretty clear what kind of reception I could expect. But it's still a shock to be faced in person with this much hostility from the man I have been married to for fifteen years. Ned really does hate me.

The tension in the kitchen is tangible. It takes all my self-control not to bolt back out of the door and run after my disappearing taxi. Eleanor is stiffly polite, Ned simmering with rage; only Agness seems oblivious. If it weren't for Guy, I'd be on the next plane home.

Except this *is* home. Or it was.

I shiver, rubbing my clammy palms against my bare arms. The sleeveless silk top, high silver sandals and flimsy chiffon skirt I wore to lunch with Julia are out of place here: in every respect.

'Is it OK if I go up and find a sweater or something?' I ask, heading for the stairs.

Ned doesn't even look round, so I take his silence as

acquiescence. Upstairs, everything is so disorientingly familiar, even the usual pile of clutter on the landing: Guy's trainers, a couple of Agness's fashion magazines, a pair of comfortable pink slippers that belong to Eleanor. I have to force myself not to pick everything up out of habit.

The door to our bedroom is closed. I hesitate for a moment before opening it. Unlike the rest of the house, this room *does* look different, and it takes me a moment to realize why. Ned has removed everything that belongs to me. The Mucha print over the bed. The bottles of perfume and jewellery on the dresser. Even the scatter cushions on the chaise longue by the window. It's all gone.

'I borrowed some of your make-up,' Agness says, following me into the room. 'I hope you don't mind.'

'Of course not, darling. Just don't overdo it at school, will you?'

'Mu-u-um,' Agness groans, but she's smiling.

My heart warms. Given the state of our relationship when I left home, I wouldn't have been surprised if my daughter had refused even to talk to me. But it's the old, open-hearted, generous Agness who greeted me ten minutes ago, not the hard-edged, sullen teenager I left. I know I don't deserve it, and I offer up a quick prayer of thanks.

I go to the wardrobe. My neat piles of sweaters and folded T-shirts are no longer there. Instead, the shelves are crammed with messy heaps of Ned's pullovers. I check the chest of drawers. It, too, is filled with Ned's clothes.

Another slap in the face.

Did you expect him to preserve everything untouched the way you left it, on the off-chance you might come back?

'I'm sorry I was such a bitch before you left,' Agness says suddenly. 'It was way uncool. I've really changed, Mum, I promise. I came top in school last term, and I tidy my own room now and everything . . .'

I cup her sweet face between my hands. 'Agness, sweetheart, I didn't leave because of you. You're not to think that.'

'I know,' she says awkwardly.

'I mean it. It had nothing to do with you.'

'You're not going to go again, are you?' she asks, her voice small.

I hesitate. 'I'm not leaving *you*.'

'Are you and Dad going to get a divorce?'

'We're talking about it, yes,' I say honestly. 'But I'm not going to disappear on you again, Agness. I promise. Now, come on. We'd better get back downstairs or they'll be wondering where we are.'

I ask Ned where he's put my clothes, and am relieved to discover they're in the loft, not the bin. He stares defiantly at me like a truculent child, and I want to slap him. Our son is *missing*, and all he can do is play these ridiculous games. It's the same when we discuss sleeping arrangements. Once again, it's left to Agness to settle things by insisting I stay here. To my complete astonishment, Eleanor offers to put fresh sheets on Guy's bed for me. I can't remember my mother lifting a finger to help around the house in all her life.

'You don't have to do that,' I say, touched.

'Of course I do.' She squeezes my arm, and my throat tightens. Her support is all the more precious because it was unlooked-for. 'It's good to have you home, Katherine.'

Ned smoulders in the corner of the kitchen. Despite – or perhaps because of – his obvious animosity, I feel an unexpected wash of tenderness for him. He has single-handedly kept the show on the road for the past three months. Whatever mess he's made of everything else, particularly our finances, he deserves some credit for that.

'I know this is difficult,' I say carefully. 'But—'

'You can stay here till we find Guy. That's the only reason you're here, right?'

My sympathy evaporates. He hasn't changed at all. He's still the same spoilt child he always was. He still can't get past how *he* feels, even now. Not once has he asked how I am. He can't even bear to look at me.

For the first time, it truly hits me that my marriage is over.

The sound of my bedroom door opening wakes me. I struggle up from a deep sleep, assuming it must be Agness. But to my surprise, it's Ned who's silhouetted in the doorway.

I push myself up on my pillows, glancing at the clock beside the bed, which reads two-fifteen. 'Is it Guy? Have you heard something?'

'No, no. Nothing like that.' He hesitates, then comes into the room. 'I can't sleep.'

'It took me a while.'

'Can I sit down?'

Surprised by his conciliatory tone, I nod, and he perches gingerly on the edge of the bed in his T-shirt and boxers. His bare feet make him look curiously vulnerable.

'Look, Kate. I'm sorry about the way I was earlier. I didn't mean to bite your head off the second you got through the door.'

'It's OK. I deserved it.'

'No.' He shakes his head. 'You didn't. You came back

because you're worried about Guy, and instead of thanking you, I started hurling abuse. I'm sorry.'

I hesitate. 'I'm sorry, too.'

'Can we start this again?'

For a foolish moment I think he's talking about our marriage, and then I realize he just means today. 'Of course we can.'

He rubs his hands over his face in an achingly familiar gesture, and my heart turns over. Suddenly he looks no older than Guy and I yearn to reach out to him. But I no longer have the right to put my arms around him in comfort. He's been my husband for a decade and a half, but he's suddenly off-limits. I don't know how to be around him.

'Did you just stop loving me?' he says suddenly into the darkness.

'Ned . . .'

'Please. I need to know.'

'It's not that simple.'

'Because I've never stopped loving you.'

He turns to face me, moonlight gilding the planes of his face. He seems so lost, and I have to fight hard not to let the past overwhelm me. Firmly I remind myself that we're not the same people we were when we fell in love. A lot has changed in the past fifteen years. *We've* changed.

'Not for one moment,' he says earnestly. 'I know I didn't make you happy, but I can. I'll do things differently from now on. I've changed. No more gambling, I swear. I've already paid back every penny I owed. I'll quit freelancing and go back to work full-time, and I'll pull my weight around the house. I'll even move to London if you want. Whatever I did wrong, I'll put right.' He takes my hand, his eyes bright with tears. 'I love you, Kate. I've missed you so much. Please come home.'

His evident pain and sincerity catch at my heart. Even though I realize it's a mistake, my resolve starts to weaken. Love is a habit, not an impulse. And like most habits, it's hard to break, even when you know you've outgrown it.

'Ned, you filed for divorce,' I say gently.

'I was angry. Hurt. I didn't mean it, you know that. I'd never have gone through with it.'

'Divorce isn't something you do by accident, Ned.'

'I know I've screwed up. I don't blame you for leaving. But can you look me in the eye and honestly say you don't still care about me?'

I drop my gaze and stare at our hands, entwined together on the duvet. I'm still wearing my wedding ring. Why could I never bring myself to take it off?

'No,' I say quietly. 'I can't do that.'

'I don't expect things to go back to the way they were overnight,' he says eagerly. 'I know it's going to take some time. But do you really want to throw away everything we had together? Don't we deserve a second chance?'

It was so much easier when he hated me. Suddenly I don't know what I feel about him. Ned's my husband, the father of my children. He's not a bad man, nor even a weak one. Look at how he's held the fort while I've been away: the fridge is full, the laundry basket empty, the house is tidy and even the lawn's been mowed. If he's prepared to overlook the pain and humiliation I've caused him, how can I not forgive him his mistakes?

Keir.

'Do you love me?' Ned presses.

'Yes . . . but—'

255

'That's all that matters,' he exclaims joyfully. 'We can make it work, right?'

You can't love Ned and Keir. Who's it going to be?

I'm in love with Keir. It's not the same.

You're splitting hairs. What's the difference?

Time.

Suddenly Ned pulls me towards him, catching me unawares. I smell the whisky on his breath, and then he's kissing me: hot, hard kisses that arouse me despite myself. As if sensing my surrender, his hand snakes beneath the old T-shirt of Guy's that I threw on after my bath, zoning in on my breast with unerring accuracy. His knee is already pushing mine apart as he presses me against the mattress with increasing urgency.

I push against his chest. 'No, Ned, please.'

He twists my nipple, kissing my neck, my face, my hair. 'It's been so long,' he says thickly.

'Ned, stop!'

Instantly he pulls back. 'Christ. I'm so sorry. I didn't mean—'

I pull down my T-shirt and yank up the duvet like a frightened virgin. 'I can't, Ned. I'm sorry.'

'No, no, it was my fault. I shouldn't have been so insensitive.' He stands up, running his hands through his rumpled hair. 'You've only been back five minutes. And we're both frantic about Guy. I just got carried away, I'm sorry.' He gets up and backs towards the door.

I feel like I'm on a runaway train with no means of stopping. 'Ned, wait –'

'I'll go. It won't happen again. We can sort everything out after we find Guy.'

'We have to talk,' I warn.

'We will, we will. Look, sleep well. I'll see you in the morning.'

He shuts the door behind him with exaggerated care. I should've told him about Keir. It's not fair to get his hopes up. I love him, yes, but not in the way he thinks, the way he wants. It's going to be a thousand times worse now when I tell him I'm leaving again as soon as we find Guy.

I stare up into the darkness, wondering how I have managed to get myself trapped in such short order.

It's a long time before sleep comes.

Ned

I feel like punching the air as I shut Guy's bedroom door behind me, but limit myself to a double thumbs-up and a cheesy grin at my reflection in the hall mirror.

Now I know Kate still loves me, I feel better about everything. Not that I expect things to miraculously resolve themselves overnight. Like she says, we've got a lot to talk about. I need to know she's not going to run off again next time we have a row about whose turn it is to put out the rubbish, for a start. And I'm sure she's got some stuff she wants to get off her chest, too.

But my wife is home. Things are finally are getting back to normal. Well, not normal, obviously; Guy's still missing. But like the cop said, he's probably just done a runner because his head's messed up over that video. It can all be sorted out. We just need to find him before he does anything stupid. Now Kate's back, it's all going to work out fine.

I climb into our empty double bed and bunch a pillow

behind my head. With any luck, I won't have it to myself much longer.

When Kate stormed off to bed earlier, I locked myself in my office and hit the Scotch, planning to drown my bitterness at the bottom of the bottle. And it worked, to begin with. I even had a neat range of perfect put-downs ready – 'Yeah, your bum does look big in that, and frankly, fucking you is like waving a sock in a wind tunnel'. But somewhere between the third and fourth tumblers, I realized I'm tired of hating her. Tired of being angry and bent on revenge. Tired of playing hardball and divorce lawyers and all the rest of the bullshit. I just want things back the way they were. That's all I've wanted since the day she left. Suddenly my pride didn't matter nearly as much as making sure she knew I loved her.

I hadn't planned to jump her; that was the Scotch talking. But I'm glad I did. She can play the reluctant bride all she likes, but that kiss didn't lie. She wanted it as much as I did, even if she won't admit it. We've got a lot to sort out – yes, yes, I get it. But we're going to make it.

I drop off within minutes and sleep like a baby.

The next morning, energized by optimism, I get up early, knock back a couple of Alka-Seltzers and fire up the computer. There's a limited number of places a seventeen-year-old kid with no money, no transport and no credit cards can go. I've no intention of leaving it to the headless chickens down the cop shop to find him. I'm an investigative journalist, for God's sake. This is what I'm good at. Only reason I haven't found Lord Lucan yet is because I'm too busy smoking out Shergar.

A little after seven, I'm hunched over my Mac with my third mug of coffee when Kate comes downstairs.

'You found the suitcases, then,' I say, glancing up.

She looks down at herself as if surprised to find she's dressed. 'Yes. Thanks for getting them down from the loft.'

She's picked a pair of pastel striped trousers she knows I hate, and a high-necked virginal white cotton T-shirt. I hide a smile. She's clearly sending me a keep-out message, but after last night, I guess I can't blame her.

'Any news?' Kate asks anxiously.

'Not yet. Thought it would be useful if we started looking for him ourselves.' I push a printout across the table. 'Those are the places I've ruled out. He's not at Liesl's – she's been in Vietnam for the last three weeks, totally unreachable, of course. We've left messages at her hotel, but God knows if she'll ever get them. Guy obviously wasn't with you, and he's not with any of his school friends, according to all the parents I've spoken to.'

'What about this boy who bullied him? Dessler?'

'Surprisingly, he's out of the picture on this one. Been in hospital since Wednesday with a burst appendix or something. Parents were a bit vague.'

She pulls out a chair opposite me and picks fretfully at the place mat in the centre of the table. 'I still don't see why Guy ran away. I mean, lots of boys get bullied at school, don't they? Isn't it par for the course?'

'This was in another league,' I say quietly. 'Those kids were up to some pretty sick stuff.'

'What do you mean? What sort of stuff?'

'You don't need to know the details. Trust me,' I add, when she starts to protest. 'Those boys hurt Guy, and then posted a video of it online. You don't need to know any more than that. It's going to be hard enough as it is for Guy to look you in the eye when he comes back.'

Kate hesitates, then nods curtly and picks up my print-out. 'I don't see that we're any further on with this,' she says. 'All we know is where he *isn't*.'

'You have to start somewhere,' I say patiently. 'He's not hiding out with friends, which means he's on his own. No money, no car. That limits the number of places he can go.'

'Salisbury's too close,' Kate muses. 'London?'

'Yeah. That'd be my first bet. He's probably got enough for a train fare and to see him through for a week or so. Either London or the coast, I'm thinking. London's more likely – it's where all the runaways go. Still think the streets are paved with gold.'

She sighs. 'It'll be like looking for a needle in a haystack.'

'Mind you,' I add, looking up from my laptop suddenly, 'maybe we *should* think about Brighton.'

'Brighton?'

'Bit of a gay hotspot, I've always heard,' I say, striving to sound offhand. A modern father, at home with his son's alternative lifestyle.

She stares at me. 'Who told you Guy was gay?'

'Agness.' There's a long silence. 'I imagine you're OK with it? After all, it's no reflection on you . . .'

'Well, of course it isn't,' she says crossly. 'Or it wouldn't be, if Guy *was* gay.'

'You don't think he is?'

'I have no idea. More to the point, neither does Guy.' She hesitates. 'I *have* wondered, I must admit, and I'm sure he has, too. He's certainly not as far along the macho curve as most of his class. He may well turn out to be gay, or he could just be more sensitive than most men,' she adds pointedly. 'I don't see that it matters. I'm certainly not going to put a label on it.'

'I wasn't trying to,' I protest. 'It was just something Agness said—'

'Agness is fourteen years old. It's all about pigeonholes at that age. When Guy's ready to tell us how he feels, he will.'

'So London, then,' I say hastily, keen to move into safer waters. 'I've done a couple of stories on runaways in the past, and I still have a few contacts in London at some of the shelters.' I'm typing as I speak. 'There's one charity that operates directly out of King's Cross, picking up kids as they arrive from the boondocks before the bad guys can get to them. I think they cover some of the other mainline stations, like Waterloo, which is where Guy—'

'Bad guys?'

'Guy will be fine,' I say quickly. 'He's seventeen. He knows how to look after himself.'

Kate nods, but I can see in her eyes that she's thinking the same thing as me: *If he knew how to look after himself, he wouldn't have had to run away.*

'Ned,' she says carefully. 'Since you're at your computer, we should probably talk about finances . . .'

'We can get to that later,' I interrupt.

'I should at least put something into the joint account,' she offers. 'I know you had the rainy-day money to keep you going, but I could cover the mortgage payment for this month.'

No need to tell her I lost the rainy-day money on an appropriately named nag called Summer Monsoon before she even left.

'I've paid it,' I say simply.

'Well, it can go towards next month's payment then.'

'I've paid the mortgage,' I repeat. 'All of it. I've paid it off.'

A sweet moment, this: Kate Forrest lost for words.

'*All* of it? That's over two hundred thousand! You can't have done!'

'I had a couple of good wins,' I say drily.

From the expression on her face, it's lucky she's sitting down. 'You won two hundred thousand pounds in a *bet*?'

'Well, not just one bet, obviously,' I say, keen to avoid being dragged into the details. 'I had a couple of . . . tips. From an impeccable source. They came good, so I cleared our mortgage and the credit cards. I thought it best to stop while I was ahead, so there's still Eleanor's mortgage, I'm afraid, but I think we can manage that . . .'

'You promised me you wouldn't gamble again,' she accuses.

Only a woman.

'You weren't here,' I remind her, not unkindly. 'The rainy-day money ran out. I had to pay Agness's school fees before they expelled her, and the mortgage, and all the rest of it. I needed cash. I couldn't earn nearly enough to cover it all, so I did what I know best. But you don't need to worry. That was the last time. I swear on my mother's life.'

I'm not kidding. Morrison played ball once, but I'm not about go to that particular well again. I'll end up with my bloody legs broken. Or worse.

Kate looks as if she's about to say something, then thinks better of it.

'If you want some breakfast, help yourself to what's on the stove,' I say, turning back to my laptop. 'Corned beef hash. Home-made.'

She lifts the lid and peers into the iron skillet. '*You* made this?'

'It tastes better than it looks. Agness is on breakfasts tomorrow, so you might want to fill up now. Her recipe for muesli takes some getting used to.'

'I didn't know you could cook,' she says faintly.

'My repertoire's still a bit basic, but yeah, I can cook.'

'And you have a *rota*?'

'One day in four. You can cover Guy while he's away, if you like.'

'Eleanor's part of it too?' she echoes. 'Things really *have* changed.'

'I told you,' I say, holding her gaze. 'It's all going to be different from now on.'

She blushes, and I know she's thinking about last night.

She pours herself a mug of coffee from the cafetière I made earlier and sits at the table opposite me.

'Look, Ned,' she says nervously. 'I don't want you to get the wrong idea. I was tired last night, and it was all a bit overwhelming, coming back home and seeing you and everything. I shouldn't have let . . . things . . . go as far as they did.'

'I'm your husband,' I point out mildly. 'It *is* allowed.'

'Come on, Ned. Please stop acting like we can just pick up where we left off.'

I shut my laptop.

'Kate. I'm not a fool. Neither one of us wants to pick up where we left off. It wasn't exactly marital Eden, was it? You ended up so damned miserable you ran away. And I'll be honest with you, I wasn't exactly a happy camper most of the time either. You treated me like shit on the sole of your shoe. I'm not saying I didn't deserve it,' I add quickly. 'I was a fucking arsehole. I let you pull the full load and then resented the hell out of you for it. Something had to give. I told you, I don't blame you for leaving.'

She stares into her coffee. 'I shouldn't have just gone. I should have told you how I felt.'

'Yeah. You should have had the balls to stay and talk it out,' I agree. 'Christ knows, you were the only one who had a pair around here.'

'I wouldn't say that. Agness can be pretty determined when she wants to be.'

I crack a smile. 'Chip off the old block.'

'I couldn't talk to you any more, Ned. Not about . . . the baby. Or anything. And it all got on top of me: Eleanor, the way Agness was with me. My job,' she says in a sudden rush. 'I *hate* my job, Ned. I've hated it for years. I hate being the one with all the responsibility. I can't go back to it. I'm sorry, I just can't.'

It feels like having the Pope tell you he's just not that into God.

'I know it'll hit our income, but I'll find something else. Maybe not as well paid,' she adds anxiously, 'but if you've really cleared the mortgage, we won't have to sell the house. The kids can stay here in their own home with you, whatever happens.'

'With *us*,' I correct automatically.

'Either way.' A long pause. 'I was thinking of teaching. Art, probably. I know it sounds silly, but—'

'I think it's a great idea,' I say calmly.

'Really?'

'Why wouldn't I? When we met, that's what you said you wanted to do. Then you got that insane job at Forde's, the money started coming in, then Agness came along, and you stopped mentioning it.'

'I'd forgotten.'

'Do it,' I urge.

She turns her mug round and round in her hands. 'I thought you'd think I was mad. Having a mid-life crisis or something.'

'Kate. I love you. I married you because I wanted to spend the rest of my life with you. I want you to be happy. Why d'you think I've put up with you working all the hours God sends instead of spending it with me and the kids? I'd much rather have had you home at a decent time every night and skipped the summers in Tuscany, but the big career was what you wanted. At least, that's what I thought. But if you want to jack it all in and live on a kibbutz, that's fine by me, as long as I get to come too. I don't give a shit about the money. I never have. *You're* the only thing that's ever mattered to me.'

She swallows hard. 'I wish . . . I wish we could've talked like this before.'

'Me too. But maybe it took some time apart for us both to get a little perspective.'

Awkwardly, I reach across the kitchen table and give her a clumsy hug. Her head falls against my shoulder and I let it lie there, inhaling the coconut smell of her hair. *Oh God, I've missed her.*

We're both startled by the unfamiliar sound of the front door bell.

'Christ! Who the fuck is that at this time in the morning?'

Kate looks fearful. 'It must be the police. Maybe they've found Guy.'

I belt down the hall to the front door, Kate a split-second behind me. I fiddle with the locks and chains on the door for what seems like hours, all fingers and thumbs.

A kid with ginger hair is standing on the doorstep, a huge backpack hanging off one shoulder.

'Hey,' he says, sticking out his hand. 'You must be Kate's ex. I'm Keir.'

Kate

'Her *ex*?' Ned echoes, his face like thunder.

Standing on the doorstep, Keir's dramatic Celtic colouring is even more intense against the soft, washed-out tones of an English summer morning than it was in Rome: his skin whiter, his gold eyes more gleaming, his flaming red hair richer and more vibrant. He looks so vividly *alive*.

I can't believe he's here. I haven't been gone twenty-four hours, and he's come to find me. Until now, I hadn't realized how much I need to see him.

'What are you doing here?' I manage finally.

'Hey. I wasn't going to leave you to deal with this all on your own, was I?'

'She's not on her own,' Ned snaps. 'She's with *me*.'

'How did you know where to find me?' I ask Keir.

'Julia gave me your address. Soon as I picked up your message, I called her. I'd have been here sooner, but the later flights out of Rome were all full.'

Ned takes my upper arm, forcefully breaking my gaze.

'Kate, who the hell *is* this?' I can almost see the steam coming out of his ears.

'Ned, this is Keir Corcoran, a friend of mine. We met in Italy. Keir, my husband, Ned Forrest.' With an effort I recover my equilibrium and gently free my arm from Ned's death-grip. 'You must be exhausted, Keir. Come in. I'll make us all some more coffee.'

Keir throws Ned an amused look as he shifts his backpack to the other shoulder and steps past him into the house. The 'ex' crack wasn't an accident, I realize. He knows we're not divorced. He's just staking out his territory.

Ned follows us silently into the kitchen. With exaggerated courtesy, he takes Keir's backpack and then tosses it into the tangle of Wellingtons and muddy trainers by the back door.

Keir slides his hands into the back pockets of his worn jeans and lounges carelessly against the kitchen counter. He's several inches shorter than Ned and at least fifty pounds lighter, but his youth and energy fill the room. Ned suddenly seems stiff and middle-aged beside him. Not every girl gets to compare her suitors side by side, I think faintly. Ned has more substance, but Keir certainly has more style.

'I take it there's been no news?' Keir says, addressing his question to me.

'No,' Ned says shortly. He pours Keir a mug of lukewarm coffee, and hands it to him without bothering to ask if he likes it black. 'Can I ask how you know my wife?'

Keir smiles easily. 'Like Kate said. We're friends.'

'I'm not really sure why you're here,' Ned says, bristling.

'Look. I don't want to get in the way, Ned. Christ knows, you've got enough on your plate. But I've had some experience with this kind of thing, and another pair of eyes looking for your kid can't do any harm, can it?'

'What sort of experience?' He sounds like a Victorian paterfamilias interviewing a prospective son-in-law.

'I ran away when I was his age,' Keir says. 'After my parents got back from Boston. I lived on the streets in Dublin and then London for seven months. I know what it's like. I know how kids like Guy think, where they go. What can happen to them when things go wrong.'

'You never mentioned that,' I exclaim, shocked.

He shrugs. 'It was a long time ago.'

'Must be all of a couple of years,' Ned says sarcastically.

Ned's not stupid. He'd have to have the sensitivity of a rhino not to pick up on the electricity zinging between Keir and me. He must be wondering what the hell is going on. Which is fair enough, since I'm wondering the same thing. Five minutes ago, I was actually entertaining the thought that Ned and I might still have a future. There's no question I still love my husband. And he's changed in the last three months, that much is startlingly clear. It's not just what he's done – paid off the mortgage (I'm still struggling to get to grips with that), handled my mother, learnt to cook. It's the fact that he's taken responsibility for himself and this family for the first time in our marriage. He's become the husband I always wanted him to be. I just don't know if it's too late.

And then there's Keir.

'Do you mind if I wash up?' Keir asks, putting his coffee down. 'I slept at the airport all night trying to get on the wait-list for a flight, and I could really use a shower.'

'Of course. Let me show you where—'

'I'll show him,' Ned says grimly.

Keir throws me a droll look and follows Ned out of the kitchen.

I finish making a fresh cafetière of coffee and pour myself a third hit, wondering if it's too early to open a bottle of wine. If I wasn't confused before, my head is certainly spinning now. Ned and I have fifteen years of history; we share children and experience and, yes, despite everything, love. When he kisses me, I still feel passion. But just being in the same room as Keir transforms me. I feel young and vital and filled with hope and energy, as if I can take on the world and win. If I go back to Ned, I will have to give this up. And I'm not sure I can bear that.

'So,' Ned says heavily when he returns. 'It wasn't all ruins in Rome, then.'

I blush. 'I had no idea Keir was coming. I didn't even have a chance to speak to him before I left Italy. I'm sure he didn't mean to—'

'Oh, he did,' Ned says. His mouth twists in an acid smile. 'I can't blame him. He's just doing what I should have done three months ago – gone after the woman he wants.'

For a moment I'm too taken aback to speak. He's right, of course. If Ned had come to Rome to claim me as soon as he figured out where I was, we wouldn't be having this conversation.

'You are aware he's half your age, right?' Ned asks conversationally.

'I really don't think this is the—'

'He's got some kind of crush on you? That's it, isn't it? A sugar-mummy thing?'

'Ned . . .'

'I can see it would be flattering.' Ned laughs as if he's suddenly decided the only way to deal with this is to treat it as a huge joke. 'Obviously he hasn't got a cat in hell's chance, but he's got good taste, I'll give him that. Poor bastard.'

I have no idea how to respond. This is hardly the moment to confess the truth of my relationship with Keir, but letting Ned believe it's nothing more than an unrequited crush on Keir's part is basically lying by omission.

Damn the pair of them. The last thing I need right now is some kind of macho showdown between my husband and my lover. I'm suddenly furious with Keir for putting me in this position when he knows I'm worried sick about my son. He hasn't come here out of concern for Guy, but because he doesn't want to lose me. Actually, I'm *not* flattered, as Ned puts it. Keir's selfishness simply reminds me, yet again, of the huge age gap between us. What on earth does he think he's playing at, waltzing into my home, into my *family*, knowing the questions his sudden appearance must raise? Doesn't he think I've got enough to worry about?

'Mum!' Agness cries, as she flies into the kitchen. 'There's this, like, hot guy upstairs! What's he doing here? Have they found Guy yet?'

'He's a friend of mine,' I say tightly, shooting a wary glance at Ned. 'He's come to help us find Guy.'

'Is he staying? Does he have a girlfriend?'

'He's far too old for you,' Ned snaps.

'More my age,' I say, unable to resist it.

Unexpectedly, Ned grins, throwing me off-balance yet again.

The door opens and Eleanor joins us, swathed in a

voluminous paisley quilted dressing gown. To my surprise, she looks almost as lit up as Agness.

'Such a pleasant young man upstairs,' she says skittishly. 'He managed to get the bolt on the bathroom skylight closed. I've been asking Ned to do it for weeks.'

'Oh, he's quite the favourite around here,' Ned says.

'Agness, dear. Pass me a couple of aspirin, would you?' Eleanor says. 'I've got a bit of a headache.'

'Who *is* he?' Agness demands, handing her grandmother the pills.

'I told you. His name's Keir and he's come to help us find Guy.'

'But how did you find him?'

'Agness, stop nagging your mother and get dressed. You can't go wandering around the house in your pyjamas when we've got people here.'

'You let me wander around the beach in a *bikini*,' Agness gripes, but she grabs an apple and heads back towards the stairs.

Eleanor cracks a couple of eggs into a frying pan. 'So how did you and Keir meet?' she asks brightly.

'Jesus, Eleanor,' Ned groans.

'Are those eggs OK?' I ask my mother. 'They smell a little strange.'

She sniffs at the pan. 'They seem fine to me.'

'I'm going to make a few calls,' Ned says, pushing himself to his feet. 'I want to chase down some of my contacts at the shelters. Maybe this Keir of yours will be able to help us later,' he adds stiffly. 'He's not much older than Guy. He's bound to know a few places we don't.'

He takes his laptop into the study. I sit down in his place, feeling slightly queasy as the smell of fried eggs fills the kitchen. I can't stand the thought of Guy sleeping rough under an archway somewhere. Or worse. If anything happens to him . . .

'It's not your fault,' Eleanor says suddenly.

'Of course it is. If I'd been here, Guy could have come to me. He wouldn't have had to run away.'

'Maybe,' Eleanor acknowledges, folding her arms. 'Maybe not. But that's not what I meant, anyway. I don't blame you for leaving. I'm glad you did. If I'd left your father, things would have turned out very differently, for you as well as me. Staying with him was the biggest mistake I ever made. But what's done is done.' She tips the two fried eggs onto a plate, and puts the pan in the sink. 'Katherine, I know things have never been easy between us. I've been harder on you than on your sister, and I've expected more from you. But I've never loved you less. The opposite, in fact.'

'Eleanor . . .'

She pinches the bridge of her nose. 'Let me finish. I'm ashamed to admit it, but I was jealous of you. I was jealous of the freedom and choices you had, which I never did. I was born thirty years too soon. But that's no excuse.' Her lips tighten. 'I stayed with your father because it was easier; in that respect, I'm more like your sister than you. You've got more courage in your little finger than the pair of us put together. It's why I've found it so hard to watch you make the same mistakes I did, history repeating itself.'

I wait for her to continue, aware that this is the most important conversation we will ever have.

She rubs her hands against the quilted skirt of her dressing gown. 'Ned's a good man. He has his faults, but I've seen a different side to him since you left. He may not be perfect, but he's a good husband, and a good father. More than James ever was. But I'm not sure he's ever been the right man for you.'

I swallow hard, willing the nausea away.

'I'm not telling you what to do,' Eleanor says firmly. 'If Ned can make you happy, nothing would give me greater pleasure. But if that new young man is the one' – she sniffs at my look of surprise – 'I may be old, dear, but I'm not a fool. I can see what's in front of my nose. If Keir is the man you should be with, don't give him up. Not for anyone. Certainly not out of a misguided sense of duty and doing the right thing. You have a duty to be happy too.' She sighs, pressing her fingertips to her forehead. 'In the end, Kate, it's all any mother wants for her child.'

It's the first time she's ever called me Kate.

Impetuously, I fling my arms around her waist as she hovers by my chair. After a startled pause, her arms slowly close around my shoulders in the first embrace I can remember her giving me since I was a child. I want to cry, but the emotions are so tightly knotted in my throat that nothing breaks free. In the distance the phone rings, but I ignore it. Agness pounds down the stairs, but it stops after just two rings and I listen to her slow footsteps as she trudges back to her room.

Eleanor gives my back a final awkward pat and straightens up. 'Agness has got a sensible head on her shoulders,' she says, rooting around in the cutlery drawer for a knife and fork. 'She'll be fine.'

'She's another one who seems to have done better without me here,' I say shakily.

'No self-pity, please,' Eleanor says with a touch of her old asperity. 'Agness has had a chance to grow up, that's all, and not before time. I could say the same for Ned, too. You need to let go of the reins a bit more. It does no one any good if you do everything for them; you least of all.'

'I'll remember that,' I smile.

'Are you sure you don't want any—'

'Kate,' Ned says from the doorway.

It's the way he says my name. One word, imbued with fear, shock, grief and a deep, bottomless, terrible need. I know, even before he utters another word.

'They've found a body,' Ned says woodenly. 'Guy's library card was in the pocket of his jacket. The one you bought him in the States. It's not a mistake. He's got the barbed-wire scar on the back of his knee. It's him.'

Guy

I just wanted to *talk* to Dessler. Get him to take the video off YouTube. Ask him to leave me alone. Make it all go away. Shit, I don't know. I didn't really think it through, OK?

Wednesday evenings, he takes fencing lessons. Seriously. Like he's Zorro or something. After Dad blew me off, too busy with his important phone call, I figured I'd got no choice but to go and talk to Dessler myself. That's all. I *swear*.

Funny. Dessler always seemed so much bigger than me, larger than life, like the bogeyman. I didn't realize till it was just the two of us face to face, no musclemen, no teachers, that I've got twenty-five pounds and four inches on him. I could take him in a heartbeat, and as soon as he saw me waiting for him in the car park, I knew he knew it too. Only as soon as I saw the fear in his eyes, I kind of freaked. I was just so fucking steamed that this bastard, this fucking thug who'd made my life shit for the last year, who'd stalked me online and turned the entire school against me and spat

277

in my food and *shoved a fucking toilet brush up my arse*, this rich, arrogant, bullying little shit was nothing but a pathetic coward after all. Without his mates to back him up, he was *nothing*. I'd been acting like he was the Godfather or something, puking my guts up in terror every morning, bunking off school just to avoid him, when the truth was *he* was scared of *me*.

Once I started hitting him, I couldn't stop. I fucking pounded the shit out of him. I broke his nose, and when he fell to the ground, I stamped on his chest and smiled when I heard his ribs crack. I knew I was going too far, I knew I had to stop before I killed him, but I couldn't. It was like this red mist had descended and I had no control any more.

He begged and begged me to stop, but I didn't listen. His face was bloody and wet with snot and tears. He curled in a ball at my feet, and I kicked him in the kidneys, and then the spine. I didn't stop till he went quiet and I realized he wasn't moving.

I just wanted to *talk* to him.

I stare down at his still body and back away in horror. Next minute I'm ralphing till there's nothing left in my stomach and I'm retching up bile. *Jesus Christ, what have I done?*

I glance frantically around the car park. It's deserted – no one has seen or heard a thing. If I go now, there'll be no witnesses. Apart from Dessler.

He still hasn't moved. I don't know if he's alive or dead.

I can't just leave him here. But if I call an ambulance and he doesn't die, he'll tell them who did this. Maybe if I'd just broken his nose or beaten him up, he'd have kept his trap shut so all the shit he did to me didn't come out. But this is too much. Too big.

He moans suddenly and a bubble of blood and mucus comes out of his nose. *He's alive*. Thank Christ.

I want to leave him to die alone in the dark, but I can't. That would make me no better than him. I dig in my pockets looking for my phone and then remember I've left it charging at home. Adrenalin pumps through me as I bend down and search Dessler's jacket. He's breathing – harsh, ragged breaths – but he's still unconscious. I wipe the snot from my own face and flip open his phone, struggling to see the numbers through my tears.

'Ambulance,' I say when the line connects. 'Someone's been mugged.'

I give them the address and then toss the phone in front of Dessler's face. My knuckles are swollen and covered in blood: Dessler's and my own. I must've cut them on his teeth.

I've no money on me. The only thing in the pocket of my jacket is my frigging library card. Without stopping to think, I search Dessler again, empty his wallet – two hundred in cash – and then toss that near his head too. *He owes me*.

I zip up my fleece, shove my bloody hands in the pockets and walk away as fast as I dare, trying not to draw attention to myself. I can be at the station in forty minutes. In London in less than two hours.

In the distance, sirens scream.

I yank my hood over my head and hide my face as I slink out of Waterloo station, trying to avoid the CCTV. Won't take a genius to figure out where I've gone, but no point making it easier than I have to. I reckon I've got at least a couple hours' head start till Dessler comes round and the cops start looking for me. *If* he comes round.

A bloke handing out leaflets comes over as I pause, trying to decide which way to go. 'You OK, kid?'

I dig my hands deeper in my pockets and nod briefly.

'You sure?' He sounds concerned. 'It's pretty late. You need to call someone?'

'I'm fine,' I snap.

I cross the road and start walking blindly in the direction of the London Eye, praying to God he doesn't follow. I've no real idea where I am. I've only been to London a few times, on school trips and that. I'll find a park bench somewhere and grab a couple of hours' sleep till it gets light. After that, I'll figure something out.

First off, I need to put as much distance between myself and the station as I can, in case they're already looking for me. I head east, crossing the river, keeping to the shadows, where possible. I read that Britain's got the most CCTV cameras of any nation on earth. Big Brother is always watching you.

A drunk lurches out of a doorway as I pass, stinking of piss and booze, slurring abuse. I push him off me, wondering what he did to fuck up.

After a while, I lose track of time. Some dude in a flash Porsche slows to a crawl beside me and offers me fifty quid to 'show him the way' to some hotel. I give him the finger and tell him to fuck off. Something in my expression must convince him I'm not to be messed with tonight, because he doesn't hang around to argue.

It starts to rain: a warm, heavy drizzle. My fleece jacket is soon wet through, but I don't care. I keep walking, water dripping from my face and down my neck. I don't care where I'm going, or what happens to me. I should be scared, but I'm not. My life is over. How much worse can it get?

Eventually, when I'm too tired to walk any further, I find a shop doorway and hunch myself into it, hands hooked round my knees, trying to keep out of the rain. But I haven't even had time to get settled before a skinny white guy with dreads to his waist starts yelling at me to get out of his crib.

'Fuckin' asshole!' he yells as I stagger to my feet and back away. He doesn't have a single tooth left in his head.

As it gets later, most of the shop doorways I pass have occupants. I turn off the main street, hoping to find some-where off the beaten track that isn't already taken. Ten minutes later, I spot a yellow skip half covered by a tarp outside one of those fancy houses with white columns and black railings. I peer into it: it's still pretty much empty. I clamber over the side, squirming my way through a bunch of broken kitchen cupboards to the back, where it's still dry. Someone's left an old painter's cloth at the bottom. I ball myself in the cloth and close my eyes. Within seconds, I'm asleep.

The sound of workmen yelling and whistling wakes me. I open my eyes and sit up, stiff and sore. Bright sunshine streams in at the far end of the skip. I struggle free of the painter's cloth and quietly clamber over a couple of cup-boards, keeping out of sight beneath the tarp. After a bit, the voices move away: morning tea-break, at a guess.

I wait a few more moments and then stick my head over the side of the skip. Some old lady walking her dog looks freaked, but there's no one else around, so I swing myself out of the skip and brush myself down. My clothes are still damp from last night's rain and I'm covered in builder's dust, but the worst part is my hands. In the cold light of day, they're black and blue with bruises, the knuckles scabbed and raw.

I'm starving. I spot a greasy spoon a bit further down the street.

'I'd like to see the other guy,' the man behind the counter jokes when I hand over a fiver for a cup of tea and a bacon sarnie.

I yank the sleeves of my fleece down over my knuckles.

'You all right, son?' the bloke asks.

Last thing I need is him calling the cops on me. I pull off a smile. 'Got bladdered last night. Mate's birthday.'

'Been there,' he laughs. 'Go on, son. Sit down. I'll bring you something to calm your stomach.'

I slide into a booth near the door, ready to bolt if I have to. The café fills with blokes coming in for breakfast, and I relax, blending into the crowd. After a bit, the guy behind the counter slaps a thick plate of fried eggs and sausages and bacon and crusty white bread in front of me.

'Slap your gums round that,' he grins.

I tear into the food. I haven't eaten in twenty-four hours, and I'm still hungry when I finish.

I haven't figured out what to do by the time I leave the café. Last night I had some vague plan to go and find Kate, but I haven't got my passport or enough money for the Eurostar. I spend the day walking round London, half out of it, and end up somewhere in the West End. When it gets dark again, I find a doorway early and growl menacingly whenever anyone comes near me. It's not as comfortable as the skip, though, and there are a lot more freaks around here. Some bloke shoots up right in front of me, jabbing a filthy needle into his arm. Two days ago I'd have been frightened out of my skull, but now I don't give a shit.

At dawn, I start walking again. I end up by the river and follow it, since I haven't got a better idea. All those fancy office blocks and flash apartments with their million-quid views. I bet they haven't got a clue what it's really like down here.

Sometime late in the afternoon, I find a bench overlooking the river and curl up on it, cold and hungry but too fried to do anything about it. I'm starting to get why people on the street drink and do drugs. Anything so you don't have to *be*.

I'm woken by a bloke shaking my shoulder. I'm about to swing a punch when I spot the dog-collar.

'It's OK,' he says calmly. 'You don't have to run. I just want to help.'

He sits down next to me on the bench. It's already dark again. How many nights have I been out here? I'm losing track.

'I'm Father Bernard,' he says, holding out his hand. He drops it when I don't take it, but his smile doesn't falter. 'You look like you could use a friend.'

I shrug.

'I run a shelter not far from here. No names, no pack-drill. You can have something hot to eat and a bed for the night. How does that sound?'

I look up warily. 'What about the cops?'

'What brought you to this place in your life is nothing to do with me. As long as you don't cause any trouble while you're under my roof, we'll get along fine.'

'Where's this shelter, then?'

'Not far. Just over the river, in Putney.'

I shrug again and he takes it for a yes.

'Grand.' He struggles to his feet. 'I'm afraid I'm not as young as I was. I've a car parked just down the street. Would that be all right with you, Ben?'

'My name's not Ben.'

He smiles again. 'I know that. But I've got to call you something, haven't I? I'm guessing you'll not be wanting to give me your real name. And I've always liked Ben.'

He seems like he's on the level, but even if he drives me straight to the nearest cop-shop, I no longer care, so I follow him to his car.

'Seat belt,' he says as I get in.

That's what Kate always used to say. Seems like a hundred years ago.

The priest or vicar or whatever he is pulls the car out into the road and turns on the radio. I tilt my head back against the headrest and close my eyes. It's the first time I've felt warm and dry and safe in days. He's got the car heater on and I half expect my damp fleece to start steaming. The thought of drying out is such a relief.

I must have dozed off, because at first I barely notice it. A warmth on my thigh. Like water, lapping against my groin, a little higher each time. I drift into consciousness, suddenly aware of the pressure of my stiffening cock against my jeans and his hand rubbing against me.

In an instant, I snap wide awake and slap his hand away. *What the fuck d'you think you're doing?*

'Ben, now – I think maybe there's been a misunderstanding . . .'

'Stop the fucking car!'

'We're on a bridge—'

'I said, *stop the fucking car*!'

He pulls into the kerb. I'm already unbuckling my seat belt and scrabbling for the door handle. The dude grabs hold of my sleeve and for a moment we grapple, then I burst out of the car and start running.

He crawls along beside me, leaning out of his window. 'Ben, now, we can talk about this. Sure and get back in the car.'

'Get the fuck away from me!'

He stops and opens the door. I look around wildly, but there's no one around. Suddenly, I'm too tired to run. I swing one leg over the side of the bridge. There's no walkway or barrier; it's easy to do.

'Ben . . .'

'My name's not Ben!'

I can't see the water in the inky blackness below me. For a second, I hesitate. *I'm so sorry, Agness.*

I don't jump.

I just let go.

Kate

I sit on the very edge of Guy's bed, both hands clapped over my mouth, trying not to giggle. It's the shock, of course. The same thing happened when my father died.

Death is always a shock, even when it's expected. Far more so when it strikes out of a clear, cloudless sky. It's a cliché, of course, but it's the *finality* that hits home. The conversations you didn't have, the questions you didn't ask; all the times you could have, should have, said *I love you*.

I want to cry. It would be so much easier if I could just cry.

I turn as the bedroom door opens. Ned hovers awkwardly on the threshold, his face white and drawn. 'The undertaker's downstairs. Would you like me to . . .'

I shake my head. 'I'll come down.'

'You don't have to,' he says. 'I can deal with this.'

'We'll do it together,' I say.

He nods sadly and shuts the door softly behind him. He's been wonderful during the past three days; so steadfast and constant. I don't know how I'd have got through this without him.

I lever myself up from the bed, feeling about a hundred and two. Guy has no mirror in his bedroom, so I peer at my reflection in the blank computer screen on his desk. Eleanor's face looks back at me. Funny how I never saw the resemblance before.

I have a sudden memory of watching through the crack of her bedroom door as my mother put on her make-up. I couldn't have been more than seven or eight. I wasn't supposed to see her while she was dressing, but thinking about it now, I'm sure she knew I was there. For a moment, it was like the door had been opened to a hidden world full of feminine secrets. I watched in fascination as she patted foundation around her eyes with the tips of her elegant fingers and stretched her lips wide to apply her lipstick. She sprayed her scent into the air and then walked through it, so the effect would be subtle. She was like a celestial being, a goddess to me. *She must know everything*, I remember thinking. She was younger than I am now.

I pull out my hairband, scrape my fingers through my hair, then refasten the bobble tighter than before.

Three months ago, I ran away from my family because they were more than I could cope with. It serves me right if I lose them now.

The undertaker nods respectfully as I come into the sitting room. He looks too ordinary to be an undertaker, despite the black suit and grave expression. I don't know what I was expecting; a cadaverous Dickensian mourner in a top hat, perhaps.

He extends a surprisingly warm hand. 'Mrs Forrest, I'm so sorry for your loss.'

'Thank you,' I say.

Ned and I sit awkwardly together on the sofa, careful not to touch. The undertaker settles himself in an armchair opposite us and discreetly slides a brochure across the coffee table. 'I'll leave this with you so you can make your selection in your own time,' he says.

'Our selection?'

'Coffins,' Ned says.

'Oh. Yes. Of course.'

I pick up the brochure. Eleanor dealt with all of this when my father died. By the time I heard the news and came home, it had all been decided. Mahogany and solid silver handles. The most expensive in the range: *It's what he would have wanted*.

Ned has found a green company proud of their sustainable credentials. The coffins all look so pretty, like over-large picnic baskets. Willow, bamboo, banana leaf, water hyacinth, cane, loom, sea grass, all interwoven with fresh flowers and garlands. Very Celtic, I think, reminded of Keir. We'll need a druid, not a priest. On the next few pages, cardboard and recycled paper board, papier mâché, felt shrouds, Egyptian gold-leaf pods. The few wooden coffins in the back of the brochure have Forest Stewardship Council certification.

'Guy would approve of this,' I say brightly. 'He's very concerned about the environment. He spent last summer working on a school conservation project, did my husband tell you that? He had us recycling long before the council introduced all those coloured boxes—'

'Kate,' Ned says softly.

My eyes are dry and wide. 'I wish he was here,' I say.

At Ned's suggestion, Keir came with us to the police mortuary in South London three days ago. 'He flew all this way to help you,' Ned said wearily. 'Maybe this is how he needs to do it.'

We tried yet again to reach Liesl, but the hotel in Vietnam said she'd gone 'up jungle' and wouldn't be back for ten days. I envied her her blissful ignorance.

Agness we left with Eleanor. 'We're following up a lead,' Ned told them, not wanting to have to break the news just yet.

An unmarked police car collected us from the house. Keir elected to sit up front with the police driver, while Ned and I sat in the back, an ocean of leather between us, and stared out of opposite windows. None of us attempted false reassurances because we all knew they were pointless. Guy hadn't dropped his library card or had his fleece stolen. Another little boy hadn't cycled into a barbed-wire fence and scarred the back of his knee. It wasn't a mistake.

The mortuary was an anonymous-looking grey council building; it could just as well have been a school or the local dole office. I walked into it flanked on one side by my lover and on the other by my husband, and the whole situation was so alien and surreal it didn't seem strange at all.

Inside, it wasn't slick and grittily glamorous, the way it is on television. The hallway was being painted; we had to turn sideways to get past stepladders and drop-cloths. Two decorators bobbed their ears in time to whatever music filled their ears from the ubiquitous white earbuds. A couple of secretaries gossiped in the doorway of an office; I heard snatches of chat about summer holidays and drinks on Friday night as we passed. All in a day's work.

Our police driver led us through a maze of corridors which grew progressively more institutional and grey. Twice he had to stop and ask for directions: 'I don't do this very often,' he offered in apology.

'Nor do we,' Ned said.

Finally, the corridor dead-ended in a high counter. No one stood in attendance, though in the far corner of the space behind it, a secretary was finishing up her lunch as we arrived, something with mayo and avocado to judge from the smears on the greaseproof paper in front of her. Pret A Manger, at a guess. She smiled politely but didn't get up.

On the top of the counter was an old-fashioned bell. The police driver hit it hesitantly, then a second time with more confidence. 'We made good time up here,' he said conversationally while we waited. 'The A3 can be a bastard sometimes.'

'It's a Saturday,' Ned offered.

'Good point.'

Keir squeezed my shoulder. I closed my eyes and leant against him. *Sandalwood.* From the guest bathroom. Agness bought it for me last year for my birthday.

If Ned noticed, he said nothing.

Finally, a short man with a thick grey Hitler moustache appeared. He handed our escort a clipboard to which a ballpoint pen was attached with a piece of yellow twine. The police driver scribbled a few words in the required spaces and returned it.

'If you'd like to follow me,' the moustache said.

I groped for Keir's hand. Together with Ned and our

driver, we followed the moustache down yet another series of corridors and into a small, empty room. Grey floors, grey walls. There was a second door on the far side of the room; on the wall to our left was a large window curtained from the other side.

The second door opened and the moustache conferred with an unseen colleague for a few moments, then turned and handed Ned a plastic bag. 'Is this your son's jacket?'

'Can I open the bag?'

'Of course.'

Ned hesitated and then pulled the jacket out of the bag. The Duke Blue Devils fleece I bought him last year on a trip to the States. 'Yes,' he said.

'I'm so sorry,' the police driver said. He looked like he was about to cry.

'You don't have to do this,' Ned said to me. His eyes were sunk in his skull, dark pools of grief and misery. 'They don't need us both.'

'I'm his mother,' I whispered.

He nodded briefly.

I moved forward, gripping the steel window frame, literally bracing myself. The room seemed to swim – the floor was rocking as if I was on board a ship. I couldn't suck enough air into my lungs. My palms started to sweat, my fingers and feet started tingling and turning numb. I felt dizzy and sick, and my mouth went as dry as cotton wool. I was terrified I'd start to laugh again, and that this time I wouldn't be able to stop.

'You can do this,' Keir said softly.

'Are you ready?' the moustache asked.

'Just do it,' Ned said thickly.

The moustache rapped on the window. On the other

side, the curtain drew back. I pressed my forehead to the cool glass, staring at the body on the table, and started to cry. *Such a waste. Such a terrible, terrible waste.*

Keir put his arm round my waist, but it was to Guy's father I turned, burying my head in his shoulder as the sobs wracked my body. Huge, ugly, hiccoughing sobs. All the pain of the last year spilled out of me: the loss of my baby, the rift with Ned, the terrible guilt I've felt at leaving the children, the end of my marriage, and now this nightmare with Guy . . .

Ned held my head against his chest. The three of us stood there for a long moment, linked in a chain of escaping grief.

Finally Ned turned to the moustached officer. 'It's not him,' he said. 'I don't know who that poor kid is, but it's not our son.'

The undertaker gets to his feet and extends his hand again. 'We've liaised with the church you requested, and they're able to do the funeral next Tuesday, a week from today. I gather you already have a plot reserved in their cemetery.'

'Yes. Thank you,' Ned says.

'But what about Guy?' I ask anxiously. 'We can't bury his grandmother without him . . .'

'Keir will find him,' Ned says firmly. 'He promised, didn't he? He'll bring him back long before next Tuesday.'

I have an idea, Keir had said as we left the mortuary. *Give me forty-eight hours. I think I know where he might have gone.*

I watched him hail a taxi, wondering dispassionately if I'd ever see him again. I don't really expect him to find Guy. In a city of ten million people, it'll be a miracle.

'It's been three days already,' I say now, but I allow myself to be convinced, because what's the alternative?

'Your mother will be in our chapel of rest until the funeral,' the undertaker tells me kindly. 'You can come to visit her at any time.'

'Eleanor will want flowers,' I say. 'She'd want everyone to know she was missed. Can you put that in the funeral notice?'

'Flowers,' the undertaker says, making a note to himself.

While Ned sees him out, I pick up the brochure again. Eleanor was always very insistent about being buried, not cremated. The willow looks pretty, I think absently. I suspect Eleanor would prefer it to the heavy formality of traditional oak, even if the latter does carry the Forest Stewardship Council stamp of approval. But what do I really know about what she would have wanted? Death isn't something Eleanor and I ever discussed.

Ned and I came home on Saturday filled with a guilty mix of elation at our reprieve, and sadness for the unknown boy who had somehow ended up with Guy's jacket, and whose corpse remained unclaimed, to find Agness sitting at the foot of the stairs, sobbing hysterically. She'd discovered Eleanor slumped over the kitchen table, a paring knife and half-peeled apple still in her hands. Unforgivably, neither Ned nor I had answered our mobiles, having forgotten to turn them back on after we'd left the morgue. Paramedics had taken my mother to hospital, but she'd been dead before Agness had even found her. A massive aneurysm, according to the doctor who signed her death certificate. Very possibly caused by the fall she took down the stairs the day before I left for Rome.

'He seemed like a nice man,' Ned says on his return. 'The undertaker.'

'Yes,' I say.

Ned sits down on the sofa beside me, twisting his body so that we're face to face. 'Kate, I know this is the worst possible time. You've just lost your mother, and we're both frantic about Guy. But this can't wait. We have to talk.'

I nod, not really listening.

'I've done my best to understand. I've tried to give you space. And Keir seems—'

'Like a nice man?'

'Look.' He rubs his hands on the knees of his trousers. 'This isn't a conversation I want to be having right now. It's not a conversation I ever thought I'd have to have, to be honest.'

'After the funeral. Let's talk then . . .'

'If this could wait, trust me, I would.' He sighs heavily and reaches into his pocket. He pulls out a flat white plastic stick and pushes it across the coffee table towards me.

'You're pregnant,' he says.

Ned

Kate stares at the white stick on the table between us. 'Where did you find that?' she asks faintly.

'Don't worry. I wasn't going through your stuff. Bag split when I was taking out the rubbish this morning.' A nasty thought suddenly strikes me. 'Christ, it *is* yours, isn't it? Dear God, if Agness is—'

'It's mine,' Kate says.

Thank God for that, at least.

We stare at each other. Kate is the colour of cheese, except for her cheeks, which have two bright pink Aunt Sally spots of colour on them.

'Positive, isn't it?' I ask, just to be sure. 'Three white lines?'

'Three white lines?'

I point.

'Two *pink* lines. Only a man,' Kate sighs.

'How long have you known?' I ask.

'I just did the test this morning. It's probably still wet.'

'So, how far along . . .'

'It's Keir's,' she says, killing my last, desperate hope.

I can't help it: despite my resolution to be mature and adult about this, I just want to find the long-haired bastard and punch his fucking lights out. Jesus Christ! Some bloody overgrown schoolboy *screwing my wife*! Getting her *pregnant*! What am I supposed to do with that?

'This changes everything, doesn't it?' she says quietly. 'Whatever you said before.'

I want to tell her no. I want to say I still love her, no matter what she's done; that I'll forgive her anything, if only she'll come back. Three months ago – Christ, three *days* ago – I'd have thought an affair was crossing the Rubicon, no going back; but I realize now it's not true. I've already forgiven her for sleeping with Keir. If that's all it was, I'd take her back in an instant. I love her *that* much.

But she's having his baby. Maybe, in the end, I'd forgive her even that; but would I ever forgive the child? How could I love a child on those terms? How could I be a decent father to it? It wouldn't be fair. Every child deserves to grow up loved.

She's right. This changes everything.

'I'm so sorry,' Kate says, her voice shaking. 'I never meant this to happen. I had no idea it *could*. After – after we lost . . . our baby . . . the doctor said I'd never get pregnant again; my eggs were just too old.' Suddenly the words are tumbling over each other in her haste to explain. 'I've only had one period since I got to Rome, just after I arrived. I thought it must be the menopause. It never occurred to me this might happen. I can't believe I was so stupid. I would never have put you through this – put *any* of us through this.'

'Does he know?'

'No. I told you, I only found out this morning. I wouldn't even have bothered with a test at all, but the other day, when Eleanor was frying eggs, I felt so sick . . .'

'You were the same with Agness,' I say. 'One whiff.'

'I don't know what to do,' she says helplessly.

Not my problem, I think bitterly; but somehow I can't bring myself to say it. I've never known Kate like this: vulnerable, scared. She's never needed me in the whole of our marriage. But she's just lost her mother, she's scared out of her wits about our son, and now she's got herself knocked up by a teenage holiday fling. How can I kick her when she's down?

I force myself to be a friend. 'Have you thought about . . .'

'No!' she says sharply. 'I'm not getting rid of it!'

'So,' I say heavily. I spread my hands. 'This thing with Keir. How serious is it?'

I think I'm still hoping she'll tell me it was a one-off; a drunken night of madness at a weak moment, even though I've seen the way they are together, the air practically humming between them. Even though the kid got on a plane and chased her halfway across Europe rather than spend a day without her. He's clearly got it bad. What I don't know is how *she* feels about *him*.

She looks at me steadily. 'Serious,' she says.

'Do you love him?'

Her gaze drops to her lap. She twists her wedding ring round her finger, and the room grows so quiet I can hear the thrum of the cat purring on the piano stool. I feel like I'm standing on the edge of a cliff. *Say no*, I plead in my head. *Say no say no say no*.

'Yes,' she whispers.

My stomach swoops. Jesus. *Jesus*. It's really over.

'The problem is,' Kate adds wearily, 'I love you too.'

'You can't,' I say. 'You can't have it both ways.'

'I love Agness and Guy,' she protests.

'It's not the same. And even if it was,' I say angrily, 'you can't *have* both of us. You have to choose.'

'I don't think I have a choice any more,' she says.

'You're having his baby.'

'Yes,' she says.

'Then no. I don't think you do.'

She buries her face in her hands. Suddenly she looks no older than Agness. I want to put my arms round her to make it all better, but I no longer have the right. She's been my wife for a decade and a half, but she's suddenly off-limits. I don't know how to be around her.

I jerk at the sound of banging at the back door. Agness – back from seeing that Goth boyfriend of hers. I must've locked the door by mistake.

I get up and go into the kitchen. It's not Agness knocking on the glass.

'Christ Almighty,' I gasp.

Once all the hugging and kissing has died down a bit, the four of us settle awkwardly around the kitchen table with our mugs of hot sweet tea, the English panacea for all ills. Kate can't stop touching Guy, as if she's unable to quite believe he's real.

'You're sure I can't get you something to eat?' she says for the nineteenth time.

'Kate, I told you,' Guy mumbles, gently shrugging her off and tugging Keir's borrowed army jacket down over his scabbed hands. 'Keir hasn't stopped feeding me since we met.'

My son's a mess. His clothes are filthy, he's missing one trainer, and he's dropped ten pounds he couldn't spare from his already skinny frame. But he seems more comfortable in his own skin than I've seen him in years. As if the worst has already happened and nothing else can touch him now.

'I can't believe you're here,' Kate says wonderingly. 'I can't believe he found you.'

She looks like a different woman from the one sobbing on the sofa just thirty minutes ago. Ten years younger. Beyond happy. Radiant is the only way to describe her now. She's staring across the table at the ginger bastard like he's some sort of fucking *god*, and I can't say a word. I can't begrudge him his moment of glory: he found my son. He found my son, a kid he'd never even met, when his own father couldn't. I'm the bloody journalist . . . I should've thought to check Guy's history on his laptop myself. But it was Keir who saw he'd been on the Eurostar website dozens of times in the past few weeks and guessed he'd try to get to Kate. And Keir who staked out St Pancras for three days and three nights, catnapping on the concourse for a few minutes at a time so he didn't miss him.

So yes, I'm grateful to my wife's lover for that. But I'm not a fucking saint. I'd be lying if I said it didn't give me a pathetic glow of satisfaction that his heroic vigil has left him looking like a fucking hobo. Greasy hair, moth-eaten red and grey stubble (kid can't even grow a proper beard, and he's already going grey), and black bags under his eyes you could pack a tent in. He smells none too sweet when you stand downwind either. Seventy-two hours without soap, water or sleep doesn't do a lot for a bloke's sex appeal.

But he found my kid. So I get to my feet and hold out my hand. 'Bloody amazing job, mate,' I say firmly. 'Can't thank you enough.'

He hesitates briefly, then stands up and shakes my hand across the table. 'No worries. Glad to help.'

Kate looks at the two of us, a strange expression on her face. Almost as if she feels . . . left out.

'Keir told me you saw the video,' Guy says suddenly.

Keir and I glance warily at each other and sit back down.

'It's OK,' Guy says. 'I'm OK about it now. He paid for it, didn't he?'

'Who paid for what?' I ask, confused.

'Dessler. The one behind the video. I beat him up. I might even have killed him,' he adds cheerfully. 'The police are looking for me. It's OK, I don't mind. We're even now. I don't mind if I have to go to prison.'

'What the hell are you talking about?' I demand incredulously. 'According to Dessler's parents, he's in hospital with a burst appendix.'

Guy looks startled. 'Who told you that?'

'I spoke to them myself!'

'The kid's kept his mouth shut,' Keir says shrewdly. 'He's not going to shop you, Guy, or it'll all come out. He'll be in a great deal more shit than *you*, dude, if they know he's the happy-slapper behind that video.'

'But . . . but I broke his ribs! I nearly *killed* him!'

I glance at Kate. 'His parents must know more than they're letting on, or they wouldn't be covering for him with the appendix bullshit. I thought at the time they sounded odd when they told me about it.'

'John Dessler's an MP,' Kate says. 'I met him at a school fundraiser once. He's probably terrified this'll end up in the papers.'

Guy looks like someone has just given him back his life. 'They're not going to lock me up?'

'No one's locking you up,' Kate says firmly. She pushes his mug of tea across the table towards him. 'Why don't you drink your tea and tell us exactly what happened. Slowly, from the beginning.'

Her expression doesn't waver as our son describes his attack on Dessler, the nights sleeping rough, the days wandering around London like a sleepwalker. Only when he details his encounter with the priest – if the sick bastard even *was* a priest – and his subsequent jump off the bridge does she look stricken, and it's all I can do not to leap up and fling my arms round her and tell her it's all going to be OK.

Then, unexpectedly, Guy laughs. 'Only landed in the mud, didn't I?' he grins, looking for the first time like the teenager he is. 'Tide was out. Didn't even get wet. I felt like such a fucking prick – sorry, Kate. It's just, there I was, jumping off the bridge like a right bloody diva, and then I just landed up to my arse in slime. I must've looked a right tosser. Lost one of my new Nikes, too.'

'Have you any idea how lucky you were?' Kate demands rhetorically.

'The mud kind of stank, but at least it was soft. I cleaned up a bit in a McDonald's, and then just walked around till I dried off. That's when I figured I had to come and find you,' he adds, turning to Kate. 'I sort of thought, if I could just make it to Rome, I'd find you somehow. It took me a couple of days to scrounge enough money for the ticket, but I managed it in the end. There's still a lot of decent people out there,' he adds thoughtfully. 'One lady gave me five pounds, told me to go home and find my mum. Don't think she knew how far I had to go.'

Kate looks sick.

'Don't feel bad,' Guy says quickly. 'I'd probably have run off anyway, even if you hadn't left.'

'I want to kill that priest,' I hiss. 'Would you know him again if you saw him?'

Guy shrugs. 'Maybe. I'd like my fleece back. I left it in his car when I jumped out.'

I don't tell him that somehow his jacket ended up on the back of another kid who wasn't so lucky. The post-mortem said the boy was strangled. For all we know, it could've been the priest. We'll have to tell the cops, but not now. It can wait an hour or two.

'When I saw Keir at the station, I thought he was just another sicko,' Guy admits, flushing. 'He came up to me when I was queuing for my ticket. Said my mum and dad were looking for me. I thought it was just another line.'

Keir rubs his chin ruefully. 'You've got a hell of a right hook there, dude.'

'Sorry about that,' Guy mumbles.

'My own fault. Should've shown you Kate's photo right off the bat. You'd have known I was kosher then.'

I do my best to crush the jealous spike of anger at the thought of this kid with my wife's photo in his wallet.

'Dad, look. D'you mind if I go up and chill out for a bit?' Guy says with a heavy yawn. 'I'm kind of shattered. I promise I'll talk to the cops or whatever you want later, but I could so use a bed right now.'

Kate leaps up. 'Why don't you let me run you a hot bath.'

'If it's OK with you, I think I'll just crash. Later?'

'Yes, of course.' She hesitates. 'Some of my things are in your room. Just put them outside the door.'

He nods, too tired to connect the dots and ask why.

'D'you mind if I take you up on that bath before I go?' Keir says, pushing back his chair. 'If I try checking in to a hotel looking like this, they won't let me in the door.'

'You know where it is,' I say drily.

'Have you told Agness that Guy's safe?' Kate says as we're finally left alone.

'I texted her. She's on her way home. I left a message for Liesl too, telling her not to worry. Not that she has been, of course. She's missed all the excitement.'

'I suppose I'd better tell Guy about Eleanor . . .'

I put out a hand to detain her. 'Not just yet.'

We sit quietly across from one another at the kitchen table, drained by the drama. I know this is probably the last time I'll have the chance to be alone like this with my wife. She's got a new life now, and it doesn't include me.

I'm not angry; not any more. A part of me actually admires her for having the balls to break free. Our marriage had been in a persistent vegetative state for years, but I'd never have had the guts to pull the plug. Most people don't. We trudge along in the same old rut, making do, getting on with things, keeping our heads down and telling ourselves it could be worse. Don't upset the apple cart. A bird in the hand. The grass is greener. It all adds up to a life half bloody lived. But we only get one shot at this. How can I blame Kate for wanting to make the most of her life? Long before she left me, I'd stopped even noticing her. We weren't *living*, we were sleepwalking towards our graves. I can't remember the last time I told her I loved her or wondered what she was thinking. She was right to go. She deserves better.

'I love you,' I tell her suddenly.

'Oh, Ned—'

'No, wait. Wait. I'm saying it wrong.' I pause, searching for the right words, wanting to get this absolutely right. 'What I mean is that I love you, and I understand why you've got to go. You belong with Keir. He'll make you happy. I was wrong, the way I treated you. I forced you to be someone you didn't want to be. I made you take on all the responsibility and deal with all the bullshit, just so I could keep being young and carefree. I don't want you to feel sad or guilty about leaving. I just hope that, one day, you'll feel that what we had, our marriage, the fifteen years we spent together, *was* worth it. Not just because of Guy and Agness, but because the good outweighed the bad. That's all I wanted to say.'

I stand up. 'I'll come to Eleanor's funeral, of course. And we need to sort things out: the house, and everything. But I think I'll go to my study for a while now. I'd rather not actually see you leave. If that's OK.'

'Thank you,' she says simply.

I nod. I know I'm doing the right thing.

So why does it hurt so *fucking* much?

Kate

On the morning of my mother's funeral, I wake from a fitful, anxious sleep just as dawn is breaking. Climbing out of bed quietly so as not to disturb Keir, I tiptoe into the cramped hotel bathroom and close the door. Then I curl up on the cold tiled floor between the bath and the lavatory like an infant and give myself over to grief.

I don't normally cry, I'm not a crier; I've always prided myself on my self-control. But I'm suddenly overwhelmed by huge, wracking sobs such as I haven't experienced since I was a child. It's as if years and years of cumulative loss have caught up with me. All the pressure and tension and strain and responsibility, coming out now in a great tidal wave of tears. I yield to it, surrender completely. Even when the crying stops I'm not sure I'll ever feel free of it.

The door opens. Keir stands there in his T-shirt and boxers, rumpled and beautiful. He crouches down beside me and tries to put his arms round me, but I push him away.

'Oh God,' I gasp, 'Oh God, I'm so sorry, I just don't want you to see me like this—'

'Don't be sorry,' Keir says firmly. 'It's good for you to cry.'

'I don't want to cry! I want . . . I want . . .'

'I know,' he says.

I can't let myself be soothed. I pull my knees into my chest and wrap my arms around them, physically blocking myself off. 'It's so unfair!' I cry pitifully, my voice echoing around the tiled bathroom walls. 'Why did she have to die? Why now?'

'Your parents always live too long or die too soon,' Keir says painfully.

'We never got a chance to talk!' I shout furiously at him. 'I left it too late!'

'What would you have said?'

'I'd have told her I loved her, for a start!'

'She knew that.'

'I'd have said I was sorry for not spending enough time with her—'

'She knew that too.'

'I'd have asked why she was always so hard on me,' I choke through my sobs. 'I'd have asked why she couldn't just *love* me. Why she never took my side. What I did that was always so *wrong*.'

'You know the answers to that already. As much as she knew herself, anyway.'

I've been harder on you than on your sister, and I've expected more from you. But I've never loved you less. The opposite, in fact.

I was jealous of you. I was jealous of the freedom and choices you had.

You have a duty to be happy, too. In the end, Kate, it's all any mother wants for her child.

I hiccough for a long time as the storm passes, wiping my snotty face with the hem of my T-shirt. 'She called me Kate,' I say finally when I can talk again. 'The last time I spoke to her. It was the first time she ever called me that.'

'There's never a good time for someone we love to die,' Keir says softly. 'We always want more time. Five more minutes. One more conversation. A single kiss. You came back in time, Kate. You told each other all that needed to be said. Maybe that's as good as it was ever going to get.'

'She told me, if you were the man I should be with, I wasn't to give you up.'

'In that case, I'm sorry I didn't get to know her better.'

'Are you the man I should be with?' I ask.

'Yes,' he says firmly.

So different from Ned, who didn't try to fight for me until it was too late.

Tell him. Tell him tell him tell him.

What if he walks away? What if I lose him? Or worse: what if he stays with me just because of the baby?

He won't leave you. He loves you. Tell him.

'Do you love me?' Keir asks, uncannily echoing my thoughts.

I don't need to think about it. 'Yes.'

'Do you want to be with me?'

'Yes, but . . .'

'Then whatever you're about to say can wait.' He reaches out his hand, and, after a brief hesitation I take it, scrambling awkwardly to my feet. 'Come back to bed. We don't need to be up for another couple of hours.'

'Actually, I think I'll take a shower. I've got a headache and I can't sleep anyway.'

'Would you like me to . . .'

'I'll be fine on my own.'

Keir shrugs. 'OK,' he says.

'It's my mother's funeral today,' I add defensively. 'I just need to be on my own for a while.'

He smiles. 'I said, it's OK.'

I lock the door behind him and step into the tiny cubicle, standing submissively under the hot, beating water, my head throbbing with fear and anxiety. I have to tell Keir about the baby today. After the funeral. I can't put it off any longer. Ned, too. I have to explain things properly to my husband. He may not want to be part of this baby's life, but we have two other children together. For their sake, if not ours, I need to be straight with him. And the two of us need to sit down together with Agness and Guy and tell them what's happening. No more running away for either of us.

When the water starts to run cold, I get out and towel myself dry, then return to the bedroom and put on the new sleeveless black shift I've had to buy for the funeral: already none of my other suitable black dresses fit. I slip on a pair of simple court shoes and pick up the hat I wore to my father's funeral. Women can be divided into two groups, I think as I put it on: those who suit hats, and those who don't. I'm firmly in the latter camp, but Eleanor would never forgive me if I didn't wear one to her funeral.

Behind me, Keir is carelessly flinging clothes and shoes and books into his backpack. After the funeral, we'll leave the hotel where we've been staying for the past week and go to London, where Keir has a small flat in Islington. His six-month sabbatical is over; when the new academic year starts in a few weeks, he'll go back to his teaching job at the UCL Institute of Archaeology. Since I'm now unemployed, we'll have to survive on his pitifully small salary; and in a few months, there'll be three of us to support.

I've no idea how we're going to manage once we've exhausted my redundancy pay-off (a conscience-soothing gesture from Paul Forde, who waited until the day my leave ended and then summarily fired me, after fifteen years, by *email*). Maybe at some point I can take an art-history teaching course at Goldsmith's and cobble together some sort of childcare, but that's too far ahead for me to think about now.

And it all depends on Keir, of course. How he reacts to my news. It doesn't come easily to me, not knowing what's going to happen in my life a day, a week, a year from now; but I'm trying.

Keir doesn't own a suit, but has rustled up a pair of black jeans and, with his crumpled grey linen jacket, he looks appropriate in his own way. We take a taxi over to the house, where Ned and the children are waiting in the sitting room, stiff and uncomfortable in their new black clothes.

It's the first time Ned and I have seen each other since I left a week ago, though I've been back to visit Agness and Guy, of course. We greet each other awkwardly, exchanging harmless comments about the weather – muggy and threatening rain – and Eleanor's reactionary WI choice of hymns for the service. Before things get too sticky, we're saved by the arrival of the hearse and stream thankfully outside to take our places in the two limousines that will make up the cortège. It's already been decided that Keir and I will travel with my sister Lindsay and her eight-year-old son in the first car; Ned, Agness and Guy will take the second. Very diplomatic; very modern.

Agness still can't quite look at me, I notice. I have no idea what Ned has said to her about our separation, although he promised he wouldn't break the news about the baby. I expected her to pull away from me again, but, to my surprise, she seems to be trying to understand. She's sad for her father, of course. As am I.

Guy puts his arm round my shoulder and gives me a quick hug as we sort ourselves out by the cars. 'Chin up, Mum,' he whispers.

I smile gratefully at him. He's like a different person since he came home. He's grown up and developed a confidence in himself that's a joy to see. I know instinctively that there'll be no more trouble for him at school, whatever choices he makes with his life. He's got the measure of himself now.

'I'll be fine,' I whisper back. 'And so will you, Guy. Whatever happens. Whatever – *who*ever – you choose.'

Our eyes meet in understanding. 'Thanks,' he says simply.

I watch him climb into the car with Ned and his sister, my heart full. I came so close to losing this fine young man. It's not a mistake I intend to repeat. My children may be almost grown, but they need me now more than ever. I won't leave them again.

'I meant to ask you,' my sister says chattily as we settle into the back of our limo. 'My car died last week. The garage says it's going to cost more to fix it than it's worth.'

She waits for me to leap in and offer to buy her a replacement, as I always do. I open my mouth and then close it again. I hear Eleanor in my head: *It does no one any good if you do everything for them; you least of all.*

Lindsay turns to stare huffily out of the window and refuses to talk to me for the rest of the journey.

When we arrive at the old church just outside Salisbury where Eleanor attended services most Sundays, the family regroups in the churchyard. Black-clad mourners are already filing into the church, greeting each other with self-conscious nods.

Keir melts tactfully towards the back of the church as we go in, taking his place in the last pew next to a man in his early sixties wearing army uniform and a chest full of medals. I wish Keir could sit beside me, but I can't do that to Ned and the children. They've got enough to cope with today.

Eleanor's willow coffin looks beautiful on the catafalque. Sweet William and freesias – her favourite flowers – are entwined around the sides, and a traditional arrangement of lilies spills from the top. No 'Gran' spelled out in chry-santhemums; she'd spin in that basket like a top if we dared do anything she'd consider common.

I know the funeral service is beautiful because I put it together, but I don't take any of it in. It's like your wedding day: it passes by in a blur, and afterwards you wonder if you were really there. We listen to 'Jerusalem' and 'Faith of Our Fathers'; Henry Scott Holland – 'Death is nothing at all' – and the twenty-third psalm. Ned gets up and gives a very surprising, moving eulogy, and I smile at him through a mist of tears as he sits down.

And then the pall-bearers are picking up the picnic-ham-per coffin, and we're all filing out of the church – the old soldier has tears streaming down his cheeks, I notice – and round the back towards the crowded graveyard. New 'cli-ents' are no longer accepted, but Eleanor reserved her place years ago, next to James; doing the proper thing in death, as she always did in life.

Agness's odd boyfriend appears from behind a gravestone, looking strangely at home for once amid the sea of black. I notice a flash of silver as they link hands. Agness informed me last week that they've both signed up to the Silver Ring Thing and pledged celibacy until marriage. Given that she's only fourteen, the fact she's even thinking about sex has me coming out in hives. I suppose I'd better have a serious talk with her about birth control soon. Not that I'm in any position to throw stones.

My sister starts to howl as Eleanor's coffin is lowered into her grave. Ned sweetly moves to put his arm round her as her young son looks on, bewildered and confused. Eleanor was right: he *is* a good man. Maybe even the right man for me. Just at the wrong time.

Afterwards, as I turn away, the old soldier is there.

'Robert Cooper,' he says formally, holding out his hand. 'Forty years ago, I loved your mother very much. I wish I'd had the chance to tell her one last time.'

For a moment I'm too startled to respond, then, belatedly, I return his handshake.

'You look like her,' he says wistfully. 'It's your eyes.'

Eleanor never mentioned another man. She never even discussed how she met my father. I always knew better than to ask.

'What happened?' I ask, too curious to be polite. 'Between the two of you?'

'She chose you,' he says with a small, sad smile.

If Keir is the man you should be with, don't give him up. Not for anyone. Certainly not out of a misguided sense of duty and doing the right thing.

I watch him as he turns and walks stiffly away, his back ramrod straight. I have no idea what he meant. Did they have an affair after I was born? Did Eleanor stay with my father, for my sake? Was she warning me not to make the same mistake? I'll never be able to ask her; and perhaps it no longer matters. Whatever Eleanor's secrets were, they've died with her.

'Are you OK?' Keir asks.

I nod. 'Just give me a few minutes.'

I thread my way through the tall, moss-covered Victorian gravestones. They did things so much better then, I think, eyeing the garish modern headstones on the fringe of the cemetery. No Hallmark inscriptions or gilt engravings. Just names and dates carved into the weathered stone and granite.

I'm contemplating a family plot – husband, wife, four children who died before their first birthdays, a son who lived to be a hundred and one – when Ned approaches.

'I don't want to disturb you,' he says as I turn round.

'It's OK.' I smile. 'Your eulogy was beautiful. Thank you.'

'Eleanor could be a piece of work, but funnily enough, I miss having her around. She kept me on my toes, if nothing else.' He reaches into his jacket pocket and pulls out a padded envelope. 'I wanted to give you this.'

I look quizzically at him for a moment and then open it. Inside is a single photograph of Eleanor and me. I recognize it instantly, though I don't think I've ever seen it before. It was taken a few days after Agness was born. My mother and I are sitting on the low wall by the kitchen garden, pink June roses in full bloom on the trellis behind us. She has her arm around my shoulders, and the two of us are laughing at something two-year-old Guy, just out of shot, has said. We look happy and relaxed in each other's company. Like any mother and daughter.

'Where did you find this?' I ask wonderingly.

'I got some boxes down from the loft. I knew it was in there somewhere.'

I trace my finger over the photograph. I know the state of our cardboard archives: Ned must have spent hours looking for this. The same man who gave me garage flowers on our anniversary and a fax machine for my last birthday.

'Thank you,' I say inadequately.

'It's too easy just to remember the bad times. I wanted you to remember how good it could be too.'

I realize he's no longer talking about my relationship with Eleanor.

'I know it's too late now,' Ned says matter-of-factly. 'But there's something I want you to know. I *would* have loved that baby. He or she will be a part of you, and there's nothing about you that I don't love. You loved Guy because he was mine. I realized after you left last week that this is no different. If you'd wanted to stay with me, your baby would have become ours. Of course it would. I'd have loved it just as much as Guy or Agness. I know it doesn't make any difference now, but I just need you to know that.'

I stare at Ned, at this man whose face is as familiar as my own, a man I've known and loved for two-thirds of my adult life, and who still has the capacity to surprise me. Who hasn't *stopped* surprising me, if I'm honest, since I came back eleven days ago. I expected him to be bitter and angry on my return; I *welcomed* it, almost. It assuaged the guilt and made my decision so much easier. I was totally unprepared for Ned to forgive me so readily, to be so generous about Keir. I watched him shake my lover's hand across the table after Guy's miraculous return and realized with a shock that I've never known Ned *not* do the right thing, however much it cost him. Even to the point of being prepared now to take on another man's child. He's made mistakes, yes – mistakes that have threatened our home and family; but so have I. Just because I've always treated him like a child doesn't mean he is one. He'd never run away from his responsibilities the way I did. For all his faults, he never gave up on me. On *us*. Still hasn't, in fact.

I never expected to find myself having to choose between two men I love equally, albeit in very different ways. All my life I've bought into the received wisdom that we all have a soul mate, one person with whom we're *meant* to be; that all our other relationships are no more than mistakes along the way. But the truth is, love's a lot more complicated than that.

I never stopped loving Ned. I just lost sight of it for a while.

'Kate,' Keir says behind me.

I turn. On the other side of the Victorian family plot, Keir is watching the two of us, his expression unreadable. His hair flames in the late July sunshine, and his amber eyes burn with intensity as he looks at me. But when he speaks, his voice is calm. 'The car's waiting, Kate.'

'Oh,' Ned says awkwardly. 'Since we're hosting the wake at the house together, I thought you might want to come back with me.'

I'm literally caught in the middle. On one side, Ned. On the other, Keir. One last time, I have to choose.

Love familiar, comfortable, comforting. Not perfect, far

from perfect, but committed and tested and true. A flawed man who has forgiven me abandonment, an affair, who'll accept a rival's child. Steadfast and loyal. And love impassioned, intense, fresh and exciting, from a man who already seems to know me better than I know myself, who allows me to be someone new. Whatever my choice, I lose as much as I gain.

And then I realize. The extravagant gesture I looked for throughout my marriage, the gesture that would tell me Ned and I *did* have passion after all: there it is.

'I'm so sorry,' I say, turning to Keir. 'I'm so very sorry.'

Ned wants me not because of the baby but despite it. It's enough.

It's everything.

'Go with him,' Keir says quietly. 'It's OK. Go with Ned.'

Still nobody moves.

Keir finally breaks the deadlock, stepping carefully around the old stones and putting his hands on my shoulders. 'When I met you, it was just you,' he says softly. 'There was no Ned, no Agness and Guy. You were free to be with me. But you're not any more. Maybe you thought you'd left them behind, but you're still part of your old family and your old life, and that's a *good* thing.' He grips my arms, his voice catching. 'It's not that I don't want to fight for you, Kate. God knows I do. But I wouldn't want to be the one to destroy something good. I couldn't build my own happiness on so much misery.'

'I do love you,' I whisper, choking on the words.

'I know you do. And I love you. But it's not always that simple, is it? There are other people involved. You have a responsibility to love them, too.'

'Keir—'

'I don't have a voice here,' he says. 'I've known that since I arrived. The pull of the past was too strong.' He kisses me gently on the cheek. 'You've made your choice. Be happy.'

I know I'll never see him again. I watch him walk away, the pain of losing him as real and raw as if I'd sliced a sharpened knife-blade across my palm. As it would have been if I'd said goodbye to Ned instead. Grief is the price we pay for love.

'Kate,' Ned says, quietly. 'Kate, what are you going to do about the baby?'

I didn't want anyone to know I was pregnant. Not after the miscarriage in February. I wanted to be sure this baby was going to make it before I threw all our lives into needless turmoil. But when Ned found the pregnancy test stick, the decision was taken out of my hands. And in a way, it made leaving him a little easier for both of us to bear. We could tell ourselves that circumstances had forced my hand; it gave him an excuse, and me a reason, for the decision.

Would I have chosen Keir if it wasn't for the baby? I still don't know. I love them both. It was like asking me to choose between my children.

But there *was* a baby. And I did choose Keir. I was sure he'd be supportive about the pregnancy, perhaps even happy. But I didn't *know*. And even if he'd stood by me, everything between us would have changed irrevocably with the news. I didn't want to tell him until I had to, until I was absolutely *sure*.

So yesterday afternoon, with a sense of weary déjà vu, I went for my first scan. It was the same sonographer who, five months previously, had broken the news that my baby was dead. If she was surprised to see me back so soon, she didn't let on.

I lay back on the couch as she smeared cold gel over my stomach, bracing myself for the worst.

'When was your last period?' she asked.

It's too small. Hasn't developed. Dead already.

'Twenty-third of April. St George's Day. Why?'

'Was it normal?'

I frowned, trying to remember. 'Maybe a day shorter than usual. But they've been all over the place since my miscarriage, it's hard to know what normal is any more.'

'Lighter?'

I pushed myself up on my elbows. 'Look, I'd rather know. Is it dead?' I asked bluntly.

She laughed. 'No, your baby's fine. Listen.'

She fiddled with a dial, and the next moment, a rich, vibrant *thump-thump-thump* filled the room.

'A hundred and sixteen beats per minute. Your baby has a nice, strong, healthy heartbeat. It's fine, I promise.'

I sank back in relief as the sonographer clicked and measured. My baby had a healthy heartbeat. It was going to be OK. My baby was going to be fine.

'It's just the dates I have a problem with,' the sonographer added casually. 'You're not twelve weeks along, Kate. More like sixteen.'

'*Sixteen?*'

'Give or take a day or two.'

'Are you sure?' I said faintly.

'Oh, yes. No question. Actually, I'm surprised you haven't felt the baby move.'

'I don't understand. I had a period! How—'

'It happens quite often.' Smiling, she slotted the probe into its holster at the side of the machine and wiped the gel from my stomach. 'Quite a few women bleed early on in their pregnancy, particularly around the time they would have got their period. It's just hormones. It won't affect the pregnancy. I promise you, Kate, there's nothing to worry about.'

'I only found out I was pregnant last week,' I said, feeling panicked, still struggling to take it in. 'I haven't taken any supplements. And I had a glass of wine at lunch . . .'

'Honestly, Kate, everything looks fine. As long as you haven't been downing a bottle of vodka a night, it won't make any difference. A glass or two of wine now and again doesn't hurt, though don't quote me on that. You're too far along for CVS testing, I'm afraid, but we can do an amnio tomorrow if you're worried about Down's.' She gave my hand a quick squeeze. 'It's good news, Kate. Everything looks perfect to me. You've made it through the first trimester, which means you're very unlikely to lose the baby now. Stop worrying.'

'So when . . . ?'

She picked up a small cardboard wheel. 'I'd guess the date of conception was around the ninth or tenth of April.'

The ninth of April. Our wedding anniversary. The last time Ned and I had sex. Weeks before I'd even met Keir, let alone slept with him.

This baby wasn't Keir's.

It was Ned's.

*

It starts to rain, a light summer drizzle that softly darkens the headstones to a deep slate grey. A welcome cool breeze drifts across the grass, freshening the muggy air.

'I didn't tell Keir,' I tell Ned steadily. 'There wasn't any need.'

'But he deserves to know,' Ned protests. 'He's the baby's father, you have to—'

'He isn't the baby's father. You are.'

I watch Ned's expression, waiting for the fear, the rejection. Taking on Keir's child is a choice; accepting his own is a responsibility he can't avoid. He's no longer being noble, but *obliged*.

His face opens in a smile of pure joy. 'We're having a baby?'

'We are.'

He catches me in his arms and kisses me, a hot sweet kiss that reaches my toes and lights a flame of longing between my legs and sets my nipples tingling and makes even my earlobes throb with longing.

When neither of us can breathe, we pull apart yet stay so close we are drinking each other's breath.

'This isn't going to be easy,' Ned murmurs.

'I know,' I say.

'There'll be times I'll wish to God we'd never had another child.'

'There'll be times I'll wonder why the hell I came back.'

'I'll wonder if you're sleeping with Guy's cute college friends.'

'I'll worry you'll gamble the house away on a horse.'

'I'll forget to insure the car and miss our anniversary and dump things in your lap and expect you to take care of them.'

'I'll bail out my sister and nag you for staying out late and treat you like a half-witted child.'

There's a sudden choking noise behind us. We swing round to find Agness standing there with her fingers halfway down her throat. 'For God's sake,' she says, unable to keep the huge grin off her face, 'can't you two get a room?'

Ned and I smile at each other. 'I don't care how bad it gets,' Ned tells me, 'I'm not going anywhere.'

'I don't care how bad it gets,' I say, 'I promise I won't run away.'

And then, to the delight and disgust of our daughter, he kisses me again.

Acknowledgements

For her unparalleled wisdom, advice and friendship these many years, my gratitude and thanks to Carole Blake, agent supreme.

The sparkling and divine gift of an editor, Wayne Brookes, as warm and funny as he is shrewd and ass-kicking.

Long suffering, unsung and brilliant, Macmillan's Team Tess: Sandra Taylor and Helen Guthrie in publicity; Ali Blackburn and Louise Buckley in editorial; Rebecca Ikin, Ellen Wood and Antonia Byrne in marketing; Michelle Taylor and Emma Dalby Bowler in sales; patient and painstaking, copy-editor Juliet Van Oss.

To all at Blake Friedmann who work so tirelessly behind the scenes.

Fabio Sermonti, who opened his home in Rome to me and shared wine, pasta and friendship with extravagant generosity; I can't thank you enough.

My dear friend Simon Piggott, who as always provides legal advice with a twinkling smile; any mistakes are mine alone.

Michele Romaine, darling girl, who inspired this story fifteen years ago; don't worry, you're not in the book.

Georgie Stewart, Andrew Roberts, Peter Davis, beloved all: thank you for your endless hospitality and dear friendship.

Acknowledgements

I cannot forget the extraordinary family who bring so much to the novelist's table: sons, Henry and Matt, and daughter, Lily; brother Charles, and his family, Rachel, George, Harry and Oliver; mother-in-law Sharon; Barbara, Mummy 2.0; darling mother, Jane, missed always; and all my extended family straddling England, New Zealand, Europe and the US – probably the only way we can stand each other.

My husband, Erik, my beloved, my *bashert*, who has made me whole in ways he can never know. You carry me through.

And finally, my father, Michael, who has inspired me my entire life. Daddy, you have faced this last battle with all the courage and determination and vitality you have brought to every challenge in your life, and I'm simply awed by you. I am so lucky to have you as my father. Everything good I have ever done, everything positive I have ever achieved, is because of you.

I love you.

www.panmacmillan.com